BILLIONAIRE WOLF

KAREN WHIDDON

MILLS &
BOON

Published in Great Britain 2015
by Mills & Boon, an imprint of Harlequin (UK) Limited,
Eton House, 18-24 Paradise Road, Richmond, Surrey, TW9 1SR

© 2015 Karen Whiddon

ISBN: 978-0-263-91820-5

89-1115

Harlequin (UK) Limited's policy is to use papers that are natural, renewable and recyclable products and made from wood grown in sustainable forests. The logging and manufacturing processes conform to the legal environmental regulations of the country of origin.

Printed and bound in Spain
by CPI, Barcelona

Karen Whiddon started weaving fanciful tales for her younger brothers at eleven. Amid the Catskill Mountains, then the Rocky Mountains, she fueled her imagination with the natural beauty surrounding her. Karen lives in north Texas and shares her life with her hero of a husband and three doting dogs. You can email Karen at KWhiddon1@aol.com or write to her at PO Box 820807, Fort Worth, TX 76182, USA. Fans can also check out her website, www.karenwhiddon.com.

As always, to my beloved husband, Lonnie.

"Are you all right?"

Ryan made no attempt to hide the fact that he wanted her. Maria could see that the darkness of his eyes and every shadow in his perfectly chiseled face all attested to his desire.

"Yes," she said as she slipped off her high heels and carried them, so she could walk barefoot in the sand.

"Are you sure that's safe?" he asked.

Tilting her head up at him, Maria smiled. "I love the way sand feels between my toes. You should try it."

To her amazement, he did exactly that, removing his boat shoes. "Nice."

When he took her hand, she couldn't suppress a tiny cry at the contact. A hot ache grew in the back of her throat, making her realize what they'd all said would happen was true. Desire, want and need had the potential to morph into so much more.

"Maria?" He turned to her, and swept her into his arms. She felt her body soften as her curves molded to his hard, muscular body. Her skin tingled from the touch of his hands as his long, elegant fingers caressed her arms.

And then he kissed her.

Chapter 1

Maria Miranda had always liked her name—almost as much as she loved the sea. The melodic sound of the six syllables always made her smile. Even now, trying to fulfill the destiny she'd been given, a walk along the waves did much to soothe her frustration at her repeated failure.

All her life, she'd taken great pains to hide her beauty. Until now. She'd just turned thirty, and her father and the Drakkor Council had grown impatient. The time had come to accomplish what she'd been born to do. Somehow. So far, nothing has been as easy as it should be.

Another Friday night. She'd decided to give this place one more shot—how could she resist a bar called Sea Dragon? She took the same seat at the bar as she had the previous two Fridays and swiveled to face the crowded nightclub. Women shot her envious and sometimes downright hostile glares, while the men couldn't seem to tear their eyes from her. Not for the first time, she found herself aching to scoop her hair back into an unflattering bun and slip her oversize, tortoiseshell glass onto her nose.

Lookin' for love in all the wrong places…

Despite the hip-hop music blasting on the nightclub's speakers, the old eighties song kept running through her head. As she got up and gyrated on the dance floor with yet another handsy, overly self-confident man, she wondered why on earth she'd ever thought coming here would be a good idea.

Because desperation fueled her, that's why. Some women talked of their biological clock ticking. Well, hers had gone into overdrive. Not just because she yearned for a baby, but because her entire race's survival depended on it. Unfortunately, for her, getting pregnant was a bit complicated.

Breathing a sigh of relief as the song ended, she gazed into her escort's eyes and tried to imagine letting his lips touch her. Nope. Not feeling it. So she thanked him and turned to go. When he grabbed her arm, she pulled free, gave him a don't-you-dare-try-that-again glare and headed back toward the bar.

Immediately, several other men jostled each other, clamoring for her attention. Ignoring them all, she raised her hand to signal the bartender, but someone stepped in front of her and ordered a drink for her, his treat.

"No thank you," she said, her voice clear and cool. And discouraging. Who knew men would think that if a reasonably attractive woman came to a bar alone, it was a signal to a bunch of hungry sharks to begin a feeding frenzy?

At the lame analogy, her inner Drakkor licked its chops. Of course, the fact that she actually had come here for that reason made the irony even more delicious. And painful.

Though she wished she could be outside strolling near the waves crashing up against the seawall, she finally ordered her own drink. The bartender brought it and three more. "From the gentlemen there, and there, and over there," he said, rolling his eyes.

"No, thanks," she said again, pushing them away. The pounding beat of the music had begun to make her head ache. Once again, she surveyed the room, feeling out of place and unsettled. More and more she had come to realize that trying to meet someone in a scene like this didn't work for her.

This was the third time in as many weeks that she'd come to this place. Maybe she should give up and move on. Though she'd danced with many, there hadn't been a single man who'd generated even the faintest flicker of interest, and she knew all too well the rules governing the task ahead of her.

One last look around the bar, and she'd knock back her drink and go home. Failure, again. Though, as a consolation prize, she felt quite sure she could find something interesting to watch on television.

And then, as her gaze swept through the packed room, she saw him. Everything else—the music, the noise, the crowd, faded away.

Gorgeous, ruggedly handsome, devilishly sexy—a hundred superlatives couldn't even begin to do him justice.

Tall and athletic, with muscles rippling under his T-shirt, the sight of him quickened her pulse. He walked with a nonchalant kind of self-confidence that drew her like a magnet. She let her gaze roam hungrily over him. Hair so dark it almost seemed black. Shaggy, a bit longer than currently fashionable. His hawk-like features, for whatever reason, seemed vaguely familiar, though she knew she hadn't met him. A man like him would not easily be forgotten.

Just like in a romance novel or a sappy movie, their eyes

met. Locked. And held. She sucked in her breath, her entire body tingling.

Then she noticed the bevy of women hanging on to his side. And more, lined up three deep behind him.

Popular, wasn't he? She couldn't say she blamed them.

Lips curling, she glanced to her left and her right, and at the unwanted drinks the bartender kept depositing in front of her. If she were to drink them all she wouldn't be able to walk.

They were an equal match. Fate. It had to be fate. A shiver snaked up her spine. Finally. The one she'd been searching for had finally appeared.

The mysterious stranger noted the drinks and her smile, and dipped his chin in agreement. Then he shook off his entourage and strode across the crowded room toward her.

Heart pounding faster than the bass beat, she stood, cutting through the men who vied for a chance to talk to her or dance with her, and smiled her welcome at him as he approached.

"Have we met?" he asked, the thick Texas drawl in his sexy voice curling her toes in her four-inch heels.

"No." Leaning away from him, she took a small sip of the drink she'd purchased. "I don't think so."

One of the men who'd tried to corner her earlier sauntered up, brazenly attempting to push himself between her and her new friend.

"She's with me," he growled, giving the newcomer a back-off glare. "Don't interrupt us again."

Muttering a curse, the intruder went away.

"Well done, sir," she said. "Maria Miranda."

Mr. Tall, Dark and Handsome smiled at her, sending a swirl of guppies swimming in her stomach. He held out his hand.

She took it, noting the long, elegant fingers. Even the

shape of his hand turned her on, though the noise made it difficult to hear.

"I can't believe it," he murmured, leaning in close, his breath tickling her ear. "Until I saw you, I was bored. I'd just decided to leave when I took one last look around. Packed dance floor, check. Bodies gyrating to music played at a decibel rivaling that of a jet taking off, check. And then…you."

She laughed, a bit shaky, hoping he didn't realize that even the husky timbre of his voice turned her on. She also noticed he hadn't mentioned the bevy of beautiful women who even now intently watched his every move.

A slow song began to play. At least, without the loud thumping of the bass, hearing became slightly easier.

"This is my third time here," she said, resisting the urge to lean even closer. "And I have to say, probably my last. This place is all too familiar and rapidly growing old."

He nodded. "I wasn't exactly sure what drew me to this bar, especially since I could easily find a hundred just like it in any number of cities." He shrugged. "In fact, I'm not clear how what had started as an evening stroll on the beach led to this."

His gaze slid over her, as intimate as a caress. "But I'm glad it did. You're quite possibly the most beautiful woman I've ever met. Tall and graceful, curved in all the right places, and enticingly spicy."

Though her mouth had gone dry, she managed to smile back at him. "You're awfully good at flirting."

He laughed. "Only when I see something I want." Every time his gaze met hers, her heart did a flip-flop. "And I want you."

Her entire body burned. If he kept looking at her like that, she'd go up in smoke. Hello, Destiny.

"My head's beginning to hurt," she told him, lightly touching his arm. "Do you want to get out of here?"

Another slow song came on. "Let's dance instead," he said, leading her out onto the dance floor. The instant he took her in his arms, she knew. This man. *Him*. Relief warred with arousal. Finally, after years of searching. She'd found him. Or he'd found her. Fate had finally tossed her a bone.

Of course she said none of those things. Men, she'd learned, sometimes took longer to reach conclusions based on instinct or intuition. Right now, with her head spinning, relishing the way his muscular body fit against hers, she didn't really care. Life had a way of sorting things out, and being held in his arms, her curves tucked up against his hard contours, her body melting against his, pushed everything else from her mind.

He looked down at her and smiled once more. The intensity of his gaze and the beauty of his smile sent a shudder through her. Her knees went weak and she stumbled. Only his strong arms kept her on her feet. And then she felt the force of his arousal jutting against her belly as they swayed to the music. A hot ache grew inside her, nearly unbearable in its intensity.

"We need to get out of here," she managed, weak with need.

To her relief, he jerked his head toward the door. "Sure. Lead the way."

The instant the cooler air hit her overheated body, she shivered. With anyone else, the scent of salt in the breeze would have brought her back to reality. Always, the sea grounded her.

Yet with him, her body still throbbed. This was right. This was what had been foretold for her, meant to be.

She nearly pinched herself to make sure she wasn't dreaming.

"Are you all right?" He made no attempt to hide the fact that he wanted her. Desire echoed in his stance, the darkness of his eyes, in every shadow of his perfectly chiseled face.

"Yes."

In unspoken accord, they crossed the parking lot, finding the stone steps down the seawall, to walk along the beach. The instant they reached the sand, Maria slipped off her high heels and carried them, so she could walk barefoot in the sand.

"Are you sure that's safe?" he asked.

Tilting her head up at him, she smiled. "I love the way sand feels between my toes. You should try it."

To her amazement, he did exactly that, removing his boat shoes. "Nice."

When he took her hand, she couldn't suppress a tiny cry at the contact. A hot ache grew in the back of her throat, making her realize what they'd all said would happen was true. Desire, want and need had the potential to morph into so much more.

Away from the bar and the tourist areas, the beach was peaceful and quiet. Silver moonlight highlighted gentle waves, and even the ever-present screech of seagulls had disappeared for the night.

"Maria?" He turned to her, and swept her into his arms. She felt her body soften as her curves molded to his hard, muscular body. Her skin tingled from the touch of his hands, his long elegant fingers caressed her arms.

And then he kissed her. His mouth covered hers with a hunger rivaling her own. Spirals of ecstasy made her quiver, even as his mouth left hers to kiss the pulsing hollow at the base of her throat.

Again she prayed this wasn't yet another dream, that she wouldn't wake alone and unfulfilled in her empty bed. His lips recaptured hers, more demanding this time, and every cell of her being answered him, *yes*.

If he laid her down in the sand right now, she would welcome him inside her.

"Not here," he told her, making her wonder if he'd read her mind. He grinned at her expression, planting a swift kiss on the tip of her nose. "You deserve better."

She let him lead her down the beach, away from the restaurants and bars, toward the residential area. When they reached the first group of beach houses sitting high up on their stilts, he grinned at her again. She marveled at the beauty of that smile, wishing for a swift instant that he, too, was Drakkor and could change and fly up into the sky with a sweep of powerful wings.

Foolishness. She pushed the thought away as quickly as it had come. Another Drakkor would be of no use to her, and above all, she had her duty to her people to hold high.

She wanted him. And tonight she was going to give herself over to passion and quit worrying about a future over which she had little control.

"Here we are," he said, pointing toward a yellow beach house with white trim. Like all the others, the house sat up on what she'd always called stilts. High enough off the ground to protect it from a water surge. After Hurricane Ike, most of these houses had been damaged or destroyed and rebuilt to more exacting standards. She ought to know. She'd spent many hours volunteering, assisting in the rebuilding efforts.

This house appeared both well-built and huge.

"Lovely," she murmured. "I live on the other side of the island, closer to the ferry."

At the base of the steps, he turned to her and gave her

a slow series of kisses. She shocked herself at her own eager response.

"Come with me," he said, and there was never a question. They hurried up the steps. He unlocked the door and they tumbled inside, laughing. Hands all over each other, they tore at each other's clothes, until they stood naked in the silver moonlight pouring through the windows.

She thought she'd never seen a more magnificent man.

"Let me look at you," he said, the reverence in his husky voice as sensual as any caress.

So she stood, unashamed and unembarrassed by her nudity, her entire body tingling and ready. Though she didn't even know his name, she didn't want to destroy the magic of the moment. There'd be time enough for that later.

He kissed her, pulling her even closer. There was nothing gentle about the way they came together. Like waves crashing upon the seawall in a storm, he possessed her and she felt herself drowning. They came together again and again, fierce and true and honest. She'd never known lovemaking could be like this, even as she shuddered, trying to hold back her second or third release and failing just as she had on all the others before.

Her inner dragon echoed her cry. At the sound, she saw a wolf rise up, a strong, shadowy image superimposed over him as he flung back his head and gave himself over to his own release. So he was Pack then. She'd known he was some kind of Shifter from his aura.

And then, and then, he pulled her close and held her, rocking her against him as if he found her infinitely precious.

Satisfied, sated, her body nevertheless stirred at his display of tenderness.

Lying there, knowing a satisfaction of a kind she'd never known, she finally slept.

Bright sunlight streaming through the windows woke her. For a second, discomfited, she realized she was still in bed with *him*, the wonderful, mystery man whose name she didn't even know.

Slowly, she turned her head, to find him sound asleep next to her.

Her heart felt full enough to burst. She'd never thought she could feel this way, despite being aware that she must, if she wanted to accomplish her life's purpose.

Determined to fulfill her destiny, she'd been actively searching for the right man for some time now. Until meeting this one, there hadn't been any to whom she felt attracted. Not one single solitary one.

She'd actually begun to wonder if she was too picky, if her proclivity to know what she wanted was hindering her achievement of the fate that had been thrust upon her. She couldn't count how many times she'd wanted out, wanted a different life, a different future. But then, all along, she'd known she really didn't have a choice.

The choice had been made for her long before her own birth.

Destiny. And fate.

Yet such things were more difficult to find than they should have been.

Earlier tonight, she'd been fed up and tired of searching, half convinced her apparently overly selective nature would ensure she'd die alone and childless, a disappointment to her father for bringing shame upon her people.

And then this man had come along. Right now, lying so still in bed next to him, with every nerve ending in her body ablaze, she felt alive. More alive than she had in weeks, months. And hopeful, too. As if her destiny might not be unobtainable after all.

As she studied him, he opened his eyes and looked at her, his bright blue gaze compelling and magnetic.

"Mornin' Maria," he said, favoring her with that smile that made every nerve in her body thrum.

Entranced, she smiled back. "Good morning yourself."

She thought about asking him if he wanted breakfast, but it was too soon to go all domestic. Her stomach growled in response to the thought, making his smile widen.

"Come here," he told her. "I want to make sure what we shared last night wasn't a dream."

All thoughts of food were forgotten as she complied.

Later, after they'd both showered and dressed—she in the same clothes she'd worn the night before—he took her hand and lightly kissed the back of it.

Now, she thought, now would be the time to learn his name.

"Let's go to breakfast," he said, holding out his hand. "There's a great little café within walking distance."

She nodded, slipping her fingers into his. "What shall I call you?" she teased, since he hadn't seemed inclined to give her his name.

Surprise flickered across his handsome features. "Ryan," he told her. "Of course. You can call me Ryan."

"Okay, Ryan." She squeezed his hand. "Let's go have breakfast."

He locked up as they stepped out onto the porch.

When they reached the bottom of the stairs, a small crowd of people surrounded them. There were cameras and microphones, and despite Ryan's attempts to shield her, bright lights were shone in her face, at her, blinding her as the people called out questions in rapid-fire sequence, each one trying to be heard over the other.

Paparazzi? "What the…?" Maria whirled, holding back an instinctive snarl. Her dragon tried to surge to the front, to take over, but she'd spent her entire life training and knew how to hold back her inner beast.

"Ryan?" She clutched his hand, hoping he'd have an explanation.

"Who's the new woman, Ryan?" One man shouted. "Can you give us a name?"

New woman? Maria blinked.

"TMZ here," yelled another. "Care to make a statement or answer a couple of questions?"

Ignoring them, Ryan shepherded her back up the stairs and into the house. Once inside, he methodically began closing all the blinds, one by one. He didn't seem fazed or even bothered, almost as if he was used to this sort of thing.

Maria, however, could barely catch her breath. She stood frozen, shocked and stunned, watching him.

When he'd finally finished, he turned to face her. "I'm sorry about that," he said, flashing that boyish grin. "I'd hoped that wouldn't happen. Now that the paparazzi know where I'm staying, they'll be staking out the place."

Pulse still pounding, she held her hand to her throat, trying her best to contain her agitation. "Paparazzi? Why on earth were they here? What did they want?" She inhaled deeply. "Or maybe the better question would be, who are you, really? If you have paparazzi, then you must be someone famous. What did I miss?"

For the space of a heartbeat, he held her gaze. Once again she felt that tug of attraction. This time, she ignored it.

Finally, he dropped his gaze and dragged his hand through his hair. "You really don't know who I am, do you?"

"No." Wrapping her arms around herself, she tried not to despair. For once, just once, she wanted something to work out. "Who are you?" Hoping her expression didn't reveal her nervousness, she waited for him to answer.

Instead of immediately answering, he got up and went into the kitchen. "Would you like a water or a glass of orange juice? Sorry, I don't have any coffee. I haven't had time to stock the house."

"What I'd like," she said, staying put between the couch and the door, wondering if the crowd of reporters still milled about outside, "is an explanation."

"Just a sec." When he returned, he brought with him two bottles of water. "Here," he handed one to her. Though the feeling of dread intensified with every second he delayed answering, she accepted and took a small sip.

"Well?" she prompted. "I'm beginning to think I might have made a terrible mistake."

Beginning to think might have been an understatement. In fact, the longer she sat there, the more every instinct screamed at her to leave. As one of the last remaining female Drakkor, two things had been drilled into her since childhood. The first had been her destiny. The second had been the need for anonymity. Whoever he was, Ryan appeared to embody the opposite.

"A mistake?" The small lines at the corners of his bright blue eyes crinkled when he smiled. Where before she'd found his assured self-confidence attractive, now it worried her.

Every movement casual, he perched on the edge of the couch, looking even more handsome.

"Here." He handed her a magazine from under a stack of several on the coffee table. "This will do a much better job of explaining than I can."

Stunned, she stared. "Your face is on the cover," she said faintly, feeling sick. Now she understood why he'd seemed vaguely familiar. Even though she generally avoided pop culture, she'd have to have been living under a rock not to recognize this face, this man. Especially with the words Ryan Howard—America's Most Eligible Billionaire Bachelor emblazoned across the front.

"Thank you." She put the magazine down without reading it and swallowed hard, avoiding his gaze. "I'm sorry. I've made an awful blunder. Don't worry about escorting me back. I can find the way. In fact, I'll just let myself out."

And she did just that, feeling both relieved and perversely peeved when he made no move to stop her.

When she reached the bottom of the stairs, more flashbulbs exploded and the paparazzi materialized, shouting questions, asking her name. Instead of answering, she kicked off her high heels and, barefoot in the sand, began to run.

Heart pounding, Maria ran, easily settling into the familiar rhythm. Before long, the paparazzi fell behind, abandoning the chase. Though she missed her running shoes, and the heels she carried kept bumping her leg, she kept on until the reporters were completely out of sight before she slowed to a walk. She'd lucked out; she hadn't hit anything sharp or dangerous, like shards of glass or the jagged edge of a broken seashell.

Stopping long enough to slip her shoes on, she strode back toward the now closed bar. Instead of going inside, she located her car, a vintage turquoise Corvette, and got inside. The engine fired up with a satisfying throaty roar, and she heaved a big sigh as she headed home.

Disaster averted. While she had to admit that Ryan Howard appealed to her more than any other man she'd ever met, he was also a public figure—and a known playboy. She didn't have time to waste on a man like him. Not with the clock ticking. In fact, the kind of man she needed to find would be his polar opposite.

Chapter 2

As usual, the throaty purr of the Corvette's engine soothed her. One finger at a time, Maria loosened her death grip on the steering wheel. That done, she squared her shoulders and inhaled deeply. She wished…

No. If wishes were fishes, this dragon would eat. She'd made an error, plain and simple. Her foolish, rose-colored glasses had made her see something that hadn't been there. One hot man and she'd nearly melted. There'd be someone else. There had to be. She had a destiny to fulfill. And soon. She couldn't permit herself to make this type of mistake ever again.

Not only had she allowed herself to believe a notorious playboy might be *The One*, but she'd risked becoming a public spectacle, and there was a certain person who could not know where to find her. Even though Doug Polacek had been imprisoned, no one knew if he had people working for him on the outside.

For right now, she'd consider herself safe unless she learned differently. She thought of the life she'd built here in Galveston, the business she'd started and loved. She'd worked hard to make her wedding chapel successful, and she knew if she had to leave the area, leaving her business would feel like ripping out a big piece of her heart. Not to mention her need to live near the ocean.

But just as she always did, she'd continue to do what she had to do. This thing with Ryan Howard would blow over quickly so she could go back to her simple and quiet life.

Pulling into her driveway, she sighed. Her tidy frame house on a quiet residential street seemed the opposite of everything she'd just endured. After clicking the opener, she pulled into her garage, killed the engine and closed the door.

One more deep breath. As she removed the keys from the ignition, she realized her hands were shaking. Of course they were. She never, ever gave in to impulse like that. Until last night, she'd had her lists and her reason and had lived her life accordingly. Responsibility had always been her hallmark. How awful to think the one single time she'd veered from this course and acted spontaneously, she'd made such a horrible mistake.

Mentally berating herself, she got out of her car. High heels clicking on the concrete, she headed inside.

She dropped her keys onto a dish on the kitchen counter, headed into the bathroom and eyed herself in the mirror. With her color high, her normally smooth olive skin looked flushed. Her eyes were suspiciously bright, making her appear as if she might be on the verge of tears, even though she wasn't. Maria never cried if she could help it. Crying was for wimps.

Shaking her head, she washed her face, pulling her wild

mop of dark hair back into a semitidy ponytail. From now on, she'd go back to ticking things off her list.

Despite her resolve, her thoughts kept returning to the night before. The lovemaking had been…sublime. And Ryan had been just as gorgeous and sexy as he appeared on TV or in the tabloids. A Shifter too, part of the Pack, which put him a notch above a simple human, at least in her book.

Ah, well. Best to put him from her mind and continue her search. If she wasn't successful in finding a man to father her child on the island, she might have to broaden her parameters.

Never again would she allow lust to overrule reason. Too much was riding on this for her to make another mistake.

Up until the moment the sultry temptress bolted, Ryan Howard hadn't been entirely sure what to think of Maria's declaration of ignorance. In his experience, ever since his face had been plastered over numerous magazines and television interviews, women had been dreaming up increasingly inventive ways to get into his bed. There were, according to his research, only 513 billionaires in the United States. He figured he was part of a tiny percentage of them who were single. Women, usually attracted by his money, flocked to him. He'd grown so weary of the tall tales they told to get close, he'd begun to use the quality of the story as a criterion to send the woman away.

Maria's beauty combined with her lack of guile had ignited a slow burning fire inside him. He'd actually allowed himself to think that once, just once, he could enjoy a casual relationship with a woman without artifice or deviousness.

When she'd recoiled at the sight of his face on the cover

of *Persons Magazine*, he'd realized she'd been telling the truth. She really hadn't known who he was. She'd based her decision to leave the bar with him on something else, and the idea so astounded him that he understood how truly jaded he'd become.

He'd known immediately from her aura her true nature as Shape-shifter, though he hadn't been able to tell what kind. All he knew was that whatever she might be, she wasn't Pack. When the flashbulbs had gone off, for a split second she'd fought her inner beast to keep from shifting. Watching her instead of the paparazzi, he'd been curious to see what manner of creature she'd reveal.

At the last minute she'd gotten herself under control, of course. This mechanism was one of the first things all Shape-shifters learned as soon as they were able to change. Living among humans, secrecy had become paramount. The last thing any of them needed was to be caught on television morphing into something else. In fact, to do so was a sentence punishable by a swift and violent death.

Shaking his head, he drained the last of his water and picked up her still-full bottle. Why had she run away? What exactly had scared her the most—who he was or the attention he garnered?

Briefly, he considered going after her, but the knowledge that the reporter-wannabes would have a field day stopped him.

Hopefully, once she'd gotten over the shock and calmed down, everything would be okay. He definitely planned to give her a call. Because, despite the mind-blowing sex they'd shared the night before, he still wanted her. Craved her, in fact. The knowledge that she'd wanted him, too, until the paparazzi had ruined it, made his blood boil with frustrated desire. They could have gone to breakfast and then returned here. Right now, they should have been wrapped in each other's arms, making love again.

Instead, he found himself alone in his new vacation house, a virtual prisoner of the paparazzi.

Which meant he'd either need to get used to it or find another place, which would be stupid since he'd just paid cash for this one. So he'd adjust, like he always did. Still, being located so quickly was pretty damn disappointing.

When he'd bought this house, he'd been careful. Everything had been done under the name of an LLC he'd formed for real estate investments. Only he or his personal assistant Timothy had dealt with the Realtor and title company. Accordingly, he'd been pretty confident he could live here for a few weeks completely under the radar. He still had no idea how they'd found him.

Walking into that nightclub with the cool name—the Sea Dragon—might have been a mistake. Since he'd been recognized there, someone must have alerted the media. He and Maria had one peaceful night. Those damn flashbulbs and video cameras had been waiting here in the morning. Pacing the length of the living room, he considered how they'd found him. His office only knew he'd gone to vacation at the coast—he hadn't even told them what city. The only person who knew the details, his personal assistant, was someone Ryan trusted with his life. Timothy had worked for him since the beginning. These days, Ryan made sure Timothy was well compensated for keeping his life running smoothly.

He cursed. That meant there were now two mysteries to be solved. He called Timothy, even though the clock showed it wasn't yet eight, and filled him in on what had happened. A sleepy sounding Timothy promised to take care of everything that morning once he got to the office. Ryan knew he would.

Satisfied, after ending the call, Ryan focused on deciding what he wanted to do about Maria. Ever since his meteoric rise to fame, there had always been women wanting something from him. Maria Miranda was the first one who'd taken off as soon as she learned who he was. This was unusual enough to give him pause.

Why? Why had she run away? One thing he knew for sure. He would find out. He knew her name and she'd told him she owned a wedding chapel here in Galveston. It wouldn't be that difficult to find her.

After getting another water and aching for coffee, he clicked on the TV and tried to relax. But he couldn't stop thinking about her. Puzzles had always intrigued him. Figuring out where the pieces fit had enabled him to develop the software company that had made him rich. The apps and games his talented designers developed had made his business into a billion-dollar enterprise, especially when his company had gone global. Recently he'd turned down offers from both Microsoft and Apple. Even Google had approached him, especially once he'd branched out to Europe and Australia. But he'd refused to even consider selling. He loved his company, had a great staff, and wouldn't know what to do without it if he sold. Plus, he had enough money. What would he do with even more?

Though he'd planned this extended vacation with the thought that he'd do as little as possible besides relax and unwind, the prospect of untangling the mysterious Maria's secrets filled him with exhilaration and a fresh sense of purpose. He hadn't felt this excited about anything in a long, long time.

First up, though, he needed to hit the grocery store. What good was a beach house without the basic amenities like coffee and food? Once he'd gotten the necessities taken care of, he'd turn his attention to the delectable beauty.

"We'll figure this out," he vowed, out loud, even though no one else could hear him. He wasn't giving up on her, not yet.

Wedding Chapel Near the Sea. Just the name made Maria smile. Even if she hadn't been able to manage an ocean view, the salty scent of the waves permeated the air. She loved her business and had spent long hours restoring the old Victorian house until she had it exactly the way she'd envisioned. Romantic, nostalgic and tranquil.

And it worked. Even catching sight of the pale peach paint with beige trim made her happy. Every morning she drove to work and went inside with a smile on her face. Today would be no different. She refused to let what had just happened ruin her day.

"You're way too chipper for this early," her receptionist, Kathleen, groused, her usual response to Maria's cheerful "Good morning."

Maria merely smiled, just as she always did, and continued on into her tiny office. She'd painted the walls bright yellow, just because the color reminded her of sunshine, and decorated with pictures and statues of pigs, because they made her laugh.

"What do we have on the schedule today?" she asked.

"The Thompson wedding is coming by to talk dates." Kathleen appeared in the doorway, reading from a ledger. "They'll be here at ten. And the Woodards are bringing the balance of their deposit at two and will want to go over the final details."

"Anything else?"

Kathleen started to shake her head, but turned when the front door opened. "Can I help you?" she asked, heading toward the reception area. "Are you here to discuss planning a wedding?"

At that point, Maria turned on her computer, waiting for it to boot up. Kathleen was good at her job and wouldn't let a potential customer get away without being made aware of all they had to offer.

"I'm here to see Maria."

The sound of the familiar deep voice sent fire through Maria's body. She froze, hands on her keyboard, wondering how on earth *he* had found her and what he wanted.

"Do you have an appointment?" Kathleen asked, sounding slightly breathless.

"No, but I don't need one. She'll see me."

Exhaling, Maria stood. "That's okay, Kathleen," she said, pitching her voice loud enough so she could be heard. "I have a little time to talk to Mr. Howard."

At the name, Kathleen let out an audible gasp. "I'm so sorry," she gushed. "Forgive me. I wasn't entirely sure it was you. Of course, let me show you Ms. Miranda's office."

Before she could, Ryan appeared in Maria's doorway. He looked so rugged and masculine, so out of place in the pointedly delicate decor, Maria had to suppress a smile.

Instead, she put on her best professional face, praying he couldn't tell how her heart practically pounded in her chest. "What can I do for you?" she asked.

Stepping into her office, he closed the door. His sheer size made the space feel three times smaller. "Why'd you run away?" he asked. The quiet question felt much more dangerous than it would have if he'd showed anger.

Again, she couldn't help but marvel at the clean-cut lines of his face and the self-confidence he radiated. Her heart jolted, her pulse hammered, and her mouth went dry.

Nope. Not going there.

Carefully, she shrugged. "I changed my mind. And I have to say, the fact that you've shown up here, at my place of business, confirms I did the right thing."

He glowered, his dark eyes still far too beautiful and seeing way too much. "I'm not stalking you, for Chrissake. You told me you owned a wedding chapel. There are only two on the island proper—yours and The Wedding Chapel on Broadway. I figured this one would be yours, and I wanted to talk to you, so here I am."

Crossing her arms, she carefully titled her head. "And, again, what can I help you with?"

Her impersonal tone had him coming closer, dragging a hand through his hair, which only made him appear sexier. "I like you," he said, his expression serious. "And I thought the feeling was mutual. How about this? Go to dinner with me tonight. No strings. Just a nice meal and some conversation."

She didn't have to feign her horror. "No, thank you. Wherever you go, there are cameras and paparazzi. That's not my thing. At all." She flashed him her most detached smile. "I'm sure you won't have trouble finding someone else to accept your invitation. At least, judging from the admirers following you around the club last night."

His mocking smile sent a shudder down her spine. "I don't want anyone else. I want you."

Instant heat. Right there, in between her legs. Her entire body, in fact. Still, she held her ground. "I'm sorry, Mr. Howard. The answer is no."

She thought he might argue with her at the very least, or maybe say something charming, in the hope of coaxing a smile. After all, if one believed his press, he was a player of the highest degree, used to getting what he wanted, when he wanted it.

Instead, he crossed the distance between them, cupped her face with his large hand and kissed her.

Stunned and shocked, she froze. Truth be told, she didn't resist. In fact, as he slanted his mouth over hers, kissing her as if she were a precious treasure, she went with it and opened her mouth so she could properly kiss him back.

Desire spooled low in her belly, and dimly she registered there was a reason Ryan Howard was good at getting women.

That thought had the effect of ice water dashed on her. She gasped and jerked away. "Out," she ordered, her voice shaking. "Get off my property right this instant."

Hands up, he backed away, nearly to the still-closed door. "About dinner…"

"No." Sucking in air, she let a trace of her anger show in her eyes, which should have been a warning. Even though Ryan was a Shape-shifter, when he saw the red glow in her eyes, he should realize he'd better stay away. To most other Shifters, the Drakkor were only legends. Few knew they still existed. Her people had formed an alliance with his, the Pack Protectors, in order to help keep the Drakkor safe. She didn't know how many of the Pack had been informed. At this moment, she didn't actually care.

"You have a fiery temper," he said softly, the intensity in his gaze telling her he knew his comment would be like throwing kindling on the embers. When she didn't respond, he dared to prod. "Dinner?"

"Out."

Nodding, he turned to go. As he grasped the door handle, he glanced back over his shoulder and tossed a business card on her desk. "Here's my number in case you change your mind. I would never have pegged you for a coward, Maria Miranda."

And with that, he left.

More shaken than she'd like to admit, even to herself, Maria dropped back into her desk chair. Coward? Had he known he'd just issued the worst insult one could to her kind? Had his choice of word been intentional, just to draw her into his sensual web?

If so, well played. She nearly ran after him. Only Kathleen's breathless appearance in her doorway stopped her.

"Oh, my goodness, how do you know Ryan Howard?" Kathleen gushed. "I couldn't help overhearing—you know how thin these walls are, and it sounded like you and he had already met. Are you going to be in the tabloids? What do you think about him? He's every bit as sexy in person as he is on TV."

"Stop, please." Maria wearily interrupted her employee and friend. "I just met him in a bar last night and we went for a walk on the beach." She carefully omitted everything else, including the fact that they'd spent the night together. "I took off when the paparazzi showed up and started taking pictures."

"Paparazzi! Oh my goodness, you *are* going to be in the tabloids!" Kathleen squealed. "I don't believe it. I can tell all my friends I've met Ryan Howard, *Persons Magazine*'s Most Eligible Billionaire Bachelor."

Maria groaned, sinking lower in her chair. "I can't believe I…" Luckily, she caught herself in time.

Unfortunately, Kathleen had a sharp mind and good ears. "Oh, my! Did you really?"

"No." Well aware her color was high, Maria gritted her teeth and held her ground. "No, I didn't. Let's talk about something else, please."

"But—"

"It's nearly ten. The first wedding party of the day should be here soon. We need to make sure everything is ready for them."

Taking the hint, Kathleen nodded and returned to her desk.

Alone again, Maria opened her email and tried to concentrate. Her rapid heartbeat finally slowed and she gathered her scattered thoughts and made herself focus.

Who knew Ryan Howard would have such an effect on her? She'd never been one for the pretty men. However, Ryan was more than easy on the eyes. He radiated masculinity, something her dragon side required. Masculinity, sex appeal and confidence. Everything she wanted in a man.

Except Ryan was entirely too famous and popular. And a playboy as well, she reminded herself, just in case she weakened. As if she could. Anyone who dated Ryan Howard would be immediately thrust into the spotlight. She couldn't afford that. Not only would it endanger her, but her future unborn child, as well.

She laughed at herself. As if. She couldn't get pregnant with him. The other thing she needed was a man who would love her. As in, forever and always. Judging from his reputation, Ryan Howard was not capable of such a thing.

The day went quickly, as they always did. Doing work she loved ensured no days ever dragged. She booked two new weddings, finalized the details on another and had a couple of other interested parties.

All in all, a good day.

At six o'clock, when Kathleen got ready to go home, Maria decided to leave, too. Her receptionist waited while she locked up, a hundred more questions in her eyes. Maria gave her a quelling look, letting her know she had no intention of answering them.

"We're done talking about Ryan Howard," Maria said when Kathleen opened her mouth. "Seriously. I have no intention of seeing him again."

Appearing reluctant, Kathleen nodded. "I can't say I understand, but I'll try. I have to say, though, most women would give their right boob for a chance to go out with him."

Unlocking her car, Maria smiled. "But then, I'm not most women, am I?" She got inside and closed the door without waiting for an answer. Lifting her hand in a quick wave, she started the engine, loving the throaty roar, and headed for home.

That white van...

Giving another quick glance in her rearview mirror, she made an impulsive turn down a side street without signaling.

The van did the same.

Concerned, she tried to remember everything she'd heard about what to do when being followed. She knew she couldn't go home. She had to go somewhere public. The police station on 54th? Or just a crowded gas station or maybe a grocery store. A&M Grocery was only a few streets away. Decision made, she swung around and headed toward 39th.

Of course, the van kept up.

A million thoughts ran through her mind. She, along with the few other remaining Drakkor females, had one enemy. Doug Polacek, a male Drakkor rapist and serial killer who'd bragged he was to be the savior of their race. He'd been arrested and locked away. Had he somehow escaped prison? If so, how had he found her? Should she call her father? Though why worry him, when there was nothing he could do from so far away.

Heart pounding, she calculated what she'd do when she reached the store. Park, jump out, and run inside? Or stay in her car, with the doors locked and the engine running, just in case she needed to take off?

Based on what she'd heard about Polacek, he was all about capturing and holding a prisoner. So he wouldn't try to kill her, though she wouldn't put it past him to shoot a tranquilizer dart or something to immobilize her so he could throw her in the van.

On second thought, maybe the police station would be the better option, despite having it drilled into her not to involve humans in Shifter business.

There. Muttering a quick prayer, she swung into the grocery store parking lot and pulled up in front of the store, in a no-parking zone. This would be high visibility and easy escape.

And here came the van. One foot on the brake, she kept the car in drive, ready for anything.

Instead of pulling up behind her or alongside her, the van pulled in to one of the empty spots reserved for the disabled. Strange. Still, she didn't relax, watching to see who'd emerge.

The driver's-side door opened. A second later, so did the passenger side, and then the rear sliding door swung open, disgorging a man with a video camera, another with a microphone. They rushed over to her car, the man with the mic clearly a reporter of some sort.

Relieved and irritated, Maria took her foot off the brake and stomped the accelerator. Screeching out of the parking lot, she traveled the back roads, taking a convoluted route toward home.

Only once she was sure they hadn't followed her did she turn down her street.

Safe inside her garage with the door closed, she sat in her car, teeth clenched, shaking. She'd only been with Ryan Howard once, and because of that, reporters were hounding her?

Slowly, she climbed out of her car and headed into the house. Should she cut her hair, change the color, make some attempt at disguising her appearance until this blew over?

Even having to consider such nonsense made her even madder. Why should she have to deal with this? Ryan Howard needed to make it stop. She suspected he had the power to fix it.

Digging his business card from her pocket, she decided to give him a call. She wanted this harassment to end, right now. The sooner she could go back to her normal life, the sooner she could get on with her quest to fulfill her destiny.

Chapter 3

Maria Miranda had looked even lovelier than the last time Ryan had seen her. The instant she'd looked up from her desk and her caramel-colored gaze connected with his, he'd felt it like a punch to his stomach.

The way she'd acted had taken him by surprise. Damned if she hadn't made him feel like some sort of creepy stalker. Embarrassed, ashamed and, yes, fuming, he paced the length of his beach house, glad that today, at least, the paparazzi had stayed away.

If it weren't for them, Maria would never have learned who he actually was. It had been refreshing to find a woman who liked him for himself, rather than what he'd become.

The kind of sizzling chemistry between him and Maria could have been the start of something amazing. Corny as it sounded, even to him, he mourned its loss. Especially since they hadn't gotten a chance to actually explore it.

He didn't understand women—what man did?—but he usually got along with them well. He'd never lied to himself, well aware looks and money got him a lot further than he'd get if he wasn't a multibillionaire. And though he didn't usually mind, since he wasn't looking for anything meaningful, the fact that the very things other women seemed to want had been what had driven Maria Miranda away felt like the bitterest form of irony.

He could practically hear his father's voice, even though he'd been dead three long years. "Be good for you, boy. You needed taking down a peg." And then the old man would have laughed, that crusty, congested sound from too many cigarettes and not enough exercise. Lung cancer had taken him, and not a day went by that Ryan didn't miss him. His dad had been one of the few people he could count on to be honest.

These days he had no one but himself.

And if he were honest now, he completely deserved what Maria Miranda had dished out. She hadn't asked to be around his baggage. While Ryan might have gotten used to the constant attention and disruption of privacy that came with his life, she clearly wasn't, nor did she want to be.

Easily understood. Normally, under any other circumstances, he would have given her a silent salute and moved on.

Except he couldn't get her out of his mind. No matter how he rationalized it, he still wanted her. Hopefully, he'd get over that in time. There were plenty of other beautiful women.

His cell phone rang. He grinned when her name popped up on his caller ID. He jotted the number down, intending to save it as a contact once they'd finished talking.

"Hello?" he answered, as if he had no idea who might be phoning him.

"Ryan, this is Maria Miranda." She sounded out of breath. "I need you to call off the reporters."

Stunned, he frowned. "I'm not sure I follow."

"They followed me after I got off work today," she continued, ripping out the words. "When I pulled into the grocery store, they tried to ambush me with a camera and everything. I have to ask you to please make it stop."

"I wish I could. But I have no control over them." Thinking fast, he seized opportunity where he saw it. "But since they already think we're together, would you reconsider and have dinner with me?"

"No," she snapped. "Maybe once they realize it's over, they'll lose interest and leave me alone." She ended the call before he could respond.

Over. Stuffing his cell phone back into his pocket, he grimaced. Over before it had even started. Might as well forget her and get on with his summer vacation.

Except, as the days went on, he still couldn't make himself stop thinking about her. And the fact that she'd wanted him, too, made it even worse. The kind of attraction that had sizzled between them kept him in a state of constant arousal.

The first week after her rejection, he went for lonely walks on the beach, telling himself he enjoyed the solitude. To keep from being recognized, he made various attempts at wearing a disguise. Mostly he wore a baseball cap, and once he even wore a long wig that made his head itch ten minutes in. With sunglasses, he figured this would be enough of a disguise to keep him from being recognized.

And it was. Strangely enough, the paparazzi seemed to have disappeared. Maybe they'd found other, more interesting people to follow, Ryan didn't know. At least Maria had gotten her wish.

On the weekend of the second week, he found himself

back at the Sea Dragon nightclub. Taking a deep breath, he went inside, unable to keep from hoping Maria might be there. If he could get her to talk to him, maybe she'd give him a second chance. He'd come up with a plan so simple he couldn't believe he hadn't thought of it earlier.

But though he searched the crowd, she wasn't anywhere to be found. He drank his beer slowly, keeping an eye on the entrance in case she came in, but eventually he admitted defeat. The repetitive noise had given him a headache, so he hurried back outside, down the concrete seawall and back to the sand. There, he breathed a sigh of relief, briefly considering kicking off his flip-flops but keeping them on, instead, when he realized even this made him think of Maria Miranda.

What the heck had happened to him? He hadn't come to Galveston looking for a hookup, but then he hadn't expected to see a woman as gorgeous as Maria. Not only that. There was something else about her, an elusive quality that fueled his need to explore all her secrets. Though he hated to admit it, the attraction seemed to be more than simply because he found her beautiful. Which so wasn't like him. He preferred his life uncomplicated, without attachments or ties. Work and play, nothing serious. Ever.

Because he enjoyed his own company, he never got lonely; in fact, part of the appeal in coming to Galveston had been the idea of complete privacy. But since meeting her, he felt her absence keenly, as if they'd been together for years rather than hours. Which made no sense whatsoever. Especially since he had no faith in intangibles like destiny or fate.

The ocean soothed him, however temporarily. Since buying the beach house, he'd learned how much he loved the gulf. He'd expected to find the solitude relaxing, the salt-scented air healing. What he hadn't expected was missing a woman he barely knew. Yet he did. Every morning he carried his coffee out to his second-floor porch and watched the sun rise above the water. He ached to have Maria there, to turn to her and draw her close to him, to talk to her about trivial, everyday things. As if they'd been together forever.

While he didn't claim to understand how this could be so, he knew enough to recognize something wonderful when it came his way.

The longer he walked, while the surf roared ashore in the background, the more focused he became. Once he'd cleared his head, he did what he always did when he wanted something. Figured out the best way to go after it.

Ryan Howard hadn't become a successful businessman by giving up. He had to convince Maria to give them a chance, at least, and see what this thing between them could become.

He'd call her instead of showing up in person. Hopefully she'd find that less threatening.

The next morning, he took his morning jog and swam in the ocean, then returned to his beach house to shower. Once he'd dressed, he made a cup of coffee and carried it out onto his patio. There, he relaxed and let the sun and the sounds of the crashing waves and screeching seagulls fill him. When he judged the time had come for a wedding chapel to be open, he searched for the number online and called.

As soon as he told the woman who answered the phone his name, she became flustered. "Let me see if M-Mizz Miranda is available," she stuttered. When she placed him on hold, the overly sweet and sappy romantic music made him smile. Perfect for a wedding chapel.

Unfortunately, instead of Maria, the receptionist returned to the line. "I'm sorry, Ms. Miranda is not available right now," she said, sounding regretful and slightly puzzled. "May I take a message?"

Since he knew if he simply left his number, he'd never hear from Maria, he decided to leave a detailed message instead. "Do you have a pen and paper?" he asked. When she replied in the affirmative, he took a deep breath. "Then write this down. The other night when we met, we had an instant connection. I felt it and I know you did, too. I'm sorry the paparazzi ruined what might have been something beautiful. I'm asking for one more chance. Just one. No cameras, no reporters, just us. One night, the water, the stars, and us. Don't take the risk of losing what could turn out to be something special. Call me, please." And he left his number.

Sounding awestruck, the receptionist promised to pass the message on.

Satisfied that he'd done all he could, Ryan ended the call. He'd told her the truth, from his heart, and come as close to begging as he ever had.

His phone rang a half hour later. Maria. Unbelievably, his heart skipped a beat from pure joy.

"What are you doing, Ryan?" Exasperation colored Maria's voice. "You know as well as I do that we didn't have any kind of magical connection…."

"What would you call it then?" He found himself grinning.

"Sexual attraction," she drawled, the erotic rasp in her voice making his blood heat. "I wanted you, you wanted me, and if I hadn't found out who you were, we'd have spent a couple of days in bed and gotten that out of our system once and for all. Then I'd never have heard from you again. I'm well aware of how that works."

"You wound me," he teased, even though he knew she was probably right. Such had been his previous method of operating. "But I honestly still think that spark is worth exploring. Give me one more chance."

The silence stretched on for so long he wondered if she'd set the phone down.

"Maria?" he prompted.

"I'm thinking." She sighed. "Giving this the serious consideration it deserves."

His heart actually skipped another damn beat. At least she hadn't immediately brushed him off.

"Ryan, I'm sorry," she began. "While I agree the sparks flying between us were combustible, I'm not the type of person who can live her life in the spotlight. Nor am I content with being one of many. So my answer is—regretfully—no."

"Wait, don't go." Talking rapidly, as he sensed she was about to hang up, he outlined his plan. "Just us and the water. No one will be able to interrupt us."

Again she went silent while she considered. When she spoke, the hint of interest in her voice told him she would agree. "For how long?" she asked. "Are you talking a few hours or an entire day?"

Though he originally had planned for one night, he realized he wanted more than hours. "This weekend," he said. "Saturday and Sunday. Just the two of us."

"I can't. The weekends are the busiest time for me at work. I could do Monday, if we come back Tuesday."

He'd take what he could get. "Sounds perfect. Meet me at the marina at 7:00 a.m. Monday morning. And, Maria? Pack light."

Hanging up the phone, Maria wondered what she'd just impulsively agreed to do. Ryan had been right about one thing. The chemistry between them had been fantastic.

She hadn't actually ever met a man who made her melt like that. Try as she might, she hadn't managed to get him out of her head, even though the better part of two weeks had passed.

She felt a twinge of guilt. She had been given an important task and her clock was ticking. Ryan met none of the bullet points on her list. She knew she needed to be focused on her objective, but she also knew she'd never forgive herself if she let Ryan Howard disappear from her life without even giving him a chance. Even though he represented everything she didn't want and couldn't have.

As if on cue, her cell phone rang. Her father.

"How's my princess?" he asked, his cheerful voice, as usual, making her smile. "Any luck finding Mr. Right?"

She sighed. "I'm trying, I promise. I've actually met someone I like, but I don't think he'll be a candidate."

While most women might feel a little weird discussing such things with their father, she only felt tired. Her search for a mate was all they talked about these days. And she couldn't blame him. After all, his hopefulness echoed that of all of their kind. The Drakkor depended on her, and the other remaining three females, to carry the future of their dwindling race. Especially since Doug Polacek had gone crazy and tried to attack the remaining females.

Maria had never met any of the others. The remaining small group of Drakkor had been purposely dispersed to opposite ends of the earth. When Maria had wanted to move from Green Bay to Galveston once she graduated high school, it had practically required an act of congress.

"Do you want to go over your list again?" her father asked kindly. "We can see if there are any bullet points we can discard."

"No." If she had to review that list again, she thought she might scream. "I know it by heart now anyway."

"Okay. Just thought I'd ask. You know, sweetheart…" He paused. "I know you're organized, but have you ever considered you might be going about this the wrong way? Love doesn't happen because of a list."

Pushing back a twinge of defensiveness, she inhaled. "I don't know what else to do. This is too important to simply leave to chance."

"That's what love is," he said. "But you'll need to find that out for yourself."

"I know." Immediately she thought of Ryan. If only.

"Tell me about this someone promising you met."

Suddenly, the idea of even discussing Ryan Howard with her father made her break out in a cold sweat. "Let me give it a bit more time," she said. "I haven't even gone out on a date with him."

Holding her breath, she waited for him to question her. In the past, the two of them had discussed each and every man she'd dated.

But, then again, Ryan wasn't a date. He was just someone she was going to have a short, sweet fling with.

The instant the realization occurred to her, she felt relief. Until that very second, she hadn't actually decided how she would approach this. But yes, she was going to actually take a break from her exhaustive search for a mate and allow herself to have fun with a man who rang every chime she possessed.

For once.

And furthermore, her father didn't need to know about it.

"Are you sure?" Her dad sounded hurt. "I might be able to help you decide if you even want to date him."

"No, I'm fine. So what's been going on with you?" As changes in subject went, it wasn't graceful, but she didn't have a choice.

To her relief, he followed her lead. They chatted a few more minutes about the weather in Green Bay, and then ended the call. But not before he reminded her to keep him posted if anything changed.

As always, she agreed, well aware her father had to make reports to the Drakkor Council on a monthly basis.

Before he hung up, he told her good luck on meeting someone who met the criteria on her list. As usual, she wasn't sure if he was teasing.

Thinking of her list gave her a headache. Thinking of Ryan made her entire body ache.

Her cell rang. Rhonda Thepault, Maria's best friend. They used to go out once a week together, but since Rhonda had gotten married, Maria only saw her about once every couple of months.

"I saw you *TMZ*," Rhonda gushed. "Why didn't you tell me you went out with Ryan Howard?"

Crud. Maria sighed. "We didn't actually go out. We met in a bar and went for a walk on the beach." Amended, but factually true.

"That's *all*?" Rhonda practically shrieked. "The Most Eligible Billionaire Bachelor and you didn't even think to call me?"

"Nothing happened. The paparazzi showed up, and I ran away. End of story."

"You what?" Rhonda sounded dumbfounded. "Ran away, like *jogged*? In high heels?"

"No I took them off. I ran barefoot. We were on the beach, after all."

Silence while her friend digested this. "Let me get this straight. Ryan Howard wanted you to walk with him on the beach and you bailed because of paparazzi?"

"Yep. That about sums it up."

"Maria, I need to come over there and talk some sense into you." The exasperation in Rhonda's voice made Maria smile. "You're single, you've tried several online dating sites, and you've been visiting nightclubs. All of this for the purpose of meeting a man, right?"

So far, her friend was absolutely correct. Except she didn't know the whole story. She had no idea of the reasons Maria needed to find the right man so quickly.

And since Rhonda was human, she never would.

Instead, Maria figured she'd make Rhonda happy when she told her the rest. "Yes, that's true. So I guess you'll be happy to know he's been calling me. He even stopped by at work."

"What?" Rhonda went really quiet. "Tell me you are going to go out with him. Please?"

"I am."

"Oh, thank goodness! When?"

Since Ryan wanted privacy and Rhonda really liked to talk and post to Facebook, Maria decided not to tell her specifics. "Monday, I think."

"Where is he taking you?" Rhonda's hushed tone meant she was in awe. "Off the island, or are you staying here?"

"I'm not sure," Maria lied. "But whatever we do, I'm sure we'll have a good time."

"Of course you will. How could you not?"

Maria had to laugh at that. "I promise I'll fill you in on all the details after, okay?"

Mollified, Rhonda agreed. They chatted for a few more minutes about Rhonda's job and how business had been going at the wedding chapel, and finally Maria let her friend go.

Her phone rang the second she ended the call.

"Maria, I saw you on *TMZ* tonight." Lourdes Rivera had been Maria's friend since kindergarten, up in Green Bay. Once they'd been close. These days, not so much, at least not since Maria had moved to Texas and Lourdes had gone out to conquer the world as an investigative reporter. Their lives had gone in different directions and they'd drifted apart. It seemed dating a famous person brought everyone out of the woodwork.

The instant she had the thought, Maria winced. Swallowing hard, she tried for a lighthearted tone. "You haven't called me in months and that's all you have to say?"

"Hey, I've been busy." Lourdes traveled all over the world for her job. "And now I learn you're famous and you didn't even tell me."

Maria opened her mouth to respond, but before she could, Lourdes continued.

"I can't believe you gave them the scoop," Lourdes complained. "I could have done so much more with it."

"First off, there is no scoop." Maria couldn't contain her flash of anger. "Secondly, you should know better than anyone that the gossip shows and magazines are rarely even accurate."

"*TMZ* is pretty darn accurate." Lourdes sighed. "And if you're dating a billionaire, then you could have at least called me."

"Where are you?" Maria asked. "Most times, you're not even in my part of the world."

"As it so happens, I'm in Mexico. Which is not all that far from Texas. Now tell me what's going on with you and Mr. Sexy, Ryan Howard. He doesn't seem at all your type."

"He's not," Maria reassured her friend. "He's something I wanted to get out of my system."

"Ah, I get it." Lourdes laughed, the sound confident. "I've had a few of those myself. How'd you meet?"

"Are you asking as my friend or are you interviewing me?"

"Hey, that's harsh." Lourdes sounded wounded. "Come on, Maria. Dish."

They spent the next several minutes catching up. When Maria had told her friend everything she could think of about not only Ryan, but work and her family. Everything, that is, but the way the pressure kept increasing to have a child and complete her destiny. Maria had never discussed that with her friend since Lourdes wasn't Drakkor. There were some things she didn't need to know.

Finally, Lourdes wound down with a request that Maria promise to let her do the interview if anything were to come of the relationship with Ryan. This was easy enough to do, since Maria knew nothing would.

By the time she'd finished all the telephone chatting, Maria's headache had worsened. Glancing at the bright blue sky, she realized she needed to get away from everything human, and let her dragon out to play. Soaring over the ocean never failed to lift her spirits.

Out of habit, she checked the planner she kept on her desk.

Yes. Her instinct had been right. According to the careful calendar she kept, the time had come for her to release her dragon. As usual, she'd drive to the most secluded place around Galveston, Corps Woods.

Morphing into a huge, scaly beast wasn't something she could just do anywhere. She could imagine the panic if any humans were to see. Especially since she'd been told her scales glistened all the colors of the rainbow.

She drove west on Seawall, turning right at the light onto Ferry Road, then right again at the sign that read US Coast Guard. Corps Woods was about a half mile on the right, along a narrow waterway outside a levee.

The tourists rarely came here, except for the occasional bird watchers during the spring migration.

After parking, she got out of her car, satisfied no one else was around. She walked out into the woods, taking care to move quietly so not to frighten the creatures who lived there.

The sun had reached the edge of the horizon. She always had to wait until full dark to avoid being spotted. That was okay, especially during a full moon when she flew out over the ocean.

Dragons' eyes saw the world differently than people's. Everything was lusher somehow. More vibrant and colorful, almost as if the world glowed. Though history had made them into fearsome monsters, in her dragon form Maria felt nothing but pure love and full of joy at being alive.

And the tingling of the ever-present magic, fueling her flights, lifting her wings as she climbed higher and higher into the sky.

Legend held it that this magic was the reason the other Shifters feared the Drakkor and the motive for the near extermination of their kind back in humanity's dark ages.

Magic. She loved this almost as much as she loved flying. Even though her magic was untrained, she could create things—and make them vanish with a flick of her fingers. Colors, sparkles, lights, fire and ice, none of that was beyond her capabilities. She could amuse her dragon self for hours with her undeveloped magic, especially since she'd taken care to keep her abilities alive.

These days, they were expressly forbidden to use magic on humans. Maria had frequently amused herself with dazzling displays of color and light, but only when she'd flown far out to sea, avoiding the shipping channels. As soon as she spotted a freighter or a cruise ship, no matter how far in the distance, she flew as far away in the opposite direction as she could.

Giddy at the thought of becoming her dragon self, Maria

walked into the thickest part of the woods and took a seat on an old log. There, she'd meditate while waiting for the sun to sink below the horizon. Once the light had gone, she'd begin the process of allowing her Drakkor to break free. And then she'd truly fly.

Feeling restless, agitated and uncomfortable could only mean one thing. Ryan needed to change. Inside, his wolf paced, wanting to hunt, needing out right this instant.

The sexually charged atmosphere created by Ryan craving Maria, and his frustration therewith, had his wolf howling inside him. Since the beach wasn't safe and he'd done his research, he got in his Jeep and drove to Corps Woods.

At this time of the night, with only one other car in the parking lot—a sweet, turquoise-colored Corvette—the place appeared deserted. All the tourists packed the restaurants and bars on the other side of the island and all the locals were home watching television.

Here, he could let his wolf run free safely.

He got out of the car and stretched, carefully scanning the area to make certain he hadn't been followed. His fame could be annoying, but if some erstwhile paparazzi captured him changing from man to wolf, his life would be over. The Pack Protectors would clean up the mess and Ryan Howard would disappear from his former life.

He'd often thought about this, aware it would be a blessing that they wouldn't kill him. In the old days, revealing the truth to a human had been a crime punishable by death. These days, the Protectors gave a second chance and a new life.

Ryan had no intention of starting over. He'd worked too damn hard to get where he was to give it all up over something stupid.

He could hear nothing but the sound of the seagulls

screeching, but he eyed the Corvette, aware he needed to find the other person. Only once he knew their location would he be able to make a sensible decision on where to shape-shift.

Moving with exaggerated casualness, he left the parking lot and headed out onto the walking trails. He wondered if the tourists even came out this far. From what he'd read, serious bird watchers mainly frequented this area, and only during the spring migration. Even if the odd curious visitor ventured here, he imagined that would be in the middle of the day. Now, with the sun blazing a farewell trail on the edge of the horizon, everyone had finished outdoor activities. Soon only the silver ghost of moonlight would shine on the trees and the canal.

Ryan grinned, feeling savage. A perfect place, and not too far from home. Once he got settled, he planned to seek out other Pack members so he could learn where they went to hunt. In his wolf shape, he ceased being *Person Magazine*'s Most Eligible Billionaire. Then he was only another lupine hunter, one more member of the Pack.

His wolf pushed, fighting to break free. Shaking his head, Ryan kept him confined. Until he made certain he wouldn't be seen, he couldn't take the chance.

Movement ahead of him had him ducking behind a tree, crouching low. Something big, too large to be human. He kept still while he tried to figure out what the heck it could be. From this distance, it had the shape of an elephant, which wasn't even possible. Or was it?

As he watched from his hiding place, the beast rose, spreading huge, rainbow-colored wings. And then, while Ryan gaped in disbelief, the thing leaped up and took to the sky.

He watched until it became only a speck in the dark sky. What the...? Had he really seen a dragon? He'd thought he knew every species of Shape-shifter. If there were dragons, he'd certainly never heard anyone mention them.

His wolf whined, reminding him of the reason he'd come to this isolated location.

Shaking his head yet again to try and clear it, Ryan stepped into a thicket of trees and shed his clothing. Then he got down on all fours and let his beast out.

As wolf, he'd found time ceased to exist. Or, at least, it existed differently than when he was man. As he prowled the area, led by his nose, he no longer counted time in minutes or in hours. Instead, the measured footsteps he took on the soft earth, the scent of a hare and the chase, these were his clock.

He hunted and he played, dancing with tree shadows, so in tune with the earth and his wolf he found joy in every breath.

And then, as he lazily contemplated returning to the tree stump where he'd left his human clothing, he heard the distant thump of wings and knew the dragon had returned.

Caution warred with fear. As wolf, he'd just devoured a rabbit. Would the dragon view a wolf as prey? Though his teeth were sharp and his claws swift, he knew if he were to go up against a beast of that size, he'd surely lose. So, once again, he crouched low to the ground, under a bush, and tried to make himself as small as possible.

The dragon flew low, scales glistening in the moonlight. Even as he held his breath, he couldn't help but be filled with awe at the deadly beauty of this mystical creature.

He heard it land somewhere in the trees behind him. Curious, he crept in that direction, wanting to see what kind of person the dragon would change back into.

But either he moved too slowly or the beast changed with the speed of light. Long before he reached the center of the woods, he heard the throaty rumble of the Corvette's engine.

Running full out, he headed toward the parking lot. His lope covered the ground effortlessly, but all he got for his effort was the sight of the taillights as the sports car drove away.

Chapter 4

Back home, after her shape-shifting flight, Maria felt reborn. As she caught sight of herself in a mirror in the entryway, she beamed. Her skin glowed, her eyes gleamed and she appeared transported, as if she'd experienced some sort of holiness or miracle.

Becoming her dragon had a way of doing that to her. She'd flown far and low, skirting the waves at times, taking care to avoid shipping channels and any private boats. She'd visited a pod of about twelve whales, seen dolphins and sharks and watched shooting stars reflect across the endless stretch of water.

Her journey had felt sacred, reminding her that her very existence as a dragon could be considered miraculous. Which was why she could not afford to fail at her task.

This sobering thought made her shake her head. She would succeed. She'd be fine. And now, fortified by the hours she'd spent as a dragon, she could prepare for her time with Ryan without worry or fear.

After all, taking a day or two off to have a little fun could do no harm. Once all this was over, she'd go back to her focused search. She had to admit, she had some preconceived notions of how her life, once she found The One, would go. A handsome and fickle playboy who refused to settle down wasn't one of them.

She sighed. Yet her attraction to him wouldn't be denied. She probably just needed to get him out of her system. Then she could resume her oh-so-serious search for the father of her children and the rest of her life.

Monday came quickly. To her surprise, Ryan had made no further attempts to contact her after she'd accepted his invitation. Instead of leaving her car at the marina, she had Kathleen take her, swearing her receptionist to secrecy.

"I can't believe you're going to be with Ryan Howard," the older woman said for maybe the third time. "In private, just the two of you, on a *yacht*."

Yeah, about that. Maria hadn't been sure what exactly to expect when Ryan invited her to spend a few days on his yacht. Yachts were different things to different people. For all she knew, he could pilot a perfectly restored 1960s sailboat. She'd been on one of those once and found it spectacularly beautiful. If she could, she'd live on the sea. She loved it more than land.

After they parked, Kathleen wanted to hang around to get a second look at Ryan. Firmly, Maria asked her to go home. "This is a fling," she said. "Just fun. Don't be making more of it than it is."

Kathleen rolled her eyes. "A fling with Ryan Howard is something major, no matter what you think. And I really want to get a look at his boat."

"No." And Maria wouldn't relent. The last thing she needed was Kathleen gushing and building this entire thing up to be something it wasn't. "Ryan asked for privacy, and that's what he's going to get. Now thank you for giving me a ride, but please, go ahead and head back home."

Though Kathleen grumbled, she did exactly that, though she backed out of her spot with excruciating slowness, no doubt hoping for a glimpse of Maria's date before she left.

Maria waited until Kathleen's minivan had disappeared before glancing again at the piece of paper where she'd written the slip number. As she walked out along the dock, she marveled at all the beautiful boats, looking for Ryan's yacht. Even though any boat could technically be called a yacht, she figured something owned by a multibillionaire would be over the top, ostentatious and possibly gaudy.

Instead, when she reached his slip, she found herself pleasantly surprised. The sleek boat looked brand-new and was probably sixty-five feet long. Just small enough that he could captain it himself without a crew if he wanted, but not so small it couldn't handle the ocean waves out in open water.

Though she seriously doubted that they'd be leaving the gulf.

"Lazzara LXS 64," she read. A shiny thing of fiber-glass beauty, with huge windows, she figured such a yacht would cost over two million dollars. With her inexplicable need to get closer to the water, boats were her weakness, her hobby, and she never missed a boat show if she could help it. She'd shopped them all, even the yachts like this that she couldn't afford in a hundred years. That didn't matter to her. She could always dream.

She'd always loved the sea and anything that got her closer to the waves made her happy. The salt spray, the seagulls, pelicans and, most of all, the whales and dolphins. She loved soaring over the vast expanse of water in her dragon form. Though smaller birds feared her, the huge whales flipped their massive tails at her in reproach or hello as she flew overhead.

As she approached, Ryan appeared from down inside the yacht. "Welcome." The warmth of his smile started a slow burn inside her.

"This is nice," she said, meaning it. "I'm assuming you don't have to employ a crew."

"No, that's why I chose this one for this trip," he told her. "I have a couple of boats, but on those I have to hire a captain and crew. I use those because when I entertain large groups of people I can't be distracted by piloting the boat. But this time, it's just going to be the two of us."

"Even though you might be…distracted?" She couldn't resist teasing him, loving the way heat instantly darkened his eyes.

"Even so."

"As long as you're sure we'll be safe." She let her smile widen, even as she raked her gaze boldly over him. "While I have no doubt you are a capable captain, since we're getting this out of our systems, I plan to be more than a little distracting."

Something intense flared between them. "No worries." He sounded confident as he held out a hand. "Come aboard. Would you like a tour?"

She nodded, smiling back. "I'd love one." Placing her hand in his, she felt a jolt as their bodies connected. She allowed him to pull her up onto his boat, marveling at how, even now, with his hair windblown and wearing an old faded T-shirt and khaki shorts, he managed to appear like a Norse god rather than a rich businessman. Her mouth dry, she fought to keep from saying or doing something stupid.

When she looked up, he stood so close she could feel his body heat. Her heart caught in her throat as all of her senses leaped to life.

"Come on," he said, his sensual grin telling her he'd guessed her thoughts. "Let me show you the rest."

Polished teak trim highlighted the handrails, along with the floor in the small den and the cabinetry in the galley and bathroom. Everything was luxuriously appointed, including pewter fixtures and stained-glass light coverings.

The salon had a dark satin wood finished interior with wooden floors and a buttery leather sectional. Along with the 42-inch flat screen TV, she loved the wet bar with Sub-Zero refrigerated drawers. There were pleated fabric shades and a retractable sunroof.

"This looks brand-new," she mused. "Did you have it built for you?"

"No." He grinned. "But I did buy it new, even though it's last year's model. I'm the first and only owner. The sole owner."

His infectious pride made her grin back. "I like it," she announced.

"Oh, you haven't seen anything yet," he said. "Come with me."

The helm, which shared deck space with the salon, had a plush seat and a glass instrument panel. The side window opened to allow a view down the side deck. Everything had been trimmed in a rich, dark wood.

"It's got three staterooms and three heads," he announced. "Or bathrooms, in case you don't like the word. The galley has all stainless-steel appliances, a huge refrigerator, a four-burner stove, and even a dishwasher. It's made for some serious vacationing. Cookware, bakeware, utensils and even knives came standard."

His pride was infectious.

"You sound like a boat salesman," she teased.

"This was my first yacht," he replied, somewhat sheepishly. "While I own a couple, one never forgets the first."

Touched, she gave in to impulse and leaned in and kissed his jaw. His scent rocked her—sea breezes and spice—all masculine and unlike any man she'd been with before.

Lazily, he turned his head so their lips brushed. He teased her with this slow kiss, promising so much more. When he moved away, she found herself breathless.

He didn't seem to notice. "I'll show you the rest of the boat later. You can either wait here or go up on deck. There are some loungers and a table with chairs. I'm going to get this baby started and take us out."

"I'd like to watch," she told him. "So I'll go up. Unless…" Feeling bold, she nudged him with her hip. "I can come stand by you while you steer."

"Not this time." His smile took the sting from his words. "You were right. You're too damn distracting."

Taking care not to show how thrilling she found his words, she sighed. "All right then. I'll head out."

"Great. I'll let you know when you can join me."

Ryan couldn't tear his eyes from Maria as she strolled away. She wore some sort of shapeless cover-up over what he could tell was a red swimsuit. He could only imagine what the sight of her in a bikini would do to him. Even now, from just a little verbal sparring and a quick kiss, she'd aroused him to the point of pain.

Only once she'd disappeared from his view did he release the breath he'd been holding. Around her, he could hardly function, and he needed all his concentration to get his boat out of the slip and then the harbor.

Going through the motions, he soon had his twin Volvo Penta D-13 engines running. He made short work of unhooking his tie-downs, and soon he had backed out and turned to head in the right direction.

Pleased, he almost wished Maria was beside him, for a celebratory high five or, even better, another kiss.

Just thinking of recapturing her soft lush mouth with his heated his blood. He shook his head, aware he needed to get in control of this insane attraction so he could explore it at his leisure. Until then, it'd be prudent to wait until they'd reached open water before even looking at his beautiful guest.

They motored past the last sandbars, the cranes standing on one leg, the pelicans arching their long necks as they decorated the weathered piers. Taking care to stay out of the way of the larger ships, he pointed his boat toward the open water, feeling free, as he always did when out on the sea.

"Permission to enter?" Maria popped her head in the doorway, her husky voice teasing.

"Sure, come on in." He made a concentrated effort to not watch her, keeping his gaze fixed on the water outside. "The difficult part is over, now I just play Avoid the Tankers until we're past all the shipping lanes."

Several huge freighters dotted the horizon, waiting for their turn to enter the shipping channel. He navigated them past these, intent and fierce, his pulse thrumming in his neck as he kept his desire under control.

Behind him, Maria prowled the salon restlessly. Überconscious of her, he refused to glance back, letting the anticipation build in him.

"I had my chef prepare several meals in advance for us," he said, more to make conversation than anything else.

"Your chef?" She laughed. "Forget I said that. Of course you have a chef."

"Not full-time. But once you agreed to come out to sea with me I had him prepare a few things. We have to eat, and I don't cook."

"Me, either," she said, surprising him. "Though I confess I'm surprised you didn't ask."

"What kind of host would I be, to ask my guest to cook for me?" He shook his head, finally glancing at her. "I would never do anything so rude."

"Good." Her wry smile had his heart thumping. "Because heaven help the man who had to eat my cooking."

Unable to tell if she was joking or not, he turned his attention back to their course, picking up the pace until they were cruising along at thirty knots, which was pretty damn fast for a boat this big.

Finally, they were clear of everything. Nothing but water, as far as the eye could see. He slowed their speed, setting the automatic pilot and fighting the urge to turn and pull Maria up against him, bury himself deep inside her right here and right now.

Inside, his inner wolf began to pace, the edge of constant desire making him savage and restless.

Damn. Ryan had never had a woman affect him this way. He wanted her something fierce, but she merited more than a quick release of driving need. She deserved candles and moonlight and romance and wine. A plush bed in a luxurious stateroom, a silky negligee and tenderness. He had it all planned, the seduction. He would not act like a rutting bull. Even though his body wanted to.

"This thing will drive itself for a while," he said, managing a casual and hopefully friendly smile. "Let's go up on deck and take a look around."

With desire on a slow simmer, and feeling unaccountably nervous, Maria watched Ryan control the boat, glad he focused on the water rather than her. Every time the man directed that intense gaze on her, she melted inside.

Now that they were completely alone and heading for

the open water, she briefly wondered if her decision to in-dulge her craving for him had been wise. No doubt her fa-ther wouldn't approve. But then, what father would?

Truth be told, she'd grown exceedingly weary of doing the right thing. Sure, she understood her destiny, but the weight of the task she'd been charged with often felt too heavy to bear.

Some time off to recharge her batteries might be just what she needed. A fling, she reminded herself for the twentieth time since she'd decided to do this. Nothing more than a fling. Fast and fun, no strings. Back to her life, to the real world, the next day.

This kind of thinking had nearly gotten her into trou-ble before. She suspected this time would be no exception. Still, she realized she didn't care. Something told her it would be worth it.

"Hey." Ryan's voice made her blink and come out of her reverie. "Are you all right? You're not feeling queasy or anything, are you?"

"I'm good." She managed what she hoped was an easy smile. "And I've never been seasick. As far as I know, I'm fine with the waves and ocean and boats."

"Good to know." His slow and steady gaze felt like a caress. She shivered, realizing the anticipation was a kind of foreplay. Even the rocking motion of the yacht as it cut through the waves felt sensual.

"I asked you if you wanted to go topside and take a look around. With this kind of weather, the view ought to be breathtaking."

She wished she had the courage to tell him what she re-ally wanted to do—go down to that elegant master bedroom, disrobe and make wild, passionate love on that huge bed.

But then it would be over. She wasn't sure she was ready for that, at least, not yet. They'd just set off, after all.

Part of her thought she should go for it. Casual sex should be just that—casual. Simple as that.

But she knew there would be nothing casual about the way Ryan made love to her. Nothing casual at all.

Better to wait, to prolong the anticipation.

She'd been buzzing with desire ever since climbing aboard the boat. Every look, every accidental touch, merely added fuel to the fire.

Upstairs, the sea breeze kept the sun from feeling too hot.

"I've dropped anchor. Do you fish?" Grinning, Ryan produced a couple of really long fishing poles.

She thought of how she usually fished, using her razor-sharp dragon claws and swooping down to snatch them right out of the water. Human fishing would never be able to compete with that. "I might have caught fish a time or two," she said. "But if you don't mind, I'll just relax and watch you."

She'd been planning to lie out and catch some sun once they were clear of the other boats. Underneath an over-size T-shirt cover-up, she wore her favorite bikini in red. She felt both nerves and anticipation as to how he'd react at the sight of her in it. The swimsuit barely covered her, and yet somehow managed to look elegant and sexy. It had been expensive and, as far as she was concerned, worth every penny.

Of necessity, Maria had learned to become expert at showcasing her…assets. This went against everything inside her quiet, would-be modest self, but it had been drilled into her that she had no choice. If she wanted to attract a mate, she had to gain his notice. So she tried.

Even so, she knew she wasn't actually good at it. Luckily, men didn't seem to care.

This was actually the first time she'd truly wanted a

man to notice her. Which, in the long run, didn't bode well for her ultimate mission.

Right now she refused to think about anything but the here and now. She wanted Ryan Howard, a man she knew she had nothing in common with, no real future. From the single night they'd spent making love, she knew they were good together. Clearly, since one night hadn't been enough. Maybe once she did this, spent enough time with him to get him out of her system, she could go on with her life and her search for The One.

Heart pounding in her throat, she removed her cover-up, feeling naked in the tiny bikini. She heard his swift intake of breath and found she couldn't even look at him, even though she was so aroused the triangles of fabric hurt her nipples.

They came together as if they'd never been apart. Touching him, she felt herself expand, as though when their bodies joined, the universe became magnified.

Amazed, astounded, so full of joy her eyes stung, she gave herself over to him. Again and again and again, they moved together, a mating dance of passion and purpose, something she knew she never wanted to end.

She flew and soared, a dragon lifting in the air, even though she never left her body. He gave her fireworks and stars and as she clenched her body around his hardness, the thought came to her lovemaking like this might have ruined her for anyone else. A second later, her practical nature asserted itself, chiding her for considering such foolishness.

And then Ryan moved inside her and she forgot to think at all.

While Maria slept in his bed, a soft smile on her lovely face, Ryan slipped out from under the sheets and headed up to the main deck. There, he watched the water, enjoying the way the moonlight caressed the waves. He felt safe here, isolated from land and people. Though he always looked for whales, he'd never seen one, though there'd been plenty of dolphins.

He thought of the other night, when he'd seen the dragon, and found himself watching the cloudless sky. Nothing but stars and black velvet. Chiding himself for his foolishness, he found himself wishing Maria would wake and join him.

She'd been everything he'd imagined she'd be and more. Fierce and fiery, she gave as well as took, and their bodies had fit together as if they'd been made for each other.

After their explosive lovemaking, he'd actually let himself fall asleep holding her, something he never did anymore and hadn't done since college.

Somehow, he'd thought this time with her would slake his ever-present hunger for her. Instead, he felt like an addict, craving more.

Shaking his head at his middle-of-the-night flight of fancy, a movement close to the water caught his eye. His heart began pounding as he got to his feet, gripped the rail and peered intently at the dark water.

Would he finally see the whale he'd longed to see?

And then, the surface of the water exploded. A huge form burst from beneath the surface, arcing toward the sky.

But this was no whale. Not even close. While Ryan stared in disbelief, the dragon launched up, a huge fish caught in one giant claw.

Ryan shrank back against the side of his boat, praying the beast hadn't seen him. This one looked larger than the one he'd seen before, and its scales didn't glimmer with as many colors. Instead, the muddy green-and-brown color made it blend better with the ocean. The expression it wore also seemed ominous, somehow. Still, he figured he would be safe as long as the dragon didn't spot a human.

Damn. This was the second time he'd seen such an unbelievable sight. After the first incident, he'd almost managed to convince himself he'd imagined it. Now, he could no longer do that. Who knew such creatures even existed?

He made a quick mental note to do some research once he got back to land and kept his eye on the dragon, just in case it decided to come for his boat.

Luckily, the beast took off, flying toward open water with its prey still flopping in one claw. Ryan stared in the direction it had gone, long after it disappeared.

"Ryan?" Maria's voice was husky with sleep. "Where are you?"

"Out here."

A moment later she appeared, wearing only his T-shirt, her dusky skin illuminated by moonlight. In reaction, his body stirred. "Couldn't sleep?"

He shook his head, debating whether or not to tell her what he'd seen. Ultimately, he decided against it. Though her aura told him she was some kind of Shape-shifter, neither would be inclined to reveal their true nature, not without a committed relationship.

And he didn't do committed relationships.

According to Maria, neither did she. Which meant this would work out perfectly, right?

"I find the sea peaceful," he said, rather than answering her question. "Also, I'm always trying to see a whale. So far, I haven't had any luck."

She tilted her head, considering. "I know there were actually two orca sightings in the gulf. But to see the large whales, you'd need to go south, closer to Mexico."

Knowing he couldn't ask her about dragons, he nodded. "I take it you've researched this."

"Actually, I have. I love the ocean and all of its inhabitants. At one point I was going to A&M in Galveston to become a marine biologist."

Fascinating. "I didn't see that coming. How'd you go from that to a wedding chapel owner?"

"Simple. I wanted to own my own business. And there are way more limitations on marine biology than I realized. So I quit school, one year short of getting my degree, and here I am." She eyed him. "What about you, Mr. Billionaire Playboy? How'd you get to do whatever it is you do?"

"You really don't know?"

Her chuckle was answer enough. "I take it I should."

"Didn't you even read the magazine after you found out who I was?" Strangely he felt equal measures of hurt and amusement.

"No. I didn't think I needed to. I'd much rather get to know someone in person."

He couldn't help but pull her in for a kiss then. "I like you," he told her, meaning it.

"I like you, too."

At her sweet words, he felt a small premonition of warning. Things were going too well. She was his ideal woman, everything he could want, including claiming not to want a relationship. Why then did he feel as if the hammer was about to come down?

The idyllic time on the boat went way too fast, as good times often do. All too soon they pulled back into the harbor and toward the marina.

Maria knew enough about herself to understand that once she got home, she would have regrets. Tons of regrets. Almost the way a junkie repents the first time trying a drug, she should never have explored Ryan Howard. One taste of him had potentially ruined her for everyone else.

Not good, especially for a woman who felt as though she always had a ticking clock hanging over her and needed to find her mate soon.

But she refused to feel regret that their time together was over.

After Ryan had parked the boat back in his slip, she went below and grabbed her bag. Rejoining him topside, she accepted his hand as he helped her onto the dock. This time, she ignored the immediate tingle the contact brought and summoned up her friendliest smile.

"Thanks for an amazing time," she told him, her tone a bit too bright. If he noticed, he gave no sign.

"Do you have a ride home?" he asked.

Holding up her cell phone, she shook her head. "I'm about to call now."

"Don't. I'll drop you off."

Briefly, she considered declining, for the foolish reason that she wasn't sure she wanted him to know where she lived. But, she realized, he'd agreed to the parameters they'd set and wouldn't be dropping by unannounced or anything. "Thank you," she said. "I'd appreciate that."

When they pulled up in front of her modest home, she realized belatedly she wasn't sure how to say goodbye. Should she kiss his cheek or his mouth, or only shake hands? Since this had been a one-time, casual encounter and she'd never done anything like it before, she had no idea what would be acceptable.

So, instead, she did nothing. As soon as he put the car in park, she opened her door and hopped out. "Thank you so much," she began, but Ryan wasn't looking at her. He stared past her, his expression suddenly thunderous.

Turning to look, she saw a man climbing out of her bedroom window.

"Do you know him?" Ryan asked, his voice low and urgent.

"No. I think I'm being robbed." She dug in her purse for her phone so she could call 911.

But Ryan didn't wait. Pulling out a pistol, he took off running after the intruder.

As she watched, her heart pounding, the man shape-shifted into a dragon. Ryan squeezed off a few shots, but they were too late and did nothing to stop the dragon from launching himself into the sky.

Chapter 5

Stunned, Maria watched as the Drakkor flew away. All she could think of was how what he'd done was in direct violation of every law set forth by the Drakkor Council. He'd changed in front of Ryan, and while she knew Ryan was Pack, this Drakkor intruder had no way of knowing.

Plus, it was broad daylight. Anyone could have seen. Did this mean Polacek had somehow escaped from prison?

Stunned, she looked back at Ryan. He, too, stared after the dragon until the huge beast disappeared into the clouds.

"Did you…" He cleared his throat. "Did you see that?"

"I did." Unable to keep the anger and fear from her voice, she folded her arms across her chest.

"What was it?"

She took a deep breath. "You'd better come inside. Those gunshots are sure to attract attention."

He stared at her. "After all that, the one thing you're worried about is my gun?"

"I didn't say that. I'm wondering how many others saw him and, worse, what will happen if someone got a picture."

Ryan followed her into the house without saying another word. She placed her purse on the little table near the front door and tried to collect her scattered thoughts so she could figure out what to say. She knew she had to choose her words carefully.

After holstering his pistol, Ryan paced the length of her small living room. "I should call someone, don't you think? I mean, that thing is flying loose over Galveston."

"That *thing* is a Drakkor," she interrupted. "And who would you call, the Pack Protectors?"

That stopped him in his tracks. "You know what I am?"

"Of course. You wear your aura just like we all do. I saw your wolf the first time we made love."

He narrowed his eyes and studied her. "Okay. Touché. Since we're exchanging personal information, tell me what manner of Shifter you are."

"That's not necessary." Her tone let him know she refused to budge on this. "We're not in a committed relationship, so there's no need. Plus, I thought you wanted to discuss the Drakkor we just witnessed."

"How do you know what it's called?"

Now came the tricky part. "Because I've studied." Not entirely a lie. She went to her bookshelf and pulled out a well-worn book. "Here. Take a look at this."

Accepting the heavy hardback, he carried it over to the kitchen table. *"History of Shape-shifters,"* he read. "This looks like something we would have learned in school when we were young."

"It probably was." She glanced out the window. "The Drakkor are a very old and venerated people. However, that still doesn't explain what that one was doing breaking into my house."

"Or the fact that he broke every law of our kind by changing into a dragon like that."

Grimly, she nodded. "Broad daylight. It will have to be reported. By the way, why do you carry a gun?"

"It's Texas. I have my concealed handgun license. Maybe me shooting at it will make that Drakkor think twice before coming back."

"Maybe."

Ryan began paging through the book. "Here we go. The Drakkor."

While he read what was admittedly a brief and incomplete article, she hurried to her bedroom to see if she could figure out what this intruder might have taken.

Everything appeared to be exactly the way she'd left it, her bed still perfectly made, her clothes hanging in her closet. She checked her dresser drawers, but her neatly folded underwear looked untouched. The same for her T-shirts and pajamas. Even her jewelry box didn't seem to have been rifled through.

"What did he steal?" Ryan asked from the doorway.

"That's just it. I don't know." Delayed reaction had set in and she realized tears pricked the back of her eyes. Horrified, especially since she didn't cry, she took several deep breaths and wrestled her emotions under control.

Good. Now she had to call her father and report what had just happened.

"You need to leave," she said, aware her brusque tone and dismissal would seem abrupt, but beyond caring. "I'd like to make some phone calls."

He studied her for a few seconds before slowly nodding. "All right. But first, I want to check and make sure everything is locked up tight. Do you have a burglar alarm?"

"No."

"I'll have one installed first thing tomorrow," he said.

Under any other circumstances, she might have argued. But right this instant, all she could do was nod. "Fine. Now please go."

He didn't move. "You can't honestly expect me to leave you alone after someone broke into your house? I think you at least need to call the police."

"And tell them what? That a Drakkor broke in but didn't steal anything?"

Again Ryan went silent. "Do you know what that person wanted? You do, don't you? That's why you don't find the entire thing absurd."

"It's frightening," she protested. "But something that needs to be handled internally."

"By who?" He took a step closer, his gaze intense. "The Drakkor Council? Is that what you are, Maria Miranda? A Drakkor?"

Frustration eclipsed her terror. "Ryan, please. Leave." She pointed at the door. "We had a good time together, but it's time to go back to our regular lives. Mine doesn't involve you, and yours doesn't include me, so please go."

Apparently this finally got through to him. Stone-faced, he shook his head and stalked to the doorway. "Have a good life, Maria. Stay safe."

As he stepped through the doorway, she braced herself, certain he'd slam the door. But he only closed it behind him. A moment later, she heard the sound of his car starting and listened as he drove off.

Then she hurried to lock the door and check every single window. Once she was certain her home was secured tightly, she called her father.

"Who could it have been?" he exclaimed, once she relayed what had occurred. "Doug Polacek's the only one crazy enough to do something like that, and he's in prison."

"Maybe you'd better check and make sure. He might have broken out."

"That would be horrible."

She took a deep breath. "What would be worse is if there's another insane Drakkor running around. We'd have to explore the possibility that insanity is spreading in our males, sort of like the disease that killed most of our females."

Silence while her father digested this. When he spoke again, his somber tone told her he understood the ramifications of either scenario. "The council will have to be notified."

"I would think so." Oddly enough, this time she used a calm, rational tone to try and soothe him rather than the other way around. "Whoever this is, he's violating ancient law. If he keeps this up, he'll destroy our entire way of living."

"The Council will be made aware. Plus, I think they need to increase the guard on Polacek, especially if this Drakkor is his accomplice. I'm sure they'll notify the Pack Protectors, as well."

Thinking of Ryan, she found herself gripping the phone way too tightly. "The Pack Protectors? I know they're helping keep us safe. Are there any here in Galveston or in the Houston area?"

"I'm sure there are. Houston is a big city. And you know they've been working closely with us ever since Polacek captured a few of their women. Only the fact that there are so few Drakkor left has kept them from exterminating him. I think that might be about to change if this sort of nonsense continues."

Maria shuddered. "I'm going to need some sort of guard."

"And you'll have it," her father promised. "I'll have the Protectors send some people immediately."

Though she had her doubts about how werewolves would fare against a magical Drakkor, she kept those to herself. She didn't want to worry her father any more than she had to.

That night, she tossed and turned, haunted by dream images of a magical battle raging in the sky while in her Drakkor form. Even though she usually didn't get up until six, after deciding she'd been staring at the ceiling long enough, she went ahead and rose at five.

Antsy and restless, she showered, dressed, ate a healthy breakfast of hardboiled eggs and an avocado, and went in to the office early.

Going through her follow-up folder, she checked out all the messages from the day before. After bringing up her calendar on her computer, she compared it with the day planner she kept on paper. Everything matched. Today promised to be a relatively quiet day, which would enable her to get caught up.

Shortly before nine, Kathleen came in and, after getting her desk ready, appeared in Maria's doorway.

"Anything interesting happen while I was gone?" Maria asked, bracing herself for a barrage of questions about how her trip with Ryan had gone.

Instead, Kathleen appeared really uneasy. Worried, even.

"Well, yes." She shifted her weight from one foot to the other. "While you were out, you had a visitor." Kathleen's voice contained a hint of nervousness, unusual for her. "A man. Nice looking, in a professional sort of way. He wasn't here to talk about planning a wedding or anything, and when I asked him if I could tell you what his visit was in regard to, he gave me the most chilling smile."

Strange. "Did he ever answer?"

"Yes." If anything, Kathleen sounded even more disturbed. "He wrote down one word, which makes no sense. He flat-out refused to elaborate, either. When I did a Google search on it, I learned it meant a mythical beast, like a dragon."

Maria froze, her blood turning to ice. Though she already knew, she had to ask anyway. "What was the word?"

"Drakkor," Kathleen answered. "I'm not entirely sure what this guy was getting at, but I didn't get a good feeling at all."

Heart sinking, Maria had a sneaking suspicion. "Did he leave his name?"

"No. He said you'd know."

Maria didn't, but she had an awful, horrible feeling. Doug Polacek must have somehow escaped captivity. "Thanks, Kathleen. Would you mind closing my door? I need to make a few private phone calls."

"Okay." The receptionist hesitated. "Maria, is everything all right?"

"Of course it is." Maria managed a laugh, though it didn't sound even slightly amused. "Don't let that weirdo bother you. If you see him again, call the police."

"I will. But I have to say I'm worried about you. First you disappear with a famous playboy for a fling, which is not like you at all. Now some strange man shows up with a cryptic message. Do you think the two might be related?"

"You watch too much *Dateline* and *48 Hours*," Maria teased. "Everything is just fine."

"Okay. But tell me, do you understand why that man left that message with just that word? You didn't seem all that surprised."

"I was. And no, I don't understand. Not at all," Maria lied. She had a pretty good idea that her visitor had left her some sort of threat, relating to the Drakkor who'd broken in to her house. What she had to figure out was why.

As soon as Kathleen closed the office door, Maria again dialed her father. Once she relayed what had happened, he cursed.

"What?" she asked. "What do you know about this?"

"You know—" he sounded furious "—I've been meaning to tease you since I saw you on television with that rich guy. But now I think that must be how you were located."

"Located? By who?"

She could actually hear him swallow.

"Polacek," he said. "I've just received a phone call telling me that Polacek escaped."

A chill went through her. "When?"

"Two days ago. Why on earth no one thought to warn us sooner, I have no idea. Our soldiers are attempting to locate him. The Pack Protectors are amassing a special unit to help us. We're trying to capture him and bring him in. He's gone rogue again."

"Rogue?" While she knew the term, she wasn't certain how it applied in this instance. "What do you mean?"

Her father sighed. "He no longer cares about our laws or traditions. In fact, we believe he doesn't give a damn if he lives or dies. That had to have been him who broke into your house."

Polacek. For the last several years, even hearing the name had sent dread coiling through her. She knew what she'd been told, how he refused to believe he—like all Drakkor men, apparently—was sterile. He'd been on a feverish search to impregnate a woman, any woman, ever since.

"I know what he's about, but why? What happened to him to make him do this?"

"His story doesn't matter. He's an insane serial killer.

He captured, raped and murdered several women. Beyond that, I don't know the details. I get tired of all the attention criminals get."

She knew this much. Before the Drakkor figured out that the disease that took most of the women had also rendered the men sterile, Doug Polacek had convinced himself he would be the savior. Met with repeated failure, he'd begun abducting and imprisoning Shifter women. He'd repeatedly raped and abused them and if they didn't conceive, he'd killed them.

Maria closed her eyes briefly. "I agree with you. This kind of evil happens too much among humans. I would have hoped the Drakkor wouldn't be capable of such things."

"Unfortunately, wickedness exists among all species."

"How did he escape?"

"That, I don't know. I believe he had not only a magical spell keeping him bound, but several Pack Protector guards, as well."

"He must be powerful then." All Drakkor were gifted with magical ability.

"I fear he is. And there's more." Her father's grim tone made her swallow hard. "The Pack Protectors believe he's going after the remaining Drakkor females."

Of which she was one. Which meant she was in danger.

"The other women are in hiding. I think you should consider this, too. He knows where you are, since you've been dating such a high-profile man."

Feeling sick, at first she couldn't respond. She took a deep breath. "He's here, in Galveston." She tried not to panic, on the verge of failing. "He must have seen me on that gossip show."

"You need to leave. Staying there is no longer safe."

For one second, she was tempted.

"This is my life," she argued. "I love my house, my business. I've worked hard. How can I let some crazy man take that away?"

"You have no choice. You know that. None of this is about you, but about our people's future. Come home. At least until Doug Polacek is captured."

"I'll think about it," Maria said, her stomach still churning. "I need a couple of hours to figure things out."

"Don't take too long," her father ordered. "You being there is no longer safe. If I don't hear from you in half an hour, I'm sending someone to collect you and bring you here to Green Bay."

After ending the call, Maria covered her face with her hands. Unlike males, female Drakkor weren't encouraged to develop their magical abilities since it was believed they had a higher purpose. Clearly, she wouldn't be capable of defending herself against an insane and powerful Drakkor wizard like Polacek. What her father said made sense. She wasn't safe. Especially since Polacek clearly knew where to find her.

But to leave this? The entire life she'd built and loved. As long as it was only temporary. Because the way it looked right now, she saw no alternative. No matter how much she hated the idea, she would need to go into hiding.

While going home to stay with her father in Wisconsin probably made the most sense, every fiber of her being resisted the idea. She had a healthy savings account. Surely she could come up with something else.

Getting up from her desk, she opened her door and managed to smile at Kathleen. "I'm not feeling well," she said, only partially lying. "I'm going to go home and lie down. Can you handle anything that comes up the rest of today?"

"Of course I can." Kathleen peered at her with concern.

"You do look a little feverish. Did you get your flu shot this year?"

"Back in November," Maria answered. Though flu season had ended a few months ago, Kathleen constantly worried about catching it. "Call me if anything comes up that you can't deal with."

"Will do."

Driving home, Maria knew she had to hammer out a quick plan. Since she couldn't drive and write, she went over a few options out loud, discarding every one of them.

As she pulled into her driveway, her cell phone rang. Ryan. She knew she shouldn't talk to him. He didn't need to be involved in any of this craziness. Even though she couldn't stop thinking about him or wanting him, the time had come to cut him out of her life.

But just like everything else she knew she should do, everything inside her resisted. Talk about foolish.

Ryan Howard, billionaire playboy and sexpot, could be a poster man for being the opposite of what she wanted and needed in a mate. She'd made sure to double- and triple-check her list, just in case there were a few items she could eliminate.

There had been, but even so, Ryan would not be a good fit. Even if he wanted to be. For starters, he was rich and famous and constantly in the spotlight. He wasn't the type of man who'd ever be content to live under the radar, unnoticed except by those closest to him. Used to being fawned over and catered to, he'd never be able to put anyone else's needs over his.

Like the kind of husband she wanted. She'd made her list years ago, adding and deleting qualities as time went on. She needed someone quiet, anonymous, someone who had deep ties to the community and his family. Someone who'd be a great dad and a supportive husband. A man who not only would make her laugh and treat her as if she was precious, but a man who'd rock her world in bed.

Okay, she admitted, Ryan did do one of those things.

Uncertain, she let the call go to voice mail, lost in her own thoughts. Due to her destiny, her life hadn't been easy, but she'd made the best of it, choosing a place to live that made her happy and opening her own business in an industry she loved.

At first, her inability to find the right man hadn't bothered her. She'd loved her life, and refused to allow her father and the Drakkor Council to ruin that. Then, as she'd celebrated each birthday, still alone, still childless, the knowledge that she was the constant focus of all the remaining Drakkor had begun to feel like a sword hanging over her head. The only thing that made her feel better was that the other females, save one, were also childless. The lone pregnant woman was mentioned with the sort of reverence reserved for deities.

As her thirtieth birthday approached, Maria had asked to meet the other Drakkor women. She'd had the idea that they could support and help each other. Instead, she'd been told that they would not be allowed to occupy the same space and must be kept as far apart as possible.

She hadn't understood. Until she'd learned of Doug Polacek, the idea that someone might want to hurt, capture or exterminate them had never occurred to her. Even now, knowing he was out there, she still didn't understand his thought process.

Of course, sane rarely understood crazy.

Even worse, in the middle of all this, she was supposed to locate a man she could love and who would love her in return. Really? Impossible. Yet this mystical, magical union was the only way she could conceive. Which she must do so the Drakkor would not die out.

On top of all that, every single day, sometimes more than once, she fought the urge to pick up the phone and call Ryan. Or worse, show up at his beach house so they could make wild, passionate love.

Spending more time with him had been a mistake. Rather than slaking her appetite for him, she only craved him more.

As if he knew she'd been thinking about him, the phone rang again. Ryan. He wasn't giving up.

This time, Maria picked up. She figured now would be as good a time as any to end things with him once and for all. The only way she was ever going to be able to focus on another man was to get Ryan out of her life.

Hoping she sounded normal, she answered.

"Maria? Are you all right? I just heard that crazy Drakkor has escaped," Ryan said, his tone low and urgent. "He may have been the one we saw breaking into your house. My friend who's a Pack Protector says they're putting together a Special Forces unit to find him."

"I already heard." She decided to fill him in on what her father wanted her to do. He'd wonder why she'd disappeared otherwise. "Even worse, I've got to leave town and go into hiding."

"What?" She'd shocked him. "Maria, what aren't you telling me? What does this crazy guy want with you?"

Though she knew she should keep her mouth shut, since she'd involved him she figured he had a right to know. "Your guess the other day was correct. I'm Drakkor. If you did your research, you'll know I'm one of the few remaining Drakkor females. Doug Polacek wants to rape me and impregnate me or, if that fails, which it will, he will kill me."

Stunned silence while he digested her words. Then he cursed. "I don't understand, but I get why you need to go into hiding. I'd like to help. Do you have any idea where you are going to go?"

Grateful for his immediate acceptance of such a bizarre scenario, she swallowed. Good thing he was a Shifter since there was no way a human would have even begun to understand. "That's the tricky part. I'm not entirely sure. I'm working on coming up with a plan now."

"Stay put. I'm on my way over there," he said, his tone brooking no argument.

"Wait—" She started to argue, but he'd ended the call.

If she admitted the truth to herself, she felt relieved to have someone else to share all of this with.

Wandering into her kitchen, she made herself a cup of tea. She knew she should start packing, but couldn't motivate herself yet. "I don't think I can do this anymore," she said out loud, even though no one was there to hear. Needing the comfort of some sort of familiarity, she got out her worn list and began trying to go over the bullet points. But she couldn't focus. Not now.

The doorbell rang, making her jump. Though she knew Polacek wouldn't do something as civilized as ring the bell, she still peered through the peephole.

When she realized Ryan stood on her front doorstep, she unlocked the dead bolt and let him inside.

As soon as she closed the door behind him and turned the lock, he pulled her into his arms. Startled, she held herself stiffly. He smelled the same—of sea breezes and spice, and felt just as wonderful, but she didn't know if her overloaded brain could take one more thing.

"Come stay with me at my beach house," he said. "I can hire security and make sure you're protected."

Shaking her head, she pulled away. "How is that safe? You have paparazzi stalking your every move. It wouldn't be too long before my picture was on *TMZ* or something.

I've already had two friends call because apparently I've been on TV. Even my father knew about it. Publicity would make it really easy for Polacek to find me."

He shrugged. "So? I told you, I'll hire security. He won't be able to get through them."

"But he will. I take it you didn't finish reading that book about the Drakkor. They—we—have magic. Some more than others. And this rogue Drakkor apparently has quite a bit of it." She walked the short distance to her sofa, and dropped down onto it. "So, thank you for offering, but I'm going to have to decline."

He eyed her, his shuttered expression revealing nothing of his thoughts. "If Drakkor have magic, why can't you use your own magic to protect yourself?"

Ah, the sixty-million-dollar question. "Because I don't know how. The men train for years to strengthen their magic. The females don't." She didn't tell him the rest of it. No one thought the few Drakkor women remaining needed to waste time perfecting their magic. They needed to breed, nothing more, nothing less.

Thinking about it like this made her realize it was wrong. Still, now was a little too late to start pondering the injustices in her people's way of life.

"What about the ocean? We can go out on my yacht," he began.

Again, she shook her head. "That's fine for a vacation, but Drakkor can fly. We'd be sitting ducks on a boat all alone in the middle of the ocean."

He considered her, his blue eyes dark. "You sound like you've given up."

"No, I haven't," she protested. "Not at all." If only he knew. She couldn't give up. Not with the entire future of her people riding on her and her as-yet unconceived child. "My father wants me to go stay with him in Green Bay."

"Wisconsin? That's too far."

"I know. But there are several elder Drakkor there. Together, they'd be able to combine their magic and make a strong enough shield to ward off any threat."

Crossing his arms, he studied her. "I think a better idea would be for them to train you in magic. You say you have some inside you. Learn how to use it. That way, you can handle anything. You won't have to rely on anyone else."

The idea was brilliant, but she knew since every single Drakkor had become so consumed with the idea of the females procreating, the Council would find this plan ridiculous. Now she could see it wasn't. She was so much more than a breeding vessel.

"You know what? You're right. I'll bring that up with my father when I get there." She took a deep breath, steeling herself for what she had to do. "Ryan, you need to leave. There's too much going on and you complicate things. The time we've had together has been amazing, but I don't think you need to try and see me again."

Chapter 6

Maria held her breath, waiting to shatter until after Ryan left. But he didn't move. Instead, he gazed at her with such kindness in his eyes she melted a bit inside.

"I know you're frightened."

"I'm not—" she began. But then she let her false denial die on her lips. There was no more point in lying.

"Please, at least think about what I've said," Ryan continued, moving closer. "You're a strong woman. Why not develop your full potential? I don't know why your people won't let females learn how to use their magic, but I'd think they'd make an exception in a situation like this. Call your father and find out."

Though she hated to admit it, she liked the idea. In fact, the more she considered, the more the possibility of her reaching inside to her own strength appealed to her.

"And, Maria?" He touched her arm, the lightest of touches, just enough to send a shiver through her. "Even though you keep sending me away, I'm not going anywhere until I know you're safe. Whichever course you choose."

Fighting the urge to lean into him, she didn't protest. How could she, when his presence made her feel secure? Deceptively so, she knew, and she wasn't foolish enough to think Ryan could challenge Polacek and win. Of course, if he managed to get off a lucky shot...

No. She couldn't risk him. This was a Drakkor battle. No reason for Ryan to be involved.

"I need to think," she told him, turning away for her own sanity. It actually hurt to look at him. Even now, in the midst of all this turmoil, his male perfection made her ache.

Which both perplexed and infuriated her. She'd never been one to be ruled by her body. Of course, she'd never been so attracted to a man, or desired one the way she craved him. She'd been proud of the strength of her mind, and her body had been a distant second. The future had always blazed bright with endless possibilities.

Until the day she'd learned she, as one of the last remaining Drakkor females, had been tasked with the continuation of their race. The burden of such a Herculean duty had grown heavier with each passing year.

No. She couldn't allow herself to wallow in self-pity or regret—she'd already tried that and she'd accomplished nothing. Once again, she had to remind herself not to dwell on the way things were. Especially as she could do nothing to change them. While it might have stung just a little, the way everyone suddenly regarded her as little more than a breeder, a prize piece of livestock, she told herself she understood. Her people's hope would one day reside within her body.

Meanwhile, her own optimism had begun to slowly die. Until now. Until Ryan's comment made her realize she could be more. His words made sense. The more she considered the idea, the more she wondered why her own people hadn't seen the wisdom of better equipping the females of their kind to defend themselves.

Maybe for the same reason they'd refused to believe the males were the ones who were sterile.

She took a deep breath and before she lost her courage, she dialed her father's number.

"Well?" His terse greeting told her how much he was worried. "What have you decided?"

"I want to go to Eyrie," she declared, her heart skipping a beat. "I want to be trained in how to use my magic."

Though she half expected her father to either outright refuse or worse, laugh, to his credit he did none of those things.

"I don't know if I can get the Council to agree to that," he said. "I confess, I've often thought the rules allowing only males to receive training should be changed. Especially since the continuation of our race is dependent on you women."

"Call them and ask, please. With Polacek on the loose, there's no time to waste. And, Dad, tell them this. If they don't agree, I will refuse to even attempt to complete the task they've asked of me. If nothing else will convince them, this should."

"I'll call you back." And he hung up without another word.

Truly, she held all the cards. Satisfaction mingled with trepidation as she dropped her phone on the table. When she looked up, Ryan watched her, his sharp gaze intense.

"What task are they asking you to complete?" he asked, his quiet tone serious.

Without dropping her gaze, she slowly shook her head. "That's not something I can discuss with you, I'm sorry.

All I can tell you is it's my destiny. I would tell you more if I could."

Just like that, his expression went remote. "I understand," he said. But she knew he didn't.

To fill the awkward silence, she muttered something about needing to pack and hurried to her room. She kept her rolling duffel bag under the bed. After dragging it out, she placed it on her bed and began placing clothes inside.

Her father called back just as she'd zipped the now-full bag closed. "What's up?" she asked.

"They wanted to call a Council meeting and take a full vote," he said. "But when I told them we didn't have time, they promised to give me an answer in thirty minutes."

"I believe I will take that as a yes," she declared, the resolve hardening inside her. "I'm going to get in the car and head toward Colorado."

His sharp intake of breath told her she'd startled him. "How do you know where Eyrie is located?"

"Everyone knows. Growing up, all the kids made up stories about that place. It's in the foothills above Boulder. I'm sure I can find it." And she also knew her magic would draw her there. Magic always attracted magic. This was one of the most basic laws in existence, even for those without any formal training. Her father knew this.

"I'm not going to argue with you," he told her. "But what are you going to do if you get there and they turn you away?"

"They won't," she replied, wondering where her sudden strength had come from. "I won't let them."

Promising to call her back as soon as he knew more, her father rang off.

Hefting her bag up onto her shoulder, Maria turned to find Ryan standing in her doorway.

A smile ghosted across his rugged face. "You're really going to do this. Good. I'm proud of you."

Despite her newfound steely resolve, she felt a warm glow at his words. "Yes, I am. Thank you so much for all of your help."

Staring at him, trying to pretend his nearness didn't overwhelm her, she swallowed. This was the part where she wasn't sure if she should kiss him goodbye, hug him or merely shake his hand. Heck, if she had her way, she'd push him back on the bed and have her way with him.

At the thought, her entire body flushed.

Gaze darkening, he eyed her, smiling as if he knew her thoughts. "You can't get rid of me that easily. I'm not going anywhere, Maria."

"What?" Gaping at him, she tried hard not show her relief. "Didn't you hear? I'm driving to Colorado."

"And I'm going with you. At least—" he swallowed hard "—if that's okay with you. I can't let you make the trip alone, not with that monster out there."

There were a hundred reasons she should tell him no and send him away. But she realized she didn't care. For all she knew, Doug Polacek could capture her tomorrow. At least for a little while, she was going to live her life the way she wanted.

And she wanted Ryan. Even though she knew her heart would be broken when he left, which he would.

"Do we need to stop by your place so you can pack some clothes?" she asked. "I want you to make sure and bring your gun."

He rewarded her with a grin that sent heat through her veins. "Nope. I keep a packed bag in my Jeep. I never know when I might have to head in to the company for some sort of emergency. And I always keep a pistol with me."

"Well, grab it and your bag." She couldn't resist tossing

her hair. "Because we're taking my vehicle. I'm driving the first shift."

His grin broadened. "Sounds good."

"I'm bringing my Ruger," she said, unable to keep from smiling at the way his eyes widened. "Yes, I also have my concealed handgun license. I thought it would be a good idea, since I'm often alone at my business. And I'm a pretty decent shot. Just because he's Drakkor doesn't mean he's impervious to bullets."

"Then why'd you act so shocked that I had a pistol?"

She shrugged. "I don't know. You just don't seem the type. I guess I figured you'd hire bodyguards or something."

"Now there's a thought," he said, grinning. "Maybe when we get back."

She punched the garage door opener, letting the sunlight reveal her sports car. Ryan stopped short, eyeing her vehicle.

"That's yours?" he asked.

"Yep." She loved seeing his stunned reaction. Just about everyone liked her car, men and women both. Of course, what's not to like?

"I saw that Corvette the other night," he said slowly. "There can't be two painted that same turquoise color. It was parked out at Corps Woods."

She froze. "Okay." She didn't know what else to say.

"That night, I changed and hunted. While still in wolf form, I saw the most beautiful dragon. The scales were every color in the rainbow."

She nodded, struck dumb. Heat coiled inside her at the realization that he'd found her beautiful.

"Was that you?" he asked quietly.

Law warred with common sense. At this point, Ryan already knew she was Drakkor, just as she knew he was Pack.

"Yes," she finally answered. "I go out there to shift into my dragon. I didn't see you, though. I always make sure no one else is around."

"You were already there when I arrived." He went outside to his Jeep and retrieved his bag and his pistol. Climbing into the passenger side of her car, he stowed the bag in the backseat and the weapon in the glove box, next to hers.

She felt strangely lighthearted as she backed out of her driveway. Both she and Ryan automatically glanced up at the cloudless blue sky. Luckily, the only flying thing above them were seagulls.

Colorado. Ryan guesstimated Boulder would be an eighteen- or nineteen-hour drive from Galveston. Of course, a lot of that depended on traffic.

Getting through Houston would be half the battle.

Maria drove with a quiet competence, her skill with the souped-up car attesting to her familiarity with it.

She looked good driving the Corvette, too. The turquoise custom paint job and the sleek lines matched her dusky beauty and wild curves. He feasted his eyes on her while she focused on the road.

She fascinated him. Not only because of her beauty and the way his body reacted to hers, but because of her nature. He couldn't help but feel envious at her ability to change into a dragon and fly. What must it be like, to soar above the earth without the aid of machines?

Slowly, bit by bit, he would unravel her mystery. He wondered what Herculean task her people asked of her. Whatever it might be, the fact that she could refuse to do it appeared to carry quite a bit of leverage with her Council. He didn't understand why the Drakkor, one of the oldest paranormal species still in existence, would have different standards for males and females. In the Pack, women were highly regarded. Many led local and state councils.

He wanted to ask Maria about magic, but decided to wait until the right time. The topic fascinated him, especially since he considered himself a man of science. He hadn't really known magic actually existed. In fact, he still wasn't sure it did. He was going to have to see some proof.

All in good time. For now, he'd stick to basics.

"I take it you and your father are close?" he asked.

"We are," she agreed, her hands casual on the steering wheel. "My mother died when I was young. She caught some sort of incurable disease right after I was born." She didn't tell him that was the reason the Drakkor had so few women. A disease had torn through the female population, killing almost all of them—elderly, adult, and very young. Maria had been one of the lucky ones who'd appeared to have a built-in immunity.

"Where did you grow up?" he asked. "You don't have a Texas accent."

The way her slow grin blossomed on her face made him want to kiss her. "Wisconsin. I may not be a native Texan, but I got here as fast as I could. What about you?"

He loved the way she appreciated his native state. "I'm a born and raised Texan. I grew up in Austin, which is where I still live today."

Grin fading, she nodded. "I know you own some tech company. Have you always worked in that field? Admittedly, I have no idea what you actually do."

"My company develops software, apps and games. I've always tinkered with that kind of thing. However, as a teenager I did the obligatory stint working in fast food."

"What about your family? Are you close to them?"

Family. He caught himself clenching his teeth. That one particular subject had been deemed off-limits to every interviewer and every woman he'd ever dated. "That's the one piece of myself I prefer to keep private," he began. Then, to his amazement, he continued. "My parents were divorced when I was fifteen." He left out the years of bitterness and vitriolic hatred each of them exhibited toward the other, even now, twenty years later.

"I have one brother. He's ten years older than I and mentally impaired. He's never going to be capable of living on his own. I promised my parents he'd always be taken care of. I've set up a trust, to ensure there's always enough money to pay the facility where he lives."

The warmth in her caramel eyes embarrassed him. "That's admirable of you."

"No. There's nothing admirable about it. I love Mark. He loves me. We're family. I visit him often. And I never discuss my family with the press, understand? I'd really appreciate it if you didn't, either."

Her stunned expression told him his last sentence might have hurt her. "I don't intend on discussing you at all with anyone," she said. Then she reached over and turned up the radio, signaling she didn't want to talk anymore.

Leaning his seat back, he closed his eyes. During the long drive north, he imagined they each would come to learn more about the other.

Somehow, unbelievably, Ryan must have dozed off. When he opened his eyes next, they were on that long, flat stretch of highway between Houston and Dallas.

Sitting up, he rubbed his eyes and stretched. He looked over at Maria to see her eyeing him with a sweet smile. His heart did a somersault at the sight.

"No sign of any giant flying beasts?" he asked, only half teasing.

"None whatsoever." She sounded cheerful. "You must

have been really tired. You've been asleep for over two hours."

"Really?" He covered a yawn with his hand. "I'm actually kind of surprised. I'm not usually able to sleep with someone else driving. Has your father called back to let you know what the Council decided?"

"Not yet." She didn't seem worried. "I'm sure there's a battle raging among the upper Drakkor echelon. That's okay. It will all work out. Best of all, Polacek won't know where to find me. I've turned off the GPS on my phone. Just in case, I'd suggest you do the same."

As he was messing with it to do exactly that, Ryan's cell phone rang. His assistant, Timothy. He sighed, not quite ready for a dash of cold reality. Briefly, he debated not answering, but in the end he knew he had to.

Instead of some business-related crisis, Timothy had more personal news. "Where are you?" he began. Then, without waiting for an answer, he rushed to continue. "I just heard from the Galveston Fire Department," he said. "Your beach house caught fire."

Ryan froze. "What? When? How?"

"I don't know. It sounded pretty serious." Timothy paused. "I should let you know that the guy who called mentioned an arson investigation. They want to talk to you as soon as possible. How long before you can get there?"

"I can't." Still stunned, Ryan glanced out the window. "I'm out of town—not anywhere near the island at all. Please drive out there and handle this for me."

"But…" Timothy sputtered. "What if they…"

"I'm sure you've got this," Ryan interrupted. "If you have any problems, let me know."

Shock turning to anger, he ended the call and told Maria what had happened.

"I'm so sorry," she said immediately. "Do they know what started the fire?"

"No. But my assistant said the fire department is investigating it. They mentioned arson." He shook his head, his jaw tight. "I think that Drakkor did it."

"That's possible," she said, her voice sad. "If he knows we've been together, I think you're right. And he wouldn't even have had to use an accelerant since when we're in dragon form, we can make fire with our breath."

The image she painted sounded like something from a movie. "The fire investigators want to talk to me. I'm guessing that, whatever he did, he made it look deliberate, like arson. Just his way of tightening the screws."

"I'm so sorry," she said again.

He touched her arm. "Don't. There's no reason for you to apologize. It's not your fault."

"But in a way, it is. If you hadn't met me—"

"No." With one word, he cut her off. "You didn't ask for any of this."

She stared straight ahead, wisps of dark hair framing her face while she considered his words. "Neither did you."

"Then we're equal."

Slowly, she nodded. "Still, it's a shame. I really liked that beach house."

"So did I. But no worries, it's insured." Even if it hadn't been, he could take the monetary loss. What he couldn't take was the way this act made him feel as if he was being hunted. As a wolf, he wasn't used to being prey.

"What I don't understand is why," Maria continued. "Is this revenge because he saw us together? I'm assuming he read a tabloid. Is he pissed because he knows I'm with you?"

Ryan tried to relax his jaw enough to speak. "No, I think he's trying to draw us out. He probably went to your house looking for you and then tried mine. When he didn't find either of us, he set the fire."

She reached over and squeezed his shoulder, her hand lingering. If she hadn't been driving, he would have pulled her close for a long, deep kiss. Instead, he simply nodded, and pretended to focus his attention on the passing landscape.

When they were south of Fort Worth, they went to a rest stop. Inside the huge gas station/convenience store and restaurant, Maria oohed and awed over selections of packaged food. Ryan couldn't help but notice the way every male in the place stared longingly at her. He knew exactly how they felt. Still, she was *his.* Ryan put his arm around her and pulled her close for a quick hug, amazed at his need to publicly claim her, even in this small way.

Laughing, she hugged him back. "What was that for?" she asked.

He shrugged. "Just because."

They bought a few things and when they went outside to get in the car, she handed him the keys. "Your turn," she said. "I could use a break."

A few seconds after pulling out of the parking lot, Ryan knew he'd be adding a Corvette to his stable of cars. The throaty rumble of the powerful engine, the smooth ride and the way driving it made him feel as if he'd been missing out all these years.

A quick glance at Maria, who grinned back at him, told him she knew exactly how he felt.

Up just northwest of Wichita Falls, as the sky slowly darkened from dusk to night, Ryan thought he saw a large and ominous shape coasting over the flat plains.

Damn. His heart stuttered in his chest. "Maria, look over there. Is that a dragon, flying low above those fields?"

Instantly, she turned to look where he pointed. "I don't

know." Squinting, she tried to see. "The darkness makes it hard to tell. Could it be a bird?"

"If it's a bird, it's a very large one."

"Maybe a plane? One of those crop dusters."

Briefly, he considered taking one of the dirt roads that led in that direction, but rejected the idea as fast as it came. Too dangerous. It would be much better if they continued on their way, remaining as anonymous as possible.

But as they drove, it appeared the shape kept pace with them, at least until full darkness fell and they could no longer see beyond the beams of their headlights.

Seeing whatever it was had made them both jumpy. "I think we should stop in Amarillo for the night," he said.

"I don't," she responded promptly. "I vote we continue on. As long as we keep driving in shifts, we'll be fine."

His stomach growled, right on cue. "We have to eat. Besides, we don't even know if what we saw was a Drakkor or not. It could have been anything."

The words had barely left his mouth when something— something huge—swooped low over the highway ahead. Maria gasped. Ryan stepped on the brakes, glad no other cars were behind them.

Then, just as suddenly as it had appeared, it vanished. Gently, Ryan eased down on the accelerator, wanting to keep moving.

"What the hell was that?"

"Drakkor," Maria said, her voice flat. "I only got a quick glimpse, but I'm fairly certain."

A chill snaked up his spine. "The same one from Galveston?"

"I don't think so, though of course I can't be one hundred percent sure. This one was smaller, and had more colors to its scales." She took a deep breath. "Maybe the Council sent someone powerful to guard me on the trip."

He gripped the steering wheel so tightly his hands ached. He didn't want to reveal to Maria how much the encounter had shaken him, so he continued to drive and kept his eyes on the road.

Finally they reached the outskirts of Amarillo and he breathed a sigh of relief. "Bigger city, less chance of another dragon visit," he said, sounding more confident than he felt.

Maria's weak attempt at a smile told him she knew. "I'm hungry, too. Let's stop to eat," she said, stifling a yawn. "And maybe we can stay over here for the night, as long as you think it's safe. I'm exhausted."

Though he no longer knew what was safe anymore and what wasn't, he nodded.

They stopped to eat at a Mexican restaurant. "Judging by the police cars and truckers' rigs in the parking lot, this is a good place," he said, parking near the entrance.

"Good." After she got out of the car, she stretched. "This drive is longer than I remember it."

He waited until they'd walked inside and followed the hostess to a table before asking, "You've driven to Colorado from Galveston before?"

"Of course." Opening her menu, she glanced around. "I love the way they've decorated this place. The multicolored wooden chairs are a great touch."

"It's nice." He barely spared the decor a glance. "When did you make this drive? Recently?"

The chips and salsa arrived and their drink orders were taken. They both ordered iced tea, disappointing the waiter after he'd promoted the margaritas.

"No, I was a little kid," she answered, once the waiter had left. "Before we moved to Wisconsin, we lived in Colorado and drove down to the coast a couple of times.

I think I probably slept the entire way, and that's why I thought the drive seemed shorter."

The waiter brought their drinks and took their food order. They snacked on the chips and salsa, while Ryan felt himself gradually relaxing in small increments.

To all appearances, they might have been just another couple out for dinner. But Ryan kept an eye on the door, even though he knew he wouldn't be able to identify another Drakkor if one walked into the restaurant.

Maria, too, kept turning and checking out the door.

"This is ridiculous," she finally said. "We might as well try to enjoy our meal. No one's going to change into a dragon or anything in here."

The couple in the booth behind them both turned at her words and stared. "Role-playing," Ryan said, chuckling as the woman's face turned tomato red. "We enjoy it."

Maria laughed out loud, the pure sound bringing a smile to everyone who heard it.

When their food arrived, chicken enchiladas for her, carne asada for him, they dug in. Afterward, they had sopapillas for dessert.

"I'm stuffed," Maria pronounced.

"Me, too. I think finding a motel nearby and getting some rest would be an excellent idea."

She nodded. "Who knows," she said in a loud whisper just as the other couple got up to leave. "Maybe we can have some role-playing."

The woman gasped, tugging on her husband's arm and rushing him out.

Maria shook her head, eyes twinkling. "Nothing good ever comes of eavesdropping, you know."

Watching her, so sexy and beautiful, desire stirred inside him. For the first time he wondered about their sleeping accommodations. Would they share one bed, or would Maria want two?

He took a deep breath to ask her, but the noise of the restaurant was shattered by a shrill scream from outside the front door.

Chapter 7

Ryan froze. Drakkor? He and Maria locked gazes. "Surely not," she muttered.

"Let me go check it out," he said, jumping to his feet.

When she stood, too, he shook his head. "Wait here," he ordered, and rushed outside. Of course, Maria was right behind him.

Outside, a small crowd had gathered around a hysterical woman. She alternated between crying and blubbering, pointing and trying to speak.

"What's going on?" Ryan asked a man standing on the outskirts of the crowd.

"She claims she saw a monster," he answered, rolling his eyes. "Not sure if she's drunk or on drugs."

Somehow, the upset woman heard him. "I'm neither," she said, gasping as she wiped at the mascara running down her cheeks. "I swear to you I just saw some sort of giant flying lizard. It's around here somewhere."

Which could only mean one thing. Drakkor. Whether friend or foe, Ryan guessed they'd find out soon enough.

Several people laughed. Someone must have called 911 because an ambulance arrived. The woman was loaded up into it, still babbling, and taken away to the nearest hospital.

The crowd began to disperse.

"We need to go back and settle up our bill," Ryan said. "Then we'll get a hotel room for the night."

Though she merely nodded, he could swear he'd seen a flash of desire in her caramel eyes. Wishful thinking on his part, he told himself as he headed back into the restaurant.

Later, after finding a clean, reasonably priced motel not too far from the interstate, he locked the door and eyed the side-by-side double beds. He'd specifically requested them so Maria would have a choice.

She caught the direction of his gaze and laughed. "Come here," she said. "We might as well enjoy each other while we can."

He'd just gone in for a kiss when her cell phone rang. She glanced at it and shook her head. "It's my father. I have to take this. He'll be calling with news from the Council."

He nodded, listening to her side of the conversation, watching as she wrote something down. He couldn't tell much, but whichever direction it went, she cut the conversation short.

"Well." She blew out a breath in a puff. "I have good news and bad. The Council has decided I'm in. They're going to train me in how to use and develop my magic. Dad gave me the address."

"That's great." He hugged her. "Congratulations."

After giving him a quick return embrace, she moved away. "However, they've put one stipulation on it. If I'm going to train, I can't have sexual intercourse for twenty-four hours prior to my arrival. Apparently it zaps the magical reserve or something."

For a second he stared at her, not entirely sure she wasn't joking. The serious expression she wore quickly disabused him of that notion.

"Well—" he kept his tone light to mask his disappointment "—then it's a good thing this room has two beds."

"Yes," she answered, sounding not at all bothered. "It really is."

Maria could barely sleep that night, her hyperawareness of Ryan in the bed next to her making her burn. He, on the other hand, fell asleep almost immediately. Apparently the ban on sex didn't affect him as badly as it did her.

Sometime in the early hours before dawn, she realized she'd begun to take this entire relationship a bit more seriously than it deserved. Whatever had made Ryan abandon his summer vacation on the beach and accompany her, he hadn't done so because he wanted their relationship to be closer. She gathered he enjoyed adventure, and from the way he'd been acting, he considered this entire thing entertaining. He certainly had no ties to keep him in one place; apparently his company pretty much ran itself.

She'd appreciated his protectiveness and desire to keep her safe, but she could not discount the fact that, by his very presence, he'd also prevent her from achieving her goal.

Even listening to the rhythmic sound of his breathing made her go all gooey inside.

Already she could see herself growing far too attached to him. If she didn't have a destiny with so many restrictions, she'd ride this thing out for however long it lasted, but she couldn't afford to do that.

So, as much as the idea pained her, once she was magically strong enough to defend herself, she'd have no choice but to send Ryan Howard away for good.

Finally, she fell asleep.

When she woke in the morning, Ryan was already in the shower. The image of him naked, water sluicing down his perfect body, brought another round of dizzying desire.

Somehow she made it through breakfast, which they grabbed at a fast-food place and ate in the car on their way out of town. She'd elected to let Ryan drive, and to avoid conversation she closed her eyes and pretended to sleep.

But once they reached the New Mexico border, with the ancient, stunted Capulin Volcano in the distance, she couldn't take her eyes from the scenery. Rolling earth made of fertile desert, green and brown grass dotted with black volcanic rocks, and white-tailed deer grazing on the other side of wire fences, oblivious to the vehicles driving past. Every now and then a ranch would appear, the low-slung house set back from the road, with cattle or horses dotting the fields.

Raton Pass fascinated her. The houses seemed to cling to the sides of the cliffs and the road dipped down as they passed the gas station rest stops at the base of the pass. After that, they began the climb into Colorado.

An old mission sat high above them on the left, the stucco exterior hinting at secrets long gone.

She'd heard even in the summer it could snow up here, but this time the sky remained clear and the road dry.

"Beautiful, isn't it?" Ryan asked.

When she glanced at him, his easy smile made her throat ache. "Yes, it is. Though I've been this way before, it's been a long time and I'd forgotten how spectacular the scenery can be."

Southern Colorado just kept getting more and more beautiful. They passed through Trinidad, Walsenburg,

Pueblo, and finally Colorado Springs as they drove north toward Denver.

As the road became more and more congested, Maria began to fidget. "Kind of reminds me of tourist season in Galveston."

"This is nothing." Again the irrepressible grin. "You should see the traffic in Austin."

Finally they left Denver behind. Ahead, the Flatirons dominated the landscape. "It's beautiful," she mused. "But I still miss the ocean."

Traffic got a bit heavier when they reached the outskirts of Boulder. Coming in on 28th Street, Maria punched the address she'd been given into the GPS on her phone and let the metallic voice guide them. They followed Iris west and began to climb.

"Your destination is on your right," the GPS finally intoned.

The brown-and-beige house, low to the ground with lots of windows and cedar, embodied serenity. The majesty of the city of Boulder spread out below it made the place look like an image from a postcard. Not to mention the undeniable pull of the magic radiating from inside the cedar-shake siding. Maria stopped in her tracks, impressed despite herself.

Even Ryan, who had no ties to anything magical, let loose a low whistle. "Very nice."

"Yes, it is." She couldn't seem to make her feet move. Staring at the place where the males of her species perfected their magical abilities, she realized she felt like the first female pilot must have felt on her first day of air force fighter pilot school.

In other words, extremely nervous.

"Do you feel that?" she asked, her voice hushed.

"Feel what?"

"The thrum of the magic? It feels like the earth is pulsing with it."

"No." Grimacing, he shook his head. "I don't feel anything. Other than amazement at how beautiful it is here."

"Go on." He gave her a little push in the small of her back. "I'll be waiting at the hotel for you to call me when you're finished."

Turning, she flashed what she hoped was a confident smile. "Will do. But don't wait at the hotel. There's a lot to see in Boulder. Go out to Pearl Street or up to Chautauqua. Enjoy the scenery."

He pulled her close and kissed her. Long and thoughtful and lingering, it was a kiss she could melt into. When they broke apart, she realized all her nervousness had gone.

"Thank you for that," she whispered.

"You're welcome." His impish grin made her want to kiss him again. "Now go in there and kick some butt."

Maria refused to look back as she marched to the front door. Just as she raised her hand to knock, the heavily oiled wood swung noiselessly open.

Okay. She took a deep breath and moved forward.

She'd taken one step inside before misgivings seized her. Spinning around, she sprinted back outside. "Wait!"

Ryan had just climbed into her car, though he hadn't yet started it.

"Don't go." Feeling foolish, nonetheless she stood her ground.

Instantly, he left the car and hurried over to her. "What's wrong?"

All she could do was shake her head. "I want you with me."

Gently he pulled her close. He smoothed her hair away from her face and kissed her on the top of her head. "It's natural to be nervous. Don't worry, you can do this. I have faith in you."

Gazing up at him, humbled by his belief in her, she nodded. Every second standing with him so close, her certainty grew. She'd never been one for esoteric things like intuition, but this time she knew what she needed. "I don't know why, but I have a strong instinct to keep you with me. Maybe I can't do this without you."

He glanced from her to the house, so low-key, yet at the same time vibrating with powerful energy. "I don't know if they're going to allow me inside."

"They will." Of that she felt positive. "On the drive here, I realized something I should have figured out a long time ago. Right now, I hold all the cards."

"How so?"

"And that is the one thing I can't tell you." She smiled to lessen the sting of her words. "But they want something from me. And they want it badly enough."

"Maybe." He sounded doubtful, and she couldn't blame him. "But if my presence angers them enough that they report me to the Pack Protectors, there'll be hell to pay."

She spoke with more confidence than she felt. "I can promise you it won't come to that."

"I don't know…"

His uncertainty seemed so uncharacteristic, she studied him closely. "This isn't like you at all," she observed. "This reticence. You seem so confident, I'd have thought—"

"There's a reason," he interrupted quietly. "This isn't my show, it's yours. I don't see how my being part of this can help you. In fact, as far as I can tell, my presence might actually hurt you."

She took a deep breath, looking back at the house. "Going through this alone will hurt me worse. And, no, I don't actually know what exactly this training will consist of. All I know is every instinct I possess is telling me you need to stay."

His concerned expression relaxed and he flashed his trademark grin. As always, warmth uncurled inside her at the sight.

"Fine. I came all this way with you, because I wanted to be with you in case you need me. If you want me to stay, then I will. But honey, eventually you're going to have to trust yourself."

Trust herself? She blinked, wondering if she should correct the misconception, and then realized she couldn't without saying things she couldn't.

"The door's still open." She grabbed his hand. "Come on. Let's see what exactly waits for us inside."

The instant he closed his fingers around hers, she felt the rightness of having him at her side.

Together, they retraced her steps and stepped into the foyer. As Ryan tugged the door closed behind them, she half expected to hear a disembodied voice intone some sort of cryptic welcome, à la *The Wizard of Oz*.

Instead, nothing but silence greeted them.

"This is kind of weird," Ryan murmured.

Keeping hold of his hand, she took another step forward. "Hello?" she called. "Is anyone here?"

A tall, white-haired, bearded man with austere facial features stepped around the corner. His cool gray eyes appraised first Maria, then Ryan. "Can I help you?" he asked, his tone remote and disinterested.

Frowning, Ryan opened his mouth and then closed it, glancing at her, instead. Maria drew herself up, straightening her shoulders and lifting her chin. "I'm Maria Miranda."

There was a subtle shift in the older man's posture as

he looked from her to Ryan and back again. "What is he doing here?" His mouth twisted downward.

"He's my bodyguard," she said with a straight face, proud of herself. "I know you want your valuable resources guarded."

"We can take care of our own." From that point on, he never once glanced at her, choosing instead to glare at Ryan. "Your servant can leave."

Ryan laughed. "Just so you know, buddy, passive aggression has never worked on me. If Maria wants me to stay, I'm staying."

The man stroked his long white beard. He lifted one hand and languidly wiggled his fingers. Immediately, some invisible force propelled Ryan toward the door, so quickly he appeared to be flying.

Magic. Every cell in her body tingled in response. Though rusty and long out of practice, she remembered she had dormant power of her own residing deep within her.

Her dragon rose at the threat to Ryan. So did her magic.

A low growl resonated in her throat. Flicking her fingers, she pulled Ryan to her while at the same time sending the other man hard against the wall. The old one's eyes widened as he put out his hands to keep himself from hitting the wood.

"Maria, stop. Don't hurt him." Though he appeared only slightly nonplussed, Ryan's accelerated breathing told her he wasn't as unaffected as he wanted to seem.

Reluctantly, Maria closed her hand and made a fist, releasing her captive. "And you—don't use magic against my friend."

"Well, well, well," the man said, his movements agile for someone of his age. Narrowing his eyes, he strolled over and looked Maria up and down. "You do know how to use your magic. Have you been practicing on your own?"

Glaring back at him, Maria wasn't sure whether or not to speak. In the end, since she'd come here to learn, she decided to tell him the truth.

"No. My magic came to life, but only just now. And only by instinct. I didn't want you to hurt Ryan, so I mimicked what you did and it worked. I'm not entirely sure how."

He laughed. "Either way, well done. My name is Micah."

Since he didn't offer a handshake, she dipped her chin in response. "I've already given my name. This is my friend Ryan."

Micah sighed. "And what do you propose we do with him during your lessons?"

Ryan laughed. "Exactly the point I tried to make."

Frowning, Maria shook her head. There were a hundred different reasons she didn't want Ryan to go, but none of them came from logic.

"How long will these lessons take?" she asked instead of answering.

"That depends on you," Micah replied.

Cryptic. And mildly annoying.

"Can you give me a rough time frame? And maybe more information? If I'm going to send Ryan into town to explore Boulder, he'll need to know what time to come back and get me."

"There will be no set time. You won't be leaving here until you've mastered your magic. How long this takes will be, as I said before, completely up to you."

Torn, Maria looked down.

"Maria, I'm going to take off." Cupping her chin, Ryan lifted her face to his. "I know I promised to keep you safe, but it seems you're in good hands here. I definitely don't want to interfere with your destiny." The inflection he put on the last word made her realize he was still a bit peeved that she'd refused to reveal exactly what said destiny might be.

Before she could respond, he gave her a quick kiss and hurried out the front door. "Call me when you're ready for me to pick you up," he called over his shoulder.

Only after she heard the throaty purr of her car driving away did she turn and face Micah. His stony expression seemed at odds with the cold anger in his gaze.

"What did you tell that wolf about your destiny?" he asked.

"Nothing." Crossing her arms, she held her ground. "He simply knows I have something important to do for my people. No more than that."

"Are you certain you haven't revealed anything else?"

"Absolutely positive."

"Good. Because I can tell you the truth right now. That wolf is not your mate."

Heart sinking, she jerked her head in a curt nod. She'd known this all along, of course. But to actually hear it spoken out loud by one with powerful magic still stung.

"How can you be sure?" Her plaintive question revealed too much, but she couldn't help herself. "I mean, I've suspected ever since I met him, but…"

Micah's stony expression remained unchanged. "In addition to magical abilities, some of us have the capability of foreseeing the future. I am one of those so blessed."

Ouch. "Oh, really?" She knew she sounded flippant. "Then since you're taking a look at my future, tell me this. Will I find a man I can love and who will love me back so I am able to conceive?"

He didn't even hesitate. "Most definitely."

Mingled emotions swirled through her hearing this. Relief, of course, and something else, a complex sort of sorrow she didn't want to look at too closely.

In desperate need of distraction, she took a deep breath. "Shall we get started?" she asked, rubbing her hands together. "I have a feeling I have a lot to learn."

There had been times in his life when Ryan had been alone and relished the solitude. There'd been others when he'd been surrounded by people and felt utterly alone. Driving away from the house perched on the side of a mountain above Boulder, he couldn't decide how he felt.

Maria still fascinated him. He'd ached for her the night before, but on some level he understood why she couldn't use her energy for sex. The more he got to know her, the more he wanted to know more, like peeling a ripe fruit to get to its core. Her many contradictions, the disparity between the often confident woman who ran her own business and bravely went to a bar alone, and the woman who seemed timid, almost cowed by some mysterious destiny she couldn't even discuss, intrigued him.

While she'd been clear she couldn't date him, her reasons made no sense. So she didn't want to be in the spotlight? He could work around that. A certain famous pop star and he had managed to keep their entire six-month relationship a secret. To this day, no one in the press even had a clue. He suspected Maria was aware of this possibility, as well.

Which meant she wasn't telling him everything. Since he knew her most compelling reason—at least to herself— was somehow tied up in her mysterious destiny, he knew he had to find out what it might be if he wanted to be able to overcome her objections. Which he would, with enough time.

Ryan hadn't ever met a woman like Maria, who cared nothing about fame and money. She had to know he could buy her whatever she asked for, but she'd requested nothing, unlike some of the women he'd dated in the past.

Thinking of Maria's secrets, he realized he needed to be completely honest with her, as well. He had a perfectly valid reason for avoiding commitment, one that had less to do with his parents' horrible divorce than with the sneaking suspicion that he might have inherited his father's inability to be faithful to any one woman. After seeing firsthand how much his father's constant stream of women hurt his mother, Ryan understood what he had to do. Lay the cards out up front, explain how things were going to be, and move on when the mood struck.

So far, this lifestyle had worked for him. Once he'd made his fortune, he pretty much had his pick of beautiful, sexy women. Right now, though, he only wanted Maria. Her refusal to even consider it only made him crave her more.

Putting her from his mind, he attempted to focus on checking out Boulder. The town had an eclectic, yet laid-back vibe. He strolled the Pearl Street Mall, stopped in an Irish pub and had a beer, and listened to various street musicians perform, tipping them all well.

The scenery couldn't be beat, with the jagged rocks of the Flatirons as backdrop. He took a drive up to Flagstaff, noted the gourmet restaurant and made a mental note to secure reservations and take Maria for dinner before they drove back to Texas.

He checked in with his assistant, Timothy, and learned the Galveston police had joined the fire marshall in requesting his presence. After giving instructions to stall them as long as he could, Ryan asked for his usual updates on the company. It stung slightly that it seemed to run like a well-oiled machine without Ryan's presence, but he knew that only meant he'd done a great job in choosing his top employees.

After his conversation with Timothy, Ryan read his email on his cell phone, took a look at Facebook and then drove back to the hotel. Once in the room, he wondered what Maria would learn and how long it would take her to master it.

Magic was energy. Repeating the words after Micah, Maria tried to keep from yawning. Most of what the older man said sounded like words from a new age self-help book. So far he hadn't provided one piece of concrete knowledge for her to latch on to.

Suddenly, she felt an invisible force lift her from the ground. Hovering four feet above the bamboo, she eyed Micah without speaking, wondering what he might be up to. Regardless, this action felt a lot better than listening to him drone on in one platitude after another.

Micah flipped his hand, and Maria found herself hanging upside down, feet to the ceiling, head near the floor.

What the...

He motioned again, propelling her ahead of him, down a long hallway and then down a flight of stairs. Though she struggled and tried to use her own magic to right herself and regain control over her own body, she couldn't. Maybe using it once had depleted it or something? The thing was, she didn't know.

Still, she'd never been one to give up easily. As she drifted along, she noticed the scent—not quite incense, not drugs, but something herbal. "What are you doing?" she asked, only to be ignored.

Once they reached the bottom of the basement, Micah waved his hand and sent her into a dark, windowless room.

"Enjoy your stay," he said, his mocking smile matching his voice. "At least you'll be safe here."

And he closed a door, leaving her hanging upside down like a bat in total darkness.

Chapter 8

The instant all light cut off, Maria panicked. She'd always been claustrophobic, and even at home she kept a small night-light on to sleep. Hyperventilating, she clawed at nothing and at everything, feeling as if she might black out from all the blood rushing to her head.

Working diligently, she managed to twist herself around until she'd reversed her position and no longer hung upside down. Mostly upright, she thought, though the complete and utter darkness made it surprisingly difficult to tell.

That accomplished, she got her breathing under control, pushing away the terror.

After fear, came anger. What the hell? Who did this Micah person think he was anyway? She'd come here with the Council's agreement, to learn magic. Not to be locked up in a dark basement and treated like a criminal.

He'd said she'd be safe here. Maybe so, but the question was—from whom?

At some point—maybe minutes, maybe hours—it was difficult to tell time—she realized this had to be some sort of test.

She tried to think. First, she needed light. In her dragon shape, she could breathe fire. Though normally she'd never do something like that inside a structure due to potential damage, this time she would be willing to take the risk.

Inhaling deeply, she stripped off her clothes and initiated the change to her Drakkor shape. For the first time since she'd been able to shape-shift, she struggled.

In the fight against some invisible force, she could smell her own fear and taste the faintly metallic scent of her perspiration. Still, she pushed through. With agonizing slowness, she felt her body begin to stretch, her bones lengthen and change. At this speed what was usually painful became excruciating, yet she gritted her teeth and continued.

Finally, she flexed her claws and screeched. Her dragon had fully emerged. Strength flowed through her as she reared up, still suspended above the floor. Certain she could end this, she gave one powerful beat of her wings and tried to break the spell, but nothing happened.

Tired of the blackness, she let loose a breath of fire, enough to see she'd been put into some kind of concrete bunker. At least it was fireproof, she thought grimly.

At one end she saw the door she'd come through. This door appeared to be made of wood. Once again she flapped her massive wings, striving to reach it, with no success.

She realized that if she kept on in this vein, she'd exhaust her limited reserves of strength. Plus, she suspected she'd continue to get nowhere if she didn't figure out a way to access her magic.

Was this why Micah had done this? To show her how to call on her inner magical ability?

If so, she was failing miserably.

Forcing her entire body to relax, she allowed herself to hang there, wings curled in close to her sides, while she considered her options. How long did Micah plan on leaving her here in the dark? Worse, it occurred to her this might not be a test, but rather a protest against a female insisting she be taught how to use abilities that had always been considered in the Drakkor males' domain only.

Again and again, she reached tentatively inside herself, knowing she merely needed to ignite that kernel, that tiny spark, and let it ignite into enough magic to free herself. She knew she had it; after all, she'd used her magic on Micah when he'd tried to push Ryan out the door. Surely she could do it again.

At some point, she took herself into a meditative state, aware that if she would ever be able to reach a higher level and access her magic, she could possibly do so then.

And, finally, she dozed. And began to dream.

The dream! Blinking, she opened her eyes to the all-encompassing blackness. One quick breath of flame eliminated that. She realized how she'd been able to draw forth her magic before.

Emotion. Seeing Micah push Ryan away had infuriated her. Anger had provided the spark she'd needed. She needed to get good and riled up, which shouldn't be difficult.

Especially once she started considering how she'd been treated. She'd come here believing she would receive instruction. Instead, she'd been locked up like a prisoner, or worse, a criminal. With a mighty Drakkonic roar, she let fury fill her. There. That ember down deep in her core, sparked, then blazed to life.

She roared again, uncurling her wings, breathing flames. The door went first, blazing up as she launched herself toward the opening. But the doorway was far too small for her dragon form, and she slammed into the concrete wall, making the entire house shudder.

From the rooms above, she heard shouts and the sound of running feet as Micah and his companions headed for the stairs.

Beyond caring, she shook herself off and waited for their arrival. They'd think twice before attempting to do something like this again.

The wooden door continued to burn, but apparently everything else had been made of cement, so the fire didn't spread.

Through the smoke, a shadowy figure appeared, sidestepping the blazing door. Micah flipped on a switch, and light flooded her concrete prison.

He gaped at her, clearly stunned. Pleased, Maria roared again and moved toward him, fully expecting him to change so they could fight, dragon to dragon.

Instead, he waved his hand, intending to use magic to confine her once again.

As soon as the wave of energy hit her, she batted it away with one claw. And took another step forward.

Fear showed on his face as he realized that not only had his magic somehow become useless against her, but that she could easily kill him. While he could not kill her. Females were so few and so valuable, he wouldn't dare.

"Stop," he called out. "I will train you. Don't hurt me."

She roared again, letting him hear her displeasure. And then she used her magic to levitate him, turning him upside down exactly the way he'd done to her. Once she had him magically secured in the middle of the room—even though she wasn't entirely sure how she'd done this—she changed back to human. She marched over and grabbed her clothes, turning her back to him while she dressed.

And then, in order to teach him a lesson, she left him there and went in search of his housemates.

Later, having released Micah after less than thirty minutes, Maria gathered him and the two others in the spacious kitchen.

All three of the male Drakkor were older and wore beards, though only Micah's had turned white. The youngest male, named Brandon, kept his trimmed short, and the dark brown matched his hair. The other, who'd reluctantly given his name as Roger, sported a long beard and a head of curls styled into a loose afro.

She fixed them, one by one, with a cold stare.

"I came here to learn. The Council approved this. If you three have issues, you should have taken them up with the Council. Not with me. I need to be able to defend myself against the rogue Drakkor. Surely you three can see that."

Micah glanced at the other two men and swallowed before he spoke. "To be honest, we—and many, many others—believed you should surround yourself with skilled men such as your father. There is no need to fill your head with these things. You have one task to do. Let us protect you."

His version of "don't worry your pretty little head about this" appalled her.

"This isn't the 1950s," she said. "Not only that, but since I clearly am able to defend myself against you, it doesn't appear to me that I'm asking too much. I have magic. I'm strong. And I'm not yet with child."

They all three stared at her, silent.

She took a deep breath, trying to remain calm. Now that she'd invoked it once, she recognized her magic simmering deep inside her, like a smoldering ember. "Gentlemen, I will need your answer."

In the future, assuming at least one of the pregnant females was successful in delivering girls, she understood much might be written about this pivotal moment. How sad that the women of her kind hadn't fought for equal rights, but how could they when they hadn't even realized they were oppressed?

As she eyed the three Drakkor mages, aware that if they were to join forces and combine their magic they might succeed in re-imprisoning her, she hoped they'd see reason instead.

Finally, Micah stepped forward and bowed his head in a nod. "We will teach you." He strode off, this time heading toward a staircase that led up. "Come with me and I'll show you your room. Once you've had time to refresh yourself, we will begin."

The next several days were exhausting. In fact, Maria came to consider them a sort of magic boot camp that lasted eight hours a day. They pushed her to her limits, yet she managed to forge on, determined to show them that, yes, she could do this. She learned all kinds of useful things. The ability to focus and summon up the kernel of magic inside of her without needing strong emotion as fuel. And the way to instinctively know when danger was near. This one seemed a bit trickier, but she finally felt she'd mastered it.

At the end of every day she fell into her bed, too exhausted to think about anything or anyone. She wasn't even sure she dreamed. Still, she found herself missing Ryan at odd times, and once or twice she actually pulled out her cell phone and attempted to contact him.

Every time she did—and after the first few attempts, she gave up—her phone showed No Service. Even her attempts to send him a text wouldn't go through. Eventually she gave up and focused on her training.

There were exercises, both of the body and the mind. She worked out until her clothes were soaked with perspiration and then worked out more. She practiced creating with her magic, at first pretty colorless bubbles, then clouds and finally fire. In this, magic was limited. She could not create infinite objects or living, breathing beings. Though, if magic was used wrongly, doing so could destroy them.

She progressed from tiny flames to a crackling bonfire—safely in the fireplace, of course. From levitating a few inches above the floor, to being able to fly in her human form, though not nearly as effortlessly as she did when she was dragon.

After she'd mastered everything in her human form, she had to change to dragon and do it all over again. Surprisingly, she found magic to be easier while in that form. As if the natural well it sprang from resided much closer to the surface.

She practiced and practiced, barely sleeping, eating just enough to keep up her energy.

"There is one thing more," Micah told her. "Come with us."

Immediately she got up, following him out to the car, where Brandon and Roger waited. They drove up into the mountains even though it was late at night. Brandon parked the car and they hiked up a hidden trail under the starlight. Though they apparently had no problem seeing, Maria had to use a flashlight as she brought up the rear.

Once they reached a flat rock more than halfway up the mountain, she watched as, one by one, Micah, Brandon and Roger shape-shifted into their dragon selves. They were so powerful the change seemed instantaneous. Their beasts were amazing, even to her seasoned gaze. Huge and ominous, lovely in their dark beauty, they reared back, huge heads swinging up as if reaching for the sky. She found herself holding her breath, her throat aching, as each one unfurled his wings and launched into the night sky.

Above her, they circled, waiting. She squinted up at the quarter moon, loving how each time a dragon flew over, they blotted out what little light it gave.

And then, she began her own change.

Something in the air…maybe it was a lingering trace of their power. Or perhaps her dragon responded in kind to the three other beasts in the night sky above. Whatever it might have been, she went from human to dragon almost instantly, changing faster than she'd ever done.

When the change was complete, she shuddered. Energy coursed through her, filling her with elation. In one swift motion she spread her wings and jumped, launching herself into the air.

Together, they flew off, circling, diving, tumbling through the air, the movements surprisingly graceful considering their size.

Maria mimicked their moves, reveling, full of unspeakable joy. It had been far too long since she'd been allowed to play in the sky with others. In fact, since she'd moved into adolescence, she'd flown alone.

Their playful moves taught her new nuances of flight, and what had always been a solitary time became a learning experience. She watched the way they dipped and twisted and soared, and attempted to mimic them.

They watched and guided, and soon she felt confident she could fly as gracefully as they.

And then they introduced magic.

Tiny things at first, a small fireball zinged from one to another, to be dodged and quickly returned. As she watched from the side, she realized they were playing a game. She took a deep breath, went into a dive and joined in.

She sent two fireballs, each in a different direction. Micah and Brandon easily dodged them, and while she watched this action, Roger came up behind her and zapped her with one of his own.

It hurt. One quick flash of pain before it subsided.

After that necessary bit of learning, no one succeeded in hitting her with a fireball again.

After playing for a few hours, one by one each massive dragon landed, curled his wings in close and changed back to man. Maria waited until last, keeping her eyes averted as she had no desire to see any of the men naked. Once they were all fully clothed, she flew down beside them, gesturing that they were to turn away until she, too, had changed and gotten dressed.

They shook their heads, but complied.

Becoming human also happened in a flash. Stunned and marveling, she snatched up her clothes and put them on. Once she'd finished, she cleared her throat. "Okay."

"Let's go," Micah ordered.

And one by one they filed back down the mountain. The trail seemed much steeper going down, but Maria felt too exhilarated to care.

Once they'd reached the car, she attempted to put into words some of how she felt. "I've always gloried in my dragon self, but this was extraordinary," she began.

Micah turned from the front passenger seat to look at her. "This was a lesson, as well. You needed to learn that magic can be fun. It's not all gloom and danger. Magic can be something that brings you joy."

She opened her mouth and then closed it. "Thank you," she told him, including the others in her gratefulness. "I will never forget this moment."

"Good," he told her. "When we return to the house, get some rest. We shall see you in the morning."

That night, she slept deeply and didn't remember dreaming.

When she woke, she realized it was the morning of the fifth day. After she showered and dressed, Micah, Brandon and Roger met her in the kitchen with a hot, nourishing breakfast. As she ate, Micah announced she was ready.

"We've taught you all we can," Micah said, cracking a smile for once. "Honestly, you've surprised us with your aptitude."

Even though she knew that meant they hadn't expected a woman to be able to succeed, she dipped her chin in a nod. "Thank you."

"You may call your wolf now to come collect you." Brandon came forward, his expression pleased. "I will say I've really enjoyed working with you." The surprise in his voice was its own kind of insult, but she let it go.

Since he clearly expected a response, she nodded, unable to reply in kind. The entire time they'd been pushing her, she hadn't been able to forget the way they'd locked her upside down in a dark room. She had to constantly remain on guard in case they tried anything else. Luckily for them all, they hadn't. She mentioned this, watching them closely.

"There was good reason for that," Roger said. "It taught you how to be prepared when your enemy comes."

She noted he'd said *when* rather than *if.* A chill snaked down her spine.

"Also," Roger continued. "You should know that you will find someone you can love and who will love you in return. The child born of this union will be close to perfect."

"And hopefully female," Brandon put in, unnecessarily. For as long as Maria could remember, everyone hoped the females would birth more females. If not, everything would be for nothing.

"I predict you will find your mate soon." Roger beamed at her.

"But it will not be your wolf," Micah put in sternly, repeating what he'd said earlier. The other two men looked at him, but didn't comment. Instead, they turned to eye her and nodded in agreement.

"I already knew that," Maria told them, ignoring the tightness in her chest at hearing the prediction repeated. "Long before I came here."

And if the last little remnant of hope inside her curled up and died right then, so be it.

Maria seemed oddly pensive, and Ryan wasn't exactly sure if he should try to tease her out of her mood or leave her alone.

He'd been surprised at how much he'd missed her. And by the reasons. More than the sex, he'd found himself wishing he could share something with her and made a mental note to do so once he saw her again.

When the call finally came to pick her up, five days after he'd dropped her off, he experienced myriad emotions, chief among them a confused combination of joy and relief. But within a few seconds of seeing her, he noticed that something within her had changed. The difference showed in the lack of light in her amazing caramel eyes.

When he'd arrived to collect her, the instant she appeared on in the foyer his heart did a funny little jolt. "Maria," he called, waving. He jumped out of her sports car and hurried up the sidewalk. Needing to touch her, he went in for a hug. Though she didn't sidestep him, he almost would have rather she had. Instead, she held her body stiffly, as if only barely enduring his touch.

Perplexed and slightly hurt, he released her and took a step back. "Maria? Are you okay?"

"Yes, I'm fine. Are you ready?" she asked, avoiding his gaze. "I'd like to get on the road to Texas."

"Yep." Keeping his tone cheerful, he grabbed her bag. Whatever had happened to her in this place, it clearly hadn't been good. No doubt she'd tell him all about it once they were safely headed down the road.

Except she didn't.

He tried talking to her and every question was met with either silence or worse, a monosyllabic answer. Finally, he'd had enough.

Pulling the 'Vette over to the side of the road, he turned in his seat to face her. Unbelievably, she still kept her profile averted, as if something out in the landscape commanded her attention.

"Maria?"

Finally, moving as slowly as if it hurt her, she swiveled her face and met his gaze. "Yes?"

"What's wrong?"

She stared at him, as cool and composed as if they were total strangers. "Nothing. I'm fine. Why do you ask?" Even her voice sounded robotic.

His chest tightened. "What did they do to you?" Reaching out, he gently touched her cheek. "Tell me. I've been with you all along on this, except while you were at your Eyrie. Don't treat me as if I'm nothing to you."

For one heartbeat, then two, she didn't move.

And then, all at once, it was as if a dam broke. Her perfect composure crumbled. She covered her face with her hands and let out a groan. The sound reminded him of an animal in pain. She bowed her head and her shoulders shook as she struggled to gain control over her emotions.

He undid his seat belt and pulled her close, holding her. "It's all right," he murmured. "Go ahead and cry. Let out all the feelings you've been keeping bottled up so tightly inside."

Once again, his words had the opposite effect. She stiffened and pulled away. "I don't cry," she said, her voice low. "Ever. I'm stronger than that."

"Okay." He took a deep breath. "Then do you mind telling me what's wrong? Did they hurt you?"

"It's not that," she said, her features once again composed and remote. "Apparently part of their abilities enable them to see into the future. I've been given a little glimpse of mine and it's a bit difficult to deal with."

He waited for her to elaborate.

"Anyway, I have control over my magic now," she said, clearly finished with the topic of her future. "At first, I thought I'd made a huge mistake coming to the Eyrie."

He waited, aware she needed time to collect her thoughts. "The first day was…rough. They imprisoned me with magic. It seemed more like torture. I got the feeling they were trying to make me pay for daring to ask for something they believe women shouldn't be allowed to do."

Horrified, he nodded. He clenched his jaw. To think they'd actually done this to her infuriated him.

"I went there thinking they would help me. Instead, I came to realize they were intent on showing me I didn't belong. That I needed to get back to figuring out a way to meet my destiny and not bother them. Finally, after being imprisoned for several hours in the dark, I couldn't take it anymore. Something inside me just…broke. I sort of let loose. I'm lucky no one was seriously injured."

"What do you mean, let loose?"

"My magic. It was only when I showed them—one at a time and then together—that they couldn't push me around that they finally let me learn." Her short laugh sounded painful. "Of course, at that point, they really had no choice.

Turns out I'm really powerful. I think I might be more powerful than any of them, though we never discussed it. Which is good, if I'm going to have a prayer of beating Doug Polacek."

He cursed. "I hope you made them pay for treating you that way."

"Only their pride. They couldn't actually hurt me, at least not my body. I'm far too valuable to our people."

"So instead they went for what? Your mind? Like psychological warfare?" While he waited for her to answer, he prayed she'd tell him no, that they hadn't done that.

Her expression pensive, she nodded, sending his stomach plummeting to the soles of his boots. "Sort of."

Inside, his wolf snarled. By some miracle he was able to keep his voice steady. "They can't be allowed to get away with treating you like that."

"I agree." Her cool gaze touched on his and then skittered away. "I intend to make sure the Council knows about this. My plan is to have the other females educated in magic so they can protect themselves. I don't want anyone else subjected to this kind of treatment."

"I don't blame you." Reaching out to smooth a tendril of hair away from his face, he noted the way his hand shook. Repressed fury. Those damn Drakkor were lucky the Pack didn't have magical ability or Ryan would turn this car around and head back to make them pay.

"It's all right," she told him, her voice soft. "I sense your distress. There's no need. I survived and I got what I went there for. Plus, in the end the lessons were actually fun. I can access my magical abilities now. And I'm confident I can hold my own if Doug Polacek comes for me. That's what matters."

Though he nodded, he wondered how anyone as intelligent and beautiful as Maria couldn't see what seemed so obvious to him. Her people, though they valued the remaining women because they were so few, clearly did not hold them in high regard otherwise. He didn't understand how this could be so, especially considering how few female Drakkor remained. He felt pretty damn sure that if something like that had happened in the Pack, those women would be treated like goddesses and given everything they could even think of wanting, and then some.

All of this gave him an idea for a new app. And possibly even a game. He made a mental note to pass it on to his team of talented designers. As soon as he got a chance, he needed to sketch out some of the characters that had begun to occur to him. While dragons and werewolves and wizards and witches were pretty common—even passé—in the app and gaming world, his unique little twist might just put his idea right on top.

Except he wasn't sure developing it would be ethical. The right thing to do would be to discuss it with Maria, maybe even have her sign some sort of consent form.

For now, he'd work on getting the idea developed. If it turned out to be a good one, he'd talk to Maria before releasing anything. For now, all his focus would be on keeping her safe.

Every time she glanced at Ryan, Maria's heart hurt. Maybe the knowledge that she'd need to send him away for good would take some getting used to. Even though, she reminded herself fiercely, she'd known this ever since the day she'd learned who he was.

Billionaires and dragons didn't mix.

When they finally reached Galveston after driving straight through, they both were exhausted. Each napped while the other drove, but it wasn't enough.

When they arrived at her place, he covered his yawn

with his hand. "Do you mind if I stay the night? Since my house burned, I'll need to find a hotel room or something. It's late and I'm not up to doing that right now."

"Of course." Suddenly she wanted nothing more than to go to sleep with him holding her and to wake up in his arms.

One last time. Though her mind knew Ryan would never be The One, she wanted to make love with him one last time. That memory would be one she'd hold close to her, buried deep, maybe, but there in case she ever wanted to pull it out and relive the moments she'd spent with him.

Maudlin, maybe. Foolish, most definitely. But she didn't care. Despite everything Micah had told her, her heart wanted what it wanted. Ryan would be difficult to let go. But since she had no choice, she knew she would.

Eventually. But for now, she'd let herself get lost in him. Then she'd move forward with the rest of her life.

Chapter 9

"That was nice," Ryan said, his voice rumbling through his chest to Maria's ear. She had her head there, right above his heart, loving the steady whump-whump sound.

"Nice?" Raising her head enough to look at him, she narrowed her eyes. "We made love last night, slept in each other's arms, and after we woke up, made love again. Is that the best adjective you can come up with?"

He laughed and kissed the tip of her nose. "Amazing, transcendent, superb. Is that better?"

As usual, his confident grin made her heart give that same twang. If she lived a hundred thousand days, she knew she'd never forget this moment. Ryan lying in her bed with the sunlight turning his hair golden, his posture relaxed, joy radiating from every pore as he talked and gestured with his hands to accentuate his points.

She'd never known a man could be so beautiful. But with Ryan, it wasn't just his physical attributes that attracted her. His energy, the light shining inside of him, drew her to him.

With a sense of mingled horror and disbelief, she realized she'd been fooling herself all along. Getting over this man wasn't going to be easy. At all.

"You know what," Ryan's easy tone oozed contentment. "This has been the best fling I've ever had."

Fling. Something inside her twisted. That's all she was to him, of course. A fling. And he'd had many. That last part went unspoken yet still understood.

She'd wanted something to remember, and she definitely would never forget this. The joke was on her.

Yet part of her felt grateful. He'd unknowingly made giving him up a little bit easier.

Pushing herself up and off him, she grabbed her bra and, keeping her back to him, managed to get it on. She found her shirt, pulled it on, and grabbed her panties and jeans before hurrying to the bathroom to clean up.

Once there, she took a good look at herself in the mirror. She had the wild and drowsy-eyed look of a woman who'd been thoroughly loved. Or rather, she amended hastily, a woman who'd been thoroughly made love to.

After cleaning up, she dressed and then finger combed her hair. She couldn't believe she'd actually contemplated making him breakfast and then telling him he could stay here until he found another place. Clearly, that wasn't going to work. He was a billionaire—he could find somewhere else to stay with a snap of his fingers. Heck, he could buy another house if he wanted to. It wasn't as if he'd have to live in his car.

Despite her many failed attempts to be done with him, Ryan had given her the final reason. Micah had told her he was not the one. Ryan had just proved it. Time to end this, once and for all, before she let herself get even more hurt. If such a thing was even possible.

She drew strength thinking about something else Micah had said during her training. *You are stronger than you realize. And I'm not just speaking of your magic. You will come to rely on that power in the days ahead.*

She'd find her Mr. Right, she told herself. The one she was meant to be with, the man who would father her child, a Halfling who would become one of the shining hopes of the Drakkor race.

Love—on both sides—was the only way such a miracle would happen. No magic or wishing could circumvent that fact.

Ryan was not that man. Never would be. She'd known this, deep in her gut, long before Micah had given her his vision of the truth of her future.

So why did she feel like she'd been punched in the stomach?

Taking a deep breath, she squared her shoulders and marched back into the room. Ryan still lay sprawled on the bed, his tanned skin golden against the white sheets. His amazing eyes glowed when she entered the room, almost as if he found her as beautiful as she did him. Or as inviting.

Mouth dry, she steeled herself against the immediate surge of desire. She squinted at him, suddenly uncomfortable. "If you're really a billionaire, why settle for a house on the Gulf Coast? Why not buy your own private island?"

He shrugged. "I'm frugal, sort of. Though I have been in negotiations for a small island in the Bahamas. I usually buy things for investment purposes. I'm not the type for wildly extravagant monetary expenditures."

Since she'd never met anyone as wealthy before, she wanted clarification. "What do you consider wildly extravagant? Do you own a jet?"

Slowly he nodded. "Yes. But I bought it used."

Like that made a difference. Who knew, maybe it did. What, a couple of million less?

"I know you have several yachts."

"I have a couple of boats." His clearly unapologetic smile made her feel kind of silly. "I guess some people might consider them yachts."

"I shouldn't ask this, but I'm going to anyway. How many houses do you own? How many cars?"

Instead of answering, he took a step closer, his gaze intent. "Is this some sort of interview? Because that's what it's starting to feel like. Why do you need to know all this? Possessions are just things. They aren't a true measure of who I am."

Though she tended to agree with him, for some reason she just couldn't let it go. "Maybe not, but honestly, I've never met someone so famous. Or so well-off."

Tilting his head, he continue to regard her. "Most women like it."

And that right there was the crux of the problem. A flash of irritation had her stepping back. "I'm not most women. I prefer not to live my life under a spotlight."

He moved with her. "Ah, but don't you like nice things? Pretty clothes, jewelry? Fine wines and multilayered meals? What about travel? I can take you to any location you've ever wanted to visit, no matter how exotic. We can go on an African safari, if you wish. Explore the ruins in Athens, or go to Spain to make a pilgrimage on the Camino de Santiago."

These things he held out to tempt her, as if he dangled a carrot before a hungry rabbit. While she truly enjoyed nice things every now and then, she didn't like the way he used the idea of them to try and tempt her into a relationship with him.

"Not so much," she managed, sounding flippant and feeling pretty damn proud of herself. "I'm just fine here in Galveston."

When she went to turn away, he stopped her with a light touch on her shoulder. "What can I give you to make you want to be with me?"

Despite the excited leap of her pulse at his touch, she knew going down that road with him would only lead to her being hurt. "You," she answered, her voice hoarse with repressed desire. "All the *things* you have don't really matter to me. You, the man, do. I'm attracted to you, I don't deny that. But I'm a private person. I have no desire to be constantly thrust into the public eye."

"I can always close the deal and buy us an island," he teased. At least, she hoped he was teasing.

"That's not the only reason. I'm at a stage in my life where I'm not looking for a fling. I need commitment. You've said on more than one occasion you don't know if you could ever be satisfied with just one woman for more than a couple of months."

"So you have read about me?" he asked, clearly not taking her seriously.

Ignoring his comment, she bulldozed on. "I'm not saying that's wrong, because if that's what works for you, that's you. But for me, I can't do a short-term relationship at this point in my life."

His eyes darkened, the blue almost black. "I've never had a woman turn me down for that reason before."

She had to laugh at his arrogance. "That's because you've been hanging out with the wrong kind of woman. Now you need to go away and let me get on with my life."

To her relief—and if she was completely honest, disappointment—he swung his legs over the side of the bed and stood, supremely unself-conscious about his naked-

ness. He strode over to where he'd dropped his jeans and
underwear, and tugged them on with deliberate movements. Then he pulled on his shirt, clearly preoccupied as
he dressed. Heaven help her, she watched him, even now
enthralled with the male perfection of his body.

When he'd gotten fully dressed, he turned to face her.

"I don't usually beg, but why not give us another month?
We can have a lot of fun. And that's not enough time for
anyone to get hurt."

Maybe not him, but she already cared about him far
too much.

"No. We need to stop this," she said, her voice rusty. "I
honestly think it's time we said goodbye."

He froze, the warmth fading from his gaze.

"Sorry," she said. She thought she could pull off a casual shrug. At least she could try. "We both agreed we
wanted something short, with no strings. It's time for me
to move on."

Was that hurt she saw flash across his face? No, that
would only be wishful thinking on her part. She wasn't stupid enough to expect him to jump up, declare his undying
love and propose marriage. And even if he did, would it be
enough? She could only conceive if her partner loved her
as much as she loved him, and she wasn't foolish enough
to believe he did.

"Why?" he asked again, his expressionless features and
flat tone giving her no hint of how he felt. "Why ruin a
good thing? Let this run its course and enjoy it while you
can. You can find your commitment with the next guy."

Ouch. The next guy. More proof that he didn't truly care
for her, not the way she wanted and needed.

"That's just it. I can't." She searched her mind for a be-
lievable reason. "I just turned thirty and my father is really
putting on the pressure for me to get married."

Her face heated. Not a complete lie, though not entirely the entire truth, either.

"Thirty, huh?" Sounding completely unbothered, he studied her, head tilted. "Any particular reason why your father wants you married soon?"

Now came the tricky part. She couldn't exactly tell him about her destiny. Or could she? If anything was designed to send him running for the door, this would be it. Adding the fact that she was thoroughly tired of lying, she decided she'd do it. He knew everything else about her. Why not tell him the rest of it?

"My biological clock is ticking. More than ticking. You know how all along I've talked about my destiny?"

He nodded, expression curious.

"Well, my destiny is to help the Drakkor species continue. I have to get pregnant." She took a deep breath, aware she'd blurted the information since she'd wanted to go all in before she had time to reconsider.

Then, while he gaped at her, she continued.

"Female Drakkor are the only ones able to reproduce. The same disease that killed our women made our males sterile. There are only four of us females remaining. One is already pregnant. If our line is to continue, I have to fulfill my destiny and conceive a child."

His features might have been carved from marble. "So *this* is what you kept talking about, the duty, the task? Your destiny?"

Heart pounding, she nodded. "Yes." She debated telling him the rest of it, the bit about love being a necessary ingredient, and decided against it. Since none of this involved him, he didn't need to know all the details.

"Your destiny is to get pregnant?"

Again she nodded.

"There isn't, uh, a chance that you could have…" he cleared his throat "…gotten pregnant while we, er…is there?

"No. None whatsoever."

Heaven help her, her heart shattered a little at the relief in his face.

"That's good," he said.

She didn't respond. She saw no need to tell him that birth control was the one thing she didn't need. Only if she and her partner were in love with each other would her body allow a seed to take root.

What had once seemed difficult now felt impossible.

"I supposed you have certain qualities you're looking for in the man who will father your child," he drawled.

"Yes, I do. I have a list," she said, pushing away a spark of fury. She might be close to babbling, but never more had she felt the need to fill the aching silence with noise. "I've kept it updated all the years I've been searching, but haven't had any luck in anyone even coming close."

What she didn't tell him was that even though he met very few of the bullet-point items on her list, she'd have gladly tossed the thing away for him.

More proof of just how foolish she'd allowed herself to become.

Though he pretended to be unaffected, Ryan could hardly believe what he was hearing. Maria's secret destiny was to be some sort of…broodmare? Seriously? With all her intelligence, her beauty and her strength, he'd expected something a bit loftier.

Then he reconsidered. He guessed maybe Savior of the Drakkor could be considered lofty enough. Sort of.

If he tried really hard, he could still be rational. Or so he thought. Though she had a point—he wasn't the marrying kind—suddenly the idea of her having a child with anyone else made him want to punch something.

"I have an idea," he said, before he could reconsider. "I'd be perfectly happy to father your child, if you'd give me a few days to have my attorneys draft up some sort of agreement."

A flash of anger sparked in those amazing brown eyes. "An agreement. I see. But there's no need for such a thing. I can't have children with you. It doesn't work that way."

No doubt she was just being difficult. "Then how does it work?" he asked, using his most reasonable and rational tone, even though he spoke through clenched teeth. "Explain it to me, please."

She shook her head. "Someone like you would never understand. What I need is the opposite of legal agreements and cut-and-dried arrangements. I need…"

Whatever she'd been about to say, apparently she realized she couldn't. Her lovely eyes widened and she closed her mouth with an audible snap. "Let me see if I can put this in words you'll understand. I need a mate."

A mate. Every Shape-shifter knew what this meant, even if not everyone believed such a thing could be possible. A mate was more than a partner or a spouse. A mate was the one individual fated to be with the other half of his or her soul.

Ryan was so not her mate. Or anyone's, for that matter. In fact, he privately thought the term had been cooked up by a bunch of old spinsters, sitting around discussing romance and ways to make women happy. He'd never known one single person who'd met his or her true mate, and even though he'd heard stories about someone who had, he put them in the same category as fairy tales.

Something of his thoughts must have shown in his face.

"Now you get it," she said, her voice relieved and also

sad. "That's why I can't waste any more time with this *fling*. I've got to continue my search for the real thing."

Ouch. But he couldn't blame her. "You're looking for your mate?" he asked, trying like hell to ignore the way his chest hurt at the thought of her with another man.

She took a deep breath and slowly nodded. "Yes. Ultimately, that is part of my destiny."

Bitterness soured his stomach. That this woman, this amazing, beautiful, talented woman should fixate on nothing more than finding her mate, made him want to punch a hole in the wall. He wouldn't, of course, because who was he to deride anyone's heartfelt desire?

"Let me help you," he offered, wondering if he'd lost his mind. "I might be able to introduce you to someone. Let me see your list."

After the briefest hesitation, unsmiling, she handed it over.

Once he got past the fact that there were bullet points, he began to read. As he did, he concluded that she didn't want a mate, she wanted a fictional man who, if he'd ever existed on this Earth, would have been a saint.

He started over at the beginning, just to make sure.

At first the list wasn't bad. *Good sense of humor, tall, handsome, physically active, loves animals and small children.*

All of those generalizations made sense.

Helps out with the household chores, including taking care of our children.

Most women expected that these days. He continued to read.

Donates time and money to charity.

Has empathy with others, no matter what race or religion or sexual orientation.

Puts others before himself.

All very noble qualities. And then her list got…strange.
Understands my needs without my vocalizing them.
Is able to accurately read my moods.

So, what? She wanted a man who was clairvoyant?

Several items below had been crossed out. Who knew, maybe her father had talked sense into her, or she'd realized she was asking for a man who didn't exist.

He eyed her, aching with the power of her beauty.

"I can do this," he heard himself say, inwardly wincing. "I can help you."

"Seriously?"

"Yes. You want to find a mate? Fine. I can work from this list. I have friends, contacts, business associates. Surely you can find someone to your liking among them."

Looking down, she covered her eyes with her hand. He thought, honestly believed, she'd refuse. But then she lifted her chin and looked him right in the eye. "I'd appreciate your help." The resignation in her quiet voice nearly broke him.

"Great." Best to get busy, keep busy, so she wouldn't see how much her quick capitulation had hurt him. But, then again, what had he expected her to do? Tell him she didn't need anyone else, that he was the only man she wanted?

Of course not. He wouldn't have believed her anyway. Women never expected more than a good time from him and he was always happy to meet their expectations.

Now, he'd do his damnedest to meet Maria's. His dreams and hers weren't the same anyway.

"This list," he pushed, handing it back to her, relentless in his helpfulness. When she accepted it, he clenched his teeth and forced a smile. "Can you get me a copy of it? I'll need to keep one with me for reference. I might be traveling back to Austin for business," he lied. "While I'm there, I'll see if I can find anyone suitable and bring them back to Galveston for you to meet."

Again the broodmare comparison came to mind. Wisely, he kept that to himself.

"Of course." Back stiff, she turned and left the room. "I just need to print off another copy and I'll be right back."

Marching down the hall to her room, Maria tried with every step to convince herself that this new development was actually a good thing. More than that—great, in fact. Ryan had a large social circle and knew a ton of people from every walk of life. Surely among them she could find a man she could love and who would love her in return.

If Ryan didn't find it awkward, then how could she? After all, they'd only had a fling, nothing more.

Having Ryan assist in her search for a mate made perfect sense, didn't it? Both of them had made it clear that they could never be more than friends, albeit intimate ones.

Still, she couldn't help but wish, for one fleeting second, that he'd have been willing to fight for her. That he might have found the thought of her with another man completely unpalatable.

Ah, well. It wasn't meant to be. She wondered if he planned to remain in Austin, if this asking for her list might be nothing more than a ruse. She considered calling him on it, and then decided she shouldn't really care.

Double-checking her list for the third time, she turned on her computer and waited for it to boot up. Soon, she'd be back on track. She was all ready to do what she needed to do. The last thing she needed to focus on was a too-enticing, sexy man who could never be anything more than a casual fling.

After printing out a second copy, she folded it in half and sighed.

This time, she'd make a better plan. No more bars or dance clubs. She'd sign up to do CrossFit three times a week and a writing workshop once a week, and she might volunteer to help out at the animal shelter on Fridays. She thought any of these things would be fine ways to meet her potential baby daddy. As an added bonus, she'd get in shape, exercise her creativity and help animals.

If the thought of all this made her teeth clench and her throat clog, so be it. She couldn't keep sitting around and expecting the perfect man to come to her. And even if he already had, it wasn't meant to be.

Before she lost her nerve, she marched back down the hall and handed the copy of her list to Ryan.

"Thank you." Accepting the folded paper from her, he raised one brow. "I have to admit, I'm curious about one thing. May I ask why you have bullet points?"

"Sure." She shrugged. "I like to be organized. This is too important to leave to chance."

"Why?" Gaze intense, he leaned forward. "Why is it so essential for you to find the perfect man? Surely there are any number of men who'd be willing to father a child with you."

"It just is." There were some things she couldn't vocalize. This was one of them.

"Okay. I'm sure I can help," he offered, sounding pleased. "Let me take this with me. I'm sure someone I know will fit the bill."

Though she nodded, she felt queasy. It stung that she meant so little to him he was willing to help her find another man.

Ryan paused near her front door, as if waiting for her to say or do something. She supposed he hoped she'd offer him shelter and a continuation of the friends-with-benefits relationship he clearly found so enjoyable.

"Take care," she said, to help send him on his way. "And have a safe trip back to Austin."

He nodded and opened the door. She stood staring after him as he got into his Jeep, started the engine and drove away. She'd once considered asking him why someone with his money chose to drive a Jeep, but then he probably had thirty different cars parked in a huge garage somewhere.

And now America's Most Eligible Billionaire claimed he'd help her find a mate.

The dragon inside her stirred, showing that her tension had made her beast restless. She needed to stop thinking about Ryan's offer to help and focus more on her own plan of action.

Yet she couldn't. Now that Ryan had left, she felt an empty, aching void. She wondered how she'd feel, having a man with whom she'd shared so much introduce her to one of his friends.

The ick factor seemed undeniable. Still, even as unpalatable as she found the idea, the more she thought about it, the more it made sense. What better way to get over her infatuation with him than to allow him to help her find a husband?

Her phone rang as she closed and locked her front door. Her father. Maybe he had good news. She hoped he might be calling to tell her Polacek had been captured.

Instead, it was pretty much the opposite.

"Are you all right?" he asked, sounding frantic. "Polacek has captured Tracey Beauchamp." Tracey was one of the other female Drakkor. Maria had never met Tracey or Stephanie or Tammy, though she—like every other Drakkor—knew their names.

Maria's heart sank. "How?"

"We're not sure. She disappeared. According to her father, she'd just met someone promising and was hopeful he would work out. Her friends reported her missing this morning when she didn't come home after a date with her new man."

Logic before panic. "How do you know it's Polacek?" she asked. "Any number of things might have happened."

"True. Except Polacek made a video and emailed it to the Council. I won't repeat to you what he said, but it's awful."

"I need you to contact the Council," Maria said. "Tell them they need to get the others to the Eyrie, one at a time and have Micah, Brandon and Roger teach them how to use their magic. Start with Stephanie and when she's done, send Tammy."

"Tammy's in seclusion getting ready for her baby."

Tammy had been the first and only one to get pregnant. Her surprise pregnancy had told the Drakkor they'd been wrong all along about the females being sterile. Tammy had spent hours being interviewed, and the scientists had realized how necessary love was to the equation.

"I don't care what she's doing," Maria told him. "If she can't travel, send a teacher to her. I wouldn't put it past Polacek to decide to take her out along with her unborn child. The way he thinks, he might figure it's better to take out our entire race if he can't be part of continuing it."

Her father cursed. "You're probably right. I'll reach out to them immediately. But before I go, are you safe?"

"I believe so. There were a few rough spots, but I learned my lessons well. I'm confident my magic is strong enough to defeat him." Though she felt a tiny niggle of doubt, she ignored it. The one part of the equation no one knew was exactly how powerful Polacek's magic had become. She hoped she never had to find out.

Chapter 10

Ryan drove to the seawall and parked. He sat in his Jeep, watching the beach and the waves, along with the hordes of tourists. Stunned, he took Maria's list from his pocket and slowly unfolded it. He couldn't believe he'd offered to help Maria find a new boyfriend. Worse, he couldn't believe she'd accepted.

Once again, he read over the list. He didn't understand why no one had told her how unrealistic some of the items were. Setting her up for failure made no sense. But she'd be doomed to disappointment if she expected any man—other than maybe a magical Drakkor—to be so in tune with her he could read her mind.

He thought of some of the stories he'd heard about true mates. Some said that once they'd mated they could intuitively get what the other was thinking. But he doubted this happened the instant they met. Heck, he seriously doubted it happened at all.

Disheartened, and wondering why he felt so gloomy, he pulled out from the parking lot and headed home to Austin.

Once he'd left the island, he phoned Timothy. "Any progress in dealing with the house fire?"

"Omigod, no." Timothy's voice went high, a sure sign his nerves were frazzled. "In fact, the longer you stay away, the more those people seem to think you had something to do with the fire. I pointed out to them that you could buy a hundred beach houses without batting an eye, but they didn't seem to care. I think they're trying to get a court order or something to make you appear. Why won't you? Where are you?"

"I'm on my way to Austin." Ryan spoke in a calm and level tone, the way he always did when Timothy freaked out. "I've got a few things I need to take care of at home. Plus I want to stop in at the office tomorrow. So if you have any paperwork needing my attention, have it ready."

"Will do. But, Ryan, why won't you deal with the house thing? It's gotten out of control. One visit from you would put an end to it. Those investigators keep blowing up our phone lines with their incessant calling."

Ryan sighed. "To be honest, I'd managed to forget about that fire."

"Forget? How could you forget? Your vacation house was torched."

"I've had a lot on my mind. Look, I'll talk to you tomorrow, okay?" Ryan ended the call before Timothy could protest. And then, because his assistant was absolutely right, he took the first exit, turned around and headed back to Galveston to deal with the fire. Some things did need to be handled, and once he got this taken care of his insurance could take over and see about getting his house repaired or replaced.

Plus, he hoped if he kept himself busy, he could stop thinking about the beautiful and desirable Maria Miranda.

Maria kept busy the next several days, blessedly so. Her heart wouldn't stop aching, which made her feel foolish, so she embraced the distraction to keep her mind off Ryan. Summers were the busiest time of the year at the wedding chapel and they were booked solid every single day. Her father kept her apprised of what the Council and the Pack were doing to try and locate Polacek and Tracey. So far, they'd had little success.

They had, however, followed Maria's advice and sent Stephanie to the Eyrie to train in using her magic. Maria could only hope that Micah, Brandon and Roger didn't give Stephanie as much of a hard time as they had her.

Four nights into Ryan's absence, Maria got home exhausted, her stomach grumbling from hunger. She made a quick sandwich and turned on the television, needing a few minutes of mindless entertainment so she could begin to relax.

Aimlessly clicking through television shows, Maria stopped when Ryan's handsome face flashed up on her screen.

"Everyone loves Ryan Howard," the female announcer said. "Now, we here at Additional TV are going to find out what makes America's Most Eligible Billionaire Bachelor tick."

Maria froze. Her heart flip-flopped in her chest. How was it she couldn't escape this man, even when he was out of town? She wondered when this interview had been filmed. No doubt long before she'd ever met him.

Ignoring her misgivings, Maria set the remote on the coffee table and watched.

Clearly, the host, Tiffani Martin, found Ryan attractive. But then again, Maria thought as she chowed down on her sandwich, who wouldn't? Still, the way the woman leaned in and constantly found ways to touch Ryan, began to annoy her.

"I know all our female viewers are wondering if you can describe your perfect woman," Tiffani asked, batting her false eyelashes at him.

Despite everything, Maria found herself holding her breath as she waited to hear what he would say.

"I'm not sure I actually have a perfect woman." Looking directly at the camera, Ryan smiled that confident and sexy smile that Maria knew so well. "I love women too much to be able to answer that question. They're all flawless, in my opinion."

"Nicely done," Tiffani's smile never faltered. "But surely you have a type that you're attracted to. Can you at least give us a hint of what that might be?"

Clearly, she wanted Ryan to tell her *she* was his type. Maria shook her head. No wonder Ryan never wanted to settle down. Why should he, when beautiful women fell all over themselves to get close to him?

"What I like in a woman is self-confidence," Ryan finally answered. "A woman who knows what she wants and isn't afraid to go after it."

Stunned, Maria dropped the rest of her sandwich back in the plate. She'd thought he'd say something shallow, something about curves or eyes, or the willingness to do whatever he wanted.

"Interesting," Tiffani purred, clearly aware she oozed self-confidence. "Anything else you'd like to add?"

Still smiling, Ryan shook his head. His dark hair gleamed in the studio lights. Once again, Maria's chest ached. She'd never known a man could be so dangerously beautiful.

"Well then, why don't you tell us a little bit about how you became a billionaire? Considering your past, that must have been quite a climb."

His past? Maria realized that, in all the time she'd known Ryan, he'd talked very little about himself.

His expression changed, just slightly. Not enough for the talk show host to notice, but Maria did. Clearly, he still wasn't a fan of tooting his own horn.

His tone clipped, he recited the history of how he'd started his own company, rushing along through dry facts and places and dates with the bored air of a man who has repeated himself far too many times before.

"But I'm sure your viewers know all that," he finished, relaxing somewhat as he made a show of glancing at his watch. "Unless you have more questions, I think our time is just about over."

"Not yet." When Tiffani smiled at the camera as if inviting viewers in to a private joke, her expression reminded Maria of a shark. "What about toys? I think our viewers would be interested to know what a billionaire drives. I assume you have several cars, a yacht, and what else?"

Ryan's smile had completely vanished now. "The answer to that question can easily be looked up on the internet. Yes, I have a couple of boats, and numerous cars and a private jet. I also have a few houses here and there." Again he checked his watch. "Now if you don't have anything interesting to ask, I need to be going."

Appearing completely unfazed by Ryan's lack of enthusiasm, Tiffani leaned forward and put her hand on his leg, her long scarlet nails vivid against his black pants. "I have more," she said softly, her expression serious for the first time since the interview started. "Talk about your past. Before you were rich. I understand you lived in your car for a while?"

Expression remote, he gave the slightest of nods. "I did. That was a long time ago."

"Not that long," she put in, her smooth tone at odds with the flat look in his eyes. "Not even ten years. I believe you were in college?"

"I left college. I wanted to start my own company. My father refused to help me and wouldn't let me come home. Nor would he contribute financially if I left school. I quit anyway."

"What about your mother?"

"My mother was in no condition to help me. She was sick and getting treatment."

Tiffani checked her notes. "For drug and alcohol abuse, is that correct?"

Anger hardened his features. "That is correct."

Maria swallowed a sudden lump in her throat. How brave Ryan had been. And, clearly, he'd done the right thing.

"Pretty amazing that you were able to do all this without any help." Tiffani chirped, echoing Maria's thoughts.

"If you say so. Determination and hard work got me where I am," he said, looking directly at the camera.

"And maybe a bit of luck?" Tiffani chimed in, still smiling.

"No luck came into it."

"Okay." Clearly not believing him, Tiffani took a deep breath. "And what about your parents? Did your mother recover? And what about your father? Are you still estranged from him today? Or did you kiss and make up once you became a billionaire?"

Instead of answering, Ryan pushed to his feet. "This interview is over," he said, still polite, even though clearly he was seething. "Thank you for your time."

"No, thank *you*," Tiffani gushed, watching Ryan stride

off the set. When he'd gone, she turned to face the camera her expression satisfied. "Even though he didn't answer, our producers did some research. While Ryan Howard is not close to his mother and father, who are now divorced, he did purchase his mother a lovely home in a retirement community in Florida, where she lives this very day."

The woman babbled on, glossing over Ryan's humanitarian efforts, and began showing photos of his various toys, as she'd put it.

Maria grabbed the remote and turned the television off, more than a bit stunned. While she—like most of the country, apparently—had taken Ryan as a superficial, conceited billionaire playboy, learning just this kernel of his past made her want to know more.

But then, why? She had no future with him, no matter how badly she wanted one.

Which she didn't, she told herself fiercely. The sooner she found her true mate, the better.

After dealing with the insurance adjuster and talking with both the Galveston Police Department and the arson investigator for the fire department, Ryan considered trying to find a hotel room instead of driving back to Austin. But with tourist season in full swing, he wasn't in the mood for dealing with so many people, so he left the crowded island and decided to keep driving until he made it home to Austin.

Meanwhile, he called Timothy and asked him to locate any and all material he could find on the Drakkor and have it sent to Ryan's house. Timothy, who was also Pack, at first had no idea what his boss meant, but after Ryan filled him in, Tim promised to get to work on it right away.

Satisfied, Ryan drove and considered his next move. Maria wanted to find a mate, and for whatever reason,

Ryan had offered to help her. Part of him wanted to parade as many horrible men in front of her, so she could see none of them were fit to father her baby.

And this brought another dilemma. What did Ryan want from her? Did he really want her to agree to have a kid with him? Especially since she'd made it clear she wouldn't sign any legal papers?

When he finally pulled up to his gate and typed the code so it would swing open, he felt energized. Parking in his house garage—the four-car garage that faced the twelve-car garage on the other side of the driveway—he jumped out of his Jeep and bounded inside.

Timothy had already been by. And he'd certainly been busy. The small stack of books on the entryway table made Ryan smile.

Upon closer examination, he realized several of the books were very old and possibly rare. Which meant Timothy had spared no expense to locate what his boss had asked for.

In the kitchen, he popped open a beer and made himself a sandwich. Then, carrying everything over to his kitchen table, he sat down to eat and to read.

The first few books he picked up seemed more like history books. While he enjoyed those, with their heavy, crackling pages and beautiful color illustrations of the dragons in flight, they told him little other than their history. King Arthur and his knights had hunted them nearly to extinction, and the Drakkor had been forced to go into hiding in order to survive.

Which was definitely interesting. But he needed to know about the Drakkor *now* so he could find out why Maria believed her destiny was to have a child and why it had to be with another type of being other than a Drakkor.

But sadly, there wasn't much. History, history and more

history. He got it. The Drakkor were a proud people with a long and colorful past.

As for the future, what little he could find seemed deliberately vague. Except one statement jumped out at him, repeated in every single article he read.

There were very few Drakkor remaining. Their people, despite hiding from the knights of old, were still close to extinction. Which might explain why Maria felt the need to have a baby. But the more he read, the more he wanted to know the Drakkor's secrets. Clearly, they were hiding something. He needed to find out what.

Beyond the one statement and the endless history, he realized that, due to their secrecy and dwindling numbers, little was known of the dragon Shifters. Some believed they had magic—which Ryan knew to be true—while others mentioned they could only fly after a ritual sacrifice—something patently false since Ryan had personally witnessed two Drakkor flights and there had been no sacrifice.

One other item mentioned in all the books caught Ryan's attention. Drakkor women were known for being uncommonly beautiful. Which fit Maria to a T.

Still, he knew it wasn't only her beauty that drew him to her. Her unique outlook on things and the self-confidence that grew stronger each and every day attracted him, too.

He'd promised to help her find a mate. Because he cared about her, he'd make good on that promise.

In Austin, he felt too far away. Once he'd learned it could take up to a year before the insurance company would settle, he instructed Timothy to find him another beach house. He still intended to have his summer vacation on Galveston Island, even if he'd be spending his time finding some other man to be with the woman he still wanted.

He had Timothy make a cash offer, contingent upon the closing being pushed up to next week.

He read so much about the Drakkor that when he went to sleep at night, he started seeing dragons in his dreams. The first time it happened, he wasn't surprised. He'd been studying hard, trying to learn everything he could about Maria's people.

But now the dreams came with increasing frequency. He didn't feel in danger, and had no fear of closing his eyes. He simply didn't understand the reason. It seemed almost as if his subconscious might be trying to tell him something. It would be up to him to figure out what that might be.

He didn't have time to worry about it, though. He had to get busy and fulfill his promise to Maria.

He made a list of all his friends and employees who weren't married, eliminating those who were already involved in personal relationships. Several he knew wouldn't be good fits, personality wise. Those that might, he circled and then tried to compare them to the more realistic aspects of Maria's list.

Finally, he ended up with four candidates he thought might be suitable. None of them had current girlfriends, they weren't gay and when he showed them Maria's picture on his phone, each and every one of them expressed interest in meeting her, of course. When the first guy, his friend Tom, gushed over how beautiful she was, Ryan had to physically restrain himself from snarling *mine*.

It took him a few seconds to get himself back under control. As he listened to his friend marvel over Maria's exquisite beauty, every primal instinct inside him woke. Even his wolf self, dozing until that instant, sprang awake and alert, ready to do battle. If Tom had been Pack, he would have sensed this and reacted. Luckily, he was human and had no idea.

After his friend left, Ryan had to take a few minutes and calm himself. The other potential men all worked for him. If he hadn't already scheduled the other interviews back-to-back and had the three men already waiting in the reception area, he would have taken off, driven to his favorite wooded area and changed. Letting his wolf hunt felt like the only thing that would make him feel better.

But he couldn't. And Ryan hadn't succeeded in business so well without being able to put a game face on and proceed under duress.

So that was exactly what he did.

Somehow, he made it through the rest of the afternoon without losing his cool. Two of the men were Shifters—one was Pack and the other was part of the Lion Pride. Both of them immediately detected his inner beast's agitation. Ryan brushed it off by saying he'd waited too long since his last change. They both understood this, as everyone knew too much time in between shape-shifting could make one unstable.

The instant the last guy left his office, Ryan grabbed his files and, barely pausing for a quick word with his secretary, hurried out to head toward the woods to set his wolf free.

Despite her best intentions of staying busy, with work and wedding season in full swing, many nights Maria got off work too exhausted to exercise or dance or do much of anything other than sit in front of her TV.

Her father had taken to texting her every single night with status updates on the search for Doug Polacek and Tracey. So far, neither the Pack Protectors nor the Council had had any luck.

Thinking of what Polacek must be doing to that poor woman made Maria feel sick. Since his captive apparently consumed all his time, the Council didn't feel as if he was an immediate threat to Maria or the other women.

Despite that, Maria felt better learning each woman had traveled to Eyrie to learn how to use their magic to defend themselves. Especially since she knew there might come a day when Polacek tired of Tracey or—heaven forbid, killed her—and went looking for fresh meat.

When a week went by and she hadn't heard from Ryan, she told herself she didn't care. She really hadn't expected him to follow up on his promise to help her find her mate. She couldn't blame him for putting as much distance between them as possible.

Still, when her doorbell rang at eight o'clock on Friday night, her heart skipped a beat. Peeking through the peephole, she saw her friend Lourdes on her front porch.

Yanking open the door, she went to hug her old friend. "I thought you were in Mexico City," she began.

Lourdes stepped back with an elegant move and motioned with her hand. Instantly, bright lights came on, blinding Maria.

"What the…?" Shielding her eyes with her hand, she realized Lourdes had brought a camera crew.

"I'm sorry," Lourdes said, her brilliant smile anything but as she turned and spoke to the camera. "This is Maria Miranda, who has recently been spotted with Ryan Howard. Miss Miranda and I grew up together, and when she wanted to tell her story, I was, of course, her first choice."

Stunned and hurt, Maria shook her head. "Get off my property," she said. "Leave now before I call the police."

When Lourdes stepped down off the stoop, Maria closed the door in her face and locked it.

A few minutes later, her cell phone rang. Lourdes. Whether calling to apologize or to explain, Maria had nothing to say to the woman she'd once considered her friend. She declined four calls before finally blocking the number.

Her inner dragon roared, wanting out, but Maria pushed her beast back down and got on the treadmill instead. She ran until her clothes were drenched in sweat, until she could no longer tell the difference between perspiration and the tears streaming down her face. No, not tears, since she didn't cry.

Exhausted, she took a quick shower and settled down to watch the local news at ten.

A few minutes in, the brief video with Lourdes attempting to interview her came on. Stunned, Maria watched as the two anchor people dissected it.

"Clearly, Ryan Howard's new woman wants her privacy," the woman said.

"I, for one, can certainly see how a woman who looks like that could attract a billionaire," the man responded, whistling. "I just can't believe we have a local woman as gorgeous as her and no one has noticed."

"Clearly, Ryan Howard has." The woman laughed. "We'll put the call out there. Since she lives in Galveston, if anyone captures a picture of Ryan and her, send it in to us and we'll put in on our Facebook page."

Swallowing hard, Maria punched the remote and turned the news off.

Almost immediately, her cell phone rang. This time, the caller was her friend Rhonda. For one awful second, Maria caught herself wondering how this friend would turn on her. Then, realizing she was being ridiculous, she answered.

"Are you all right?" Rhonda asked, worry coloring her voice. "I just saw that segment on the news. I can't believe Lourdes did that to you."

Maria sighed. "Me, either. I'm guessing she figured she

had a chance to get some sort of scoop. If she'd only asked me first, I could have told her she was wasting her time. I'm no longer seeing Ryan Howard at all."

"What? Why not? What happened?"

"Nothing happened." Maria tried to keep the tension out of her tone. "I told you we just got together for a casual type of thing. No commitment. As far as I know, he's gone back to Austin."

"You sound sad." Of course her best friend picked up on this.

"Maybe a little," Maria allowed. "But you know how busy work is with so many summer weddings, and I've been super busy. Even if he was still on the island, I wouldn't have time to date him."

Rhonda laughed. "Oh, that's a lie! You can't tell me you wouldn't have made time for him."

They talked for a few more minutes. Rhonda ended the call with a vague promise to get together, the way she always did.

Shaking her head, Maria got up and began turning off the lights. Time to go to bed and get some sleep. Tomorrow would be another busy day.

When her cell rang yet again, just after she'd finished brushing her teeth, she checked the caller ID. Since she didn't recognize the number, she let the call go to voice mail. At least she knew Lourdes wouldn't have given her number to any other reporters—she wouldn't want to take a chance of someone else getting the story.

Right before getting into bed, Maria decided to listen to her message. When a man's voice began speaking in a flat, menacing tone, she froze.

"By now I'm sure you've heard of me. Doug. Doug Polacek." He spoke his name as if announcing royalty. "I have a visitor named Tracey and she isn't happy."

In the background, Maria heard a woman scream. Her blood ran cold.

"I think maybe some company might cheer her up," he continued. "Would you like to volunteer?"

Panicked, Maria pushed stop. She wanted to instantly erase the message, but knew she'd better let someone— her father, the council—hear it.

Pacing, she checked caller ID, wrote down the number and phoned her dad. When she relayed the information to him, he cursed. "That's it. I'm asking that you be put under heavy guard."

"Not necessary," she shot back, pacing her room to try and relieve the tension. "I have magic now."

"Don't argue. They'll be there tomorrow."

"As long as they understand that I have a business to run and a life to lead," she told him. "I can't have them interfering."

"You'll hardly even notice they're there."

Shaking her head, she finally agreed. Not knowing what else to do, she climbed into her bed and slid beneath the sheets. Her hand trembled as she reached for her lamp and clicked it off.

Alone in the total darkness, she told herself she had no reason to be afraid. Still, she couldn't help but wish Ryan was lying next to her so she could let him hold her and banish her fears with his body.

Chapter 11

Somehow, she must have fallen asleep. When she opened her eyes again, the sun had already risen, which meant she'd overslept.

She rushed through her usual morning preparations, then grabbed a bagel and slathered it with cream cheese before jumping into her car. Backing from her garage, she saw no sign of any guards or reporters or anything different than any other morning.

Which was good, she thought. Hopefully she could have a productive day and put all this craziness behind her.

Kathleen had already begun answering the phones by the time Maria hurried in.

"What did you do now?" Kathleen asked breathlessly, putting her caller on hold. "Every gossip mag and TV show has called and requested an interview. I thought you and Ryan were over."

Accepting the sheaf of pink messages, Maria frowned. "We are. One of my former friends must have stirred things up with her attempt to corral me into an interview last night. If anyone else calls, just tell them no outright."

"Even Oprah?" Eyes huge, Kathleen watched her.

"Has Oprah called?"

"Well, no, but she might. What do you want me to do if she does?"

Hiding her sigh, Maria shrugged. "You do know this is not a big enough story to catch Oprah's eye, right?"

"Maybe, maybe not. But you never know."

"Well, if Oprah calls, just put her on hold and let me know."

This appeared to satisfy Kathleen. And since Maria knew good and well Oprah wouldn't be beating down her door anytime soon, she went on into her office.

Her guards showed up exactly one hour later.

There were four of them, dressed in military-style fatigues. Their auras proclaimed them Pack, and their muscular bodies and soldierly demeanor declared them efficient.

A thoroughly flustered Kathleen rushed into Maria's office to tell her she had visitors.

"Thanks." Maria cut her off. "Send them back. I've been expecting them."

Though Kathleen's mouth fell open in surprise, she spun around and did exactly as Maria asked.

The leader, a tall man named Colton Richards, explained two men would be stationed at the wedding chapel and two at her home. "This is nonnegotiable," he said, giving her a flat stare. "We've been completely briefed on Polacek, and are well aware of what to expect."

She shrugged, doubting that. "Fine. But your guys are going to get superbored. I live a quiet life."

His smile transformed his face, making him less intimidating, and kind of cute. Covertly, she checked his hand, disappointed to see a gold wedding ring on his third finger.

One by one, she glanced at the three other men. Two of them had ringless hands. Still, they might be involved with someone. She'd never know unless she asked.

"Listen, are any of you gentlemen..." clearing her throat, she pushed past her embarrassment "...single and unattached?"

Colton's expression went blank, then he turned to look at one of his men, a husky blond with Viking legs and shaggy hair. Maria smiled at him, approving of the speculative way he eyed her. She wouldn't have been surprised to find out his name was Thor.

"Um, I am," he told her, his tone almost apologetic. "But you're not my type."

Stunned, she wasn't sure how to reply to that.

Colton laughed. "James prefers men," he said. "Sorry."

What could she do but throw up her hands and laugh. "Ah, well, at least I tried."

The other men all laughed with her, making her feel marginally better.

"Colton's a widower," James threw in, earning a death stare from his boss. "Though he still wears his wedding ring."

"I don't believe in mixing business with pleasure," he told her. "Now, if you don't mind, ma'am, we'll be getting to work. By the way, we'll be screening all phone calls, so I'm going to need to ask you to let them go to voice mail."

Immediately she shook her head. "That will never work. This is our busiest season."

"Your receptionist can check each message the instant it has finished recording, as long as she doesn't delete it. We just need to be able to access every call."

Maria considered, well aware Kathleen wasn't going to

like this. "Fine, I'll give it a try. But I'll tell you right now, if it messes with my business, I won't be continuing it."

"Fair enough," Colton said. "We can see ourselves out. I promise you won't even notice we're here."

Ryan felt marginally better after letting his wolf run free. He ran until all four of his legs ached, hunted until his hunger had been sated and even indulged in a bit of howling at the moon. His melancholy had even carried over after he changed, though logically he had no idea why.

He decided, after sleeping on it, that he'd introduce Maria to the two men who were Shape-shifters, as he felt they'd be better candidates to be with a Drakkor. Never mind that his insides twisted at the thought. He'd told her he would help and so he would. Now all he had to do was set things up and see what happened. As soon as Timothy let him know he had a new house, Ryan would bring them to a company retreat and begin the introductions.

Then he'd make himself scarce. There was a limit to how much he could take. The idea of watching another man put his hands on Maria would be way past it.

Timothy phoned him shortly past noon. Apparently dangling cash in front of a seller had worked. "It's a much more luxurious place. Even better, you close in three days," he said, naming a title company in Houston. Ryan promised to be there.

"Perfect. I even got the seller to leave the furnishings for a nominal fee. I really think you're going to love this."

Though Ryan didn't really care, he thanked Timothy and agreed he probably would. After he hung up he got busy setting a date in a week for a mini-retreat with the two men he'd selected to meet Maria.

After the closing, Ryan drove back to Galveston, to the address on his paperwork, and eyed the beach house.

Located within the Enclaves of Pirates Cove, the place had cost him a little over two million, but it was worth it. This place actually had land and multiple decks. He made a mental note to thank Timothy again. He might actually enjoy spending his summer here.

And Maria would love it. As the thought occurred to him, he realized he still wasn't over her. Which he didn't understand. Acting like a lovesick boy wasn't in character for him, not at all. More than anyone, he knew he could never give Maria what she wanted from a man. Yet he couldn't stop thinking about her.

It had to be the way she'd brushed him off. He wasn't used to that and maybe his pride had been pricked, just a little. He'd get his mojo back in time.

After thoroughly exploring the house, he unpacked his ice chest, opened a beer and carried it out onto the patio, enjoying the view of the sun setting over the ocean.

The next morning, he phoned the wedding chapel. While he found it odd when he got the answering machine rather than a live person, he figured this must be their busiest season, so he left a message.

Maria didn't return his call.

That afternoon, he phoned her cell. Again, he got voice mail, so he left yet another message.

He waited two days, then on the third he finally admitted to himself that she wasn't going to let him make contact. Which might be for the best. At least he could say he tried. Despite his offer to help her find another man, every time he pictured her with someone else, his gut clenched. Still, since she'd been completely honest with him, and he couldn't give her what she needed, finding someone else had seemed the least he could do. Maybe now he could go on with his summer, relegating her to his memories, like any other past fling.

Except she wouldn't go. He still wanted her.

To ease his restlessness, he went out to Corps Woods and changed into wolf again, all the while watching for another sight of the beautiful dragon. He saw nothing, and more importantly, smelled nothing. The constant sea breeze had washed away any trace of a scent.

This time, the edgy feeling refused to leave him, no matter how long he remained wolf. Finally he admitted to himself that he had to see her.

He called her cell once again. This time, she answered, which so surprised him, he found himself at a momentary loss of words.

"Hello?" she asked, a trace of impatience in her voice. "Are you there?"

"I am." He spoke just as remotely. "Just a bit surprised you answered, since you never called me back."

"Why are you calling me?" Her surprise seemed genuine, which rankled him. "You know as well as I do that our fling is over."

For the first time he realized he might have hurt her with his choice of words. At least he was making an honest effort to make up for it. "Remember I promised to help you fulfill your destiny?" He considered it a minor miracle that he didn't choke on the words. "Well, I've got two candidates for you to meet. Are you up for a meeting, like, maybe this coming weekend?"

"Oh, wow." Her swift intake of air told him he'd stunned her. "Here? In Galveston?"

"Sure. They work for me. If you'd like, you and I can get together to discuss specifics."

"Ah. Sure. How about tonight, after work?"

Slightly annoyed at the way she suddenly made time for him now that he had men for her to meet, he nevertheless agreed. Just the thought of seeing her again made him feel dizzy with desire. And wonder what the hell he was doing, trying to set her up with other men.

"See you around eight," she said, and ended the call.

The rest of the day, anticipation made him impatient. Since his new house had come with a workout room, complete with equipment, he spent a couple of hours punishing his body.

After a quick shower and a protein shake, he still had several hours left to kill.

He went out for dinner, and spent some time roaming the Strand. Finally, he got in his Jeep and drove to her house, parking right in front of it.

As he opened his car door to get out, a tall, muscular man walked up in front of him, blocking him from the house. The man's aura proclaimed him Pack.

"Excuse me," Ryan said, attempting to go around.

But the man cut him off again. "State your business." He flashed an ID badge. Pack Protector.

Stunned, Ryan shook his head. "I'm here to visit Maria Miranda."

"No." The guy glared at him. "You're not. Best be moving along."

As Ryan considered arguing, another man stepped out from the shadow of a huge palm tree. "Better do as he says, buddy."

To his surprise, Ryan recognized the second man. "Colton?"

Colton squinted at him. "Ryan? I thought you and Maria were no longer dating."

Ryan laughed. "We're not. But we're friends. She's expecting me. What are the Protectors doing here?"

"Guarding her. Some crazy Drakkor snatched another woman. It appears Maria might be in danger. Her father specifically requested she be guarded 24/7."

Ryan nodded, refraining from bringing up magic. Colton wouldn't believe him anyway. "Can you call her and let her know I'm here?"

"Sure thing." The other man turned away and spoke into his cell phone. A flash of jealousy stabbed Ryan in his gut. Unbelievable. Aware of his own foolishness, Ryan shook it off.

A second later, Colton turned to him with a wide smile. "She says to let you go on in."

Thanking his friend, Ryan hurried up the sidewalk, completely unprepared for the joy that exploded within him at his first sight of her as she opened her door.

"Come on in," she said, smiling as she stepped aside so he could enter. Instead, he pulled her close for a hug, craving the feel of her body against his.

Her uneasy laugh had him releasing her just as quickly. Hounds, she looked beautiful, especially since she'd clearly washed off her makeup. Without it, she looked fresh, sexy and vibrant, with her long dark hair falling around her smooth shoulders. She wore a tight tank top and formfitting shorts, highlighting her lush curves. His body stirred as he gazed at her.

"Would you like something to drink?" she asked, turning and leading the way into her small kitchen.

"Sure." He took a seat at the kitchen bar to hide his growing arousal.

She poured them both tall glasses of iced tea. Instead of sitting next to him, she remained standing on the other side of the bar.

"I bought another house," he told her, more to break the ice than anything else.

"The problems of rich people." She shook her head. "What are you going to do with the first one once it's repaired?"

"Maybe sell it. I like this new one better. I wrote the address down in case you ever want to come and see it." He slid the paper across to her.

She accepted it without a word, putting it inside one of her kitchen drawers. "So, what do you have?"

At first, her question made no sense, until he realized he still held the manila folder with basic info on the two men he'd selected as potential mates for her.

Clenching his jaw, he slid the folder across the counter. He'd done a lot of difficult things in his life, but damned if this wasn't turning out to be one of the hardest.

Taking it, she hesitated. Meeting his gaze, she sighed. "I've got to tell you, this just feels…weird."

Oh, it felt a hundred times worse than that, he thought, nodding grimly. For a second, he wanted to tell her he'd do whatever she wanted, be whatever she needed, and he wouldn't make her sign a single document, ever.

But common sense asserted itself, and he looked away. Eventually, some other woman would come along and pique his interest and Maria would get hurt. Plus, Ryan hadn't gotten to where he was in life by making foolish, sentimental decisions. He didn't plan to lose everything he'd worked so hard for just because of his infatuation with her.

Because that's what it had to be. Infatuation. Once he met someone else, he could move on.

This idea—which unbelievably had never occurred to him—rocked him to his core. Of course. Why hadn't he thought of that? A distraction. Beautiful women always worked wonders. He just needed to find another one.

Immensely cheered, he opened the folder for her and began to tell her about Jeff, the Shifter who also was Pack.

Maria watched Ryan closely as he sat in her kitchen discussing her dating another man. At first she'd thought he'd actually come to tell her he had a problem with procuring dates for her. To her dismay, he now appeared genuinely excited about the prospect.

As she should be. Heaven knew, if she ever intended to get pregnant, she needed to meet someone. Work had kept her so busy she hadn't had time to put any of her ambitious plans to socialize into play.

She thought she made appropriate noises of approval at the first candidate, a handsome guy named Jeff. Not her type at all, if she went strictly by the photograph, but she was entirely willing to meet him in person and give him a chance.

The second man, David Morrison, looked like a nice guy, too, if a little more rough around the edges than Jeff. She heard herself agree to back-to-back dates, the first one this coming Friday night, the other on Saturday.

Once she'd agreed, Ryan closed the folder and drank his tea. With his dark hair longer and shaggier than he normally wore it, his strong features and the confident way he moved had her aching to touch him. He looked even more handsome and virile than she remembered, and perversely she was glad she hadn't tried to look her best for him. Even now, it took every bit of self-control she possessed not to go around the bar and kiss him, right there in her own kitchen. Especially since she knew how combustible the two of them were together and that they'd end up in her bed.

With every fiber of her being, she wanted this. She even took a step forward, as though his presence compelled her. Yet she managed to stop and remind herself she had duties and responsibilities. The time had come to take them seriously.

So she smiled and nodded and sipped her tea. She agreed to meet two men in whom she had no real interest, all the while aching for the one man she could never have. She'd even gone so far as to make a list—with bullet points—of the reasons. Billionaire playboys had never been in her future.

Finally Ryan left. She followed him to the door, locking up carefully once he'd gone. When she turned to go back to her kitchen, she felt as if all the oxygen had left with him.

Shaking her head at her own stupidity, she went to her room to reread her list, hoping if she did she'd feel better about letting him go. She fell asleep with the list tucked under her pillow.

The next morning all remained quiet at her little house. Despite Polacek's threats, he didn't appear, which didn't help cut through Maria's unease. Some small voice kept warning her of danger. One of the things she'd learned in Eyrie had been to pay attention to her own instincts.

She called the number Colton Richards had given her and, despite feeling slightly foolish, warned him to tell his men to be ready. Just in case.

To his credit, he didn't sound patronizing when he told her he would do so immediately.

The rest of the day, she jumped at every little sound, so much so she was driving herself crazy. Though she longed to call Ryan, she finally sat herself down in her chair and reminded herself she had enough control over her magical abilities to defend herself.

The day ended without incident, as did the next. Finally, Friday dawned, the day she'd agreed to go on a date with Jeff. She'd always hated blind dates, though she viewed them as a necessary evil considering her situation. The fact that Ryan had set this one up made it worse.

Still, she was nothing if not a trouper. Ryan had told her he'd have Jeff call her so they could discuss where they wanted to go.

* * *

Ryan hadn't realized Maria would go with Jeff to the same bar where Ryan had first met her. When Friday night arrived and he knew they'd have their first date, he'd promptly taken himself there to drown his sorrows. Though he'd initially planned to try and meet someone else, he'd been stunned to find out that the idea held no appeal for him. He wanted Maria, not any other woman.

This time, he'd taken a bit more trouble with his disguise and no one recognized him. He'd also tried to make himself as unattractive as possible to ensure he'd be left alone.

Jeff had driven down from Austin that morning and hung out with Ryan at his new beach house. Ryan had kept his jaw clenched and his mouth shut while the other man waxed poetic over how lucky he considered himself to be going on a blind date with someone as gorgeous as Maria Miranda.

Ryan fought the urge to open his front door and push Jeff out of the house.

Instead, because he'd given his word to Maria, he'd gone through with it. For whatever reason, he hoped the two of them didn't hit it off.

Either way, they'd gone on a date. Realizing he couldn't remain alone in his new house while Jeff was with her, Ryan had come here.

One drink, he'd told himself. He'd have one drink, maybe two, then he'd slip out and go take a walk on the beach.

Fighting his way through the crowd to the bar, he'd ordered a Shiner and paid. After taking a deep drink of the ice-cold beer, he turned and surveyed the room, already regretting whatever impulse had made him step inside.

And then he saw them. Jeff had his arm around her

slender shoulders, which made Ryan immediately want to knock it off.

Maria looked gorgeous, as always. She'd chosen a form-fitting, black minidress that showcased her ample curves. Her exotic, lush beauty made his mouth go dry.

Desire slammed into him. The lure of her beauty made him realize how foolish he'd been. *His.* Every primal instinct inside him woke. Even his wolf self, dozing until that instant, sprang awake and alert.

What kind of fool had he been, letting her go so easily?

Taking another pull on his beer as he seethed, Ryan watched while the two of them, unaware of his scrutiny, found a two-top on the other side of the crowded dance floor.

Jeff got up to fetch them drinks, and the instant he left, several men appeared at the table, drawn to her beauty like moths to a flame. She handled them like a pro. Though he had no idea what she'd said, it worked. Her would-be suitors melted away as if blasted by the heat of the hot Texas sun.

Ryan inclined his head in a silent gesture of respect. Kudos to her for mastering such a skill. Though he could easily understand why she drew so much masculine attention. Everything about her, from the sensual way she moved to her devastating curves and the perfect pout of her mouth, screamed sex.

Only he knew she was so much more than that.

Oblivious, Jeff got two beers and returned to her, nearly tripping over himself in his hurry to rejoin her.

Though normally not a sucker for punishment, Ryan couldn't make himself leave. He sat there, aching, and watched as the woman he craved flirted and made small talk with one of his employees.

Inside, the smoldering embers became an inferno. He'd

been foolish to think he could do this. How could he help her find somebody else when he still wanted her for himself?

Again, his wolf fought to break free. Ryan subdued the urge to change and tried to get himself under control. In the back corner of the room, he recognized the two men who were her guards.

His chest felt as though it could burst. Aware he took quick, shallow breaths, he watched her the way a wolf watches a rabbit. When Jeff got up to go somewhere, whether for more drinks or to use the restroom, Ryan seized his chance. Though he knew he shouldn't, he had to go to her.

As he wove his way through the crowd, keeping his eye on the prize, he watched her repel a second wave of admirers. And then, just as he came around to her side of the packed room, she looked up and met his gaze.

Electricity, desire, need, a thousand powerful emotions flared when their eyes locked. He stood still, his nostrils flaring, realizing he needed to smell her scent, taste her tawny skin, touch her…possess her. Right now, if he could have ordered the bar to empty, he would have.

Her lovely caramel eyes widened slightly, letting him know she recognized him, despite his disguise.

"Ryan?" She pushed to her feet, one hand to her slender throat. "What are you doing here?"

Everything he meant to say to her vanished. In one swift, almost violent motion, he had her in his arms. And then he kissed her.

Mouth hard and demanding, he tried to show her what he couldn't say. *Mine. You belong with me, no one else.*

Parting her lips, she raised herself to meet him halfway.

Everything else ceased to exist. Everything but her and him and the desire electrifying his blood. When she pressed her body into his, her curves fitting as if they'd been made for him, his sudden and violent arousal made him grin savagely.

His. At least for tonight.

"Um? Excuse me." Jeff had returned. He cleared his throat, the sound like a dash of ice water on Ryan's head. When they broke apart to look at him, Ryan had to throttle the urge to snarl at the other man to get the hell away.

"Maria?" Jeff asked, his gaze going from her to Ryan and back again. "Is this man bothering you?"

After a second of startled silence, Ryan threw back his head and laughed. He couldn't help it. "Did it look like I was bothering her?" he asked, his tone mocking.

Maria's gentle touch on his arm stopped him. "Stop." She turned to face her date, her expression apologetic. "Jeff, I'm sorry. It looks like I still have some things to work out with my ex."

Ex? Jaw tight, Ryan kept his mouth shut.

"Your ex?" Jeff shook his head. "Ryan didn't tell me about any of this," he muttered, which made Ryan realize the other man hadn't recognized him.

"Here." Ryan passed Jeff two twenties. "Catch a cab back to wherever you're staying. Maria and I have a lot to talk about."

Jeff's expression tightened. Part of Ryan wondered if the other man might be willing to fight for her. He knew he would have, if the situation were reversed. Except that kiss made a statement all its own.

Taking the money, Jeff spun around and stalked out.

Chapter 12

"What's wrong with you?" Maria rounded on Ryan, hands on her hips. "Why are you acting like you just caught me cheating on you?"

"I can't do this," he told her, fighting the urge to touch her again. "This is crazy."

She watched him closely. When she finally nodded, the relief flooding through him nearly sent him to his knees. "I agree," she said. "We need to talk. Let's get out of here."

Figuring they'd take a walk on the beach while hammering out the parameters of their relationship, he stepped aside to allow her to precede him. "Lead the way."

With his hand on the small of her back as they navigated the packed room, he couldn't help but notice how many people watched her. Men with blatant desire, women with envy. Without even trying, Maria evoked a visceral response in everyone she passed.

As they stepped outside into the humid air, he steered her down the steps toward the seawall. Beyond that was the sandy beach. Moonlight highlighted silver waves ghosting across the water, just as they had the night they first met.

He fought the urge to take her, right there on the sand, even as his inner wolf growled approval. *His*.

"Beautiful," he said, gazing at her rather than the landscape. "This night is suddenly full of potential."

"Maybe." Her noncommittal response made him smile. "I still don't understand why you interrupted my date."

Was she kidding? Narrow-eyed, he cocked his head, wondering how to put it into words if his kiss hadn't been enough to convince her.

"I can't do this, Maria." He gestured back at the noisy bar. "I know I promised to help you, but there's no way I can stand by and watch you with another man. We belong together."

He wasn't good at flowery speeches or poetry. He hoped she understood what he was trying to say.

Instead, she pulled away. "I'm serious. What are you doing? I get that I'm attractive to you because I'm probably the first woman in all of creation who isn't falling all over herself to be with you. But you need to understand me. I'm looking for something else. Something permanent." The sea breeze ruffled her long dark hair, making the silky strands appear to be caressing her face the way his fingers ached to.

"You can't deny how good we are together. Our kisses could fuse metal."

Even in the moonlight, he could see how her dusky skin colored at his words. Her quickened breathing and the delightful way her nipples pebbled against her dress told him he aroused her as much as she did him. As if either of them needed confirmation.

"Be with me. Explore this thing between us, for however long it lasts." He realized his mistake as soon as he finished speaking.

Her caramel-colored gaze swept over him, as sensual as a caress. "No," she replied, her tone furious. "And, Ryan, I agree. We can't do this. I release you from your promise to help me find someone. I'll manage on my own."

Her quiet refusal felt like a knife in the heart. Narrowing his eyes, he studied her, trying to figure out why he couldn't seem to just walk away and wash his hands of her. "What do you want from me?"

She shook her head. "Something you're not able to give. It's okay, Ryan. We had a good *fling*." She spoke the last word as if it was a curse.

"Look," he said. "I'm sorry. I didn't mean to hurt you."

She sighed heavily. "I know. You're just being who you are."

In the end, it all boiled down to this. They wanted different things. She'd said she needed commitment, which meant marriage, a house with a white picket fence, and most importantly, kids. While he wanted…he realized he wasn't sure what he wanted. The only thing he knew with absolute certainty was that he wanted her. At least right now. No one could foresee the future. Not even someone with magic.

Noise from down the beach drew their attention. A group of partiers, drunk from the sound of it, headed down the sand directly toward them.

Though his heart felt as though it might be breaking, he knew he should agree with her and let her go. It wasn't as if he was about to drop to his knee and propose marriage. Even the very word made him shudder.

He managed to look her in the eye and smile. "You're right. I'll leave you alone from now on. Can we at least be…friends?"

Though he'd nearly choked on the last word, she returned his smile and nodded. "I'd like that very much. As long as you promise not to show up on any of my dates ever again."

"That's one promise I can definitely keep," he swore vehemently. Maybe if she didn't have any luck finding her perfect, mind-reading man, she'd let their relationship be more like a friends-with-benefits type thing. In the meantime, he needed to get busy finding her replacement.

Ryan showing up on her date with Jeff had stunned Maria. Even with his ridiculous disguise on, she'd recognized him the instant his gaze met hers. She'd tried to curb the dizzying current that had electrified her at his appearance.

And then…he'd kissed her. The kiss had rocked her world. Everything about the moment his mouth touched her, the salt of the sea-scented air on his lips, his hard muscular body and that particular way he had of looking at her as if she were more precious than gold, turned her into a puddle of need.

She loved him. The certainty of it brought her pain rather than joy. She may have been lurching along, unsure and unsteady in her path, wondering how in the world she'd manage to complete her destiny, but Ryan's lips on hers made her feel more alive than she ever had.

Watching him walk away, she stood on the beach and wanted to weep. The drunken revelers reached her, swirled around her, tried to coax her into a dance or a smile, but she only shook her head, the darkness in her expression warning them away.

Yes, she loved him. Ryan Howard, billionaire playboy. A man who never wanted for anything. Right at that moment, she wished desperately that he wasn't rich or famous, that he was an ordinary man who might have been able to conceive of a future with someone like her.

She wanted one thing in a man, and clearly Ryan wasn't capable of it.

All her life she'd understood her love was a precious gift, not to be bestowed carelessly. When she'd pictured her future, she'd never really understood what love would feel like. She'd envisioned it like some romantic comedy. Lots of laughter, lighthearted kisses and an easy path full of welcoming yellow light, homemade bread and a bright future.

Loving Ryan had opened her eyes to the truth. The way she felt about him was messy and complicated. And painful.

In a daze, she walked back to her car. If she'd had a choice, she would have accepted what Ryan offered and taken as long with him as he could give.

But she couldn't. Because her love alone wouldn't enable her to conceive.

Not for the first time, she hated her destiny.

Because until recently the Drakkor had believed the women were sterile, Maria had grown up without the awful shadow of this fate hanging over her. Quite frankly, she'd adjusted to the idea she'd be childless. The disease had left few women, but Drakkor men had long gone outside their own species.

Somehow it hadn't dawned on any of them that they might be the ones with an inability to procreate, despite the fact that none of the men had been able to get any of their girlfriends or wives pregnant since Maria had been a child.

Pride, she guessed. She knew her father had been devastated when he'd learned the news.

Tammy, one of the other Drakkor females remaining, and also the oldest who had managed to escape the ravages of the disease that had taken Maria's mother, had miraculously been able to conceive. She'd fallen in love with a Fae man, and despite having worked with Polacek at one point, was now considered to be the mother of the continuation of the Drakkor species.

Focus had immediately shifted to the other females. Initially, it was believed there were only three, but then Stephanie had been located on a secluded Greek island.

After learning that everything she'd been told about her body had been false, Maria had come to realize nothing in life was absolutely certain. Okay, maybe a few things, like the fact that she could shape-shift into a dragon and fly high above the clouds, out into the ocean where no one could see her.

But the new knowledge, the truth about what she needed from a mate, at least according to Tammy, had frustrated her. Despite her relatively young age, Maria had enough wisdom to understand love couldn't be ordered up like a pizza.

Now that she'd found love, she wondered if she'd be graced with the ability to find it again. And she simply had to, and soon. The Council constantly badgered her father, which in turn made him push her.

He'd been hopeful when he'd seen her with Ryan, despite the notoriety that went with being a billionaire. "Just think of all he can do to keep you and your children safe," he'd said. "And maybe he'd be willing to fund our existing research so we can learn why all our males are sterile."

When she'd finally gotten up the courage to tell him the truth about Ryan—that he didn't believe in commitment or love—her father had been devastated.

The next few days passed in a sort of a daze. She went to work and came home, she ate and drank and showered and breathed. But in her determination to stay away from

Ryan Howard, she learned something else. Love hurt. Like hell. Clearly love wasn't all rainbows and unicorns.

Rhonda called to check on her. As soon as she learned Maria felt depressed, she arrange a girls' night out. "We'll go out to eat, then dancing and drinking. Who knows, since the island is packed with tourists, maybe you'll meet someone."

Maria's first reaction was to decline. But the time had come to rouse herself and do something, even if it was just getting out with a friend. Any distraction might help her stop thinking about a man she couldn't have.

They made plans to meet on the coming Friday. For the first time since she'd last seen Ryan, Maria felt a bit of sunshine shining through the gloom. When she finished up work Friday afternoon, she hurried home. She notified Colton Richards, who promised he would remain in the shadows and claimed she wouldn't even notice him following her.

With a sigh, Maria thanked him and headed inside her house to get ready. When she and Rhonda went out, they both wore jeans, heels and cute tops. Redoing her makeup, Maria got dressed, checking her watch impatiently. They'd decided to eat at Willie G's Steakhouse on Harborside Drive. It had been a while since she'd had red meat, and her dragon had begun to crave it.

Though Maria arrived early, Rhonda had already been seated and waved her over.

"You look amazing," Maria said, after she hugged her friend. "Marriage and motherhood clearly agree with you."

"Thanks!" Rhonda cocked her head, studying Maria. "You look wonderful, too. What have you been doing? You're positively glowing."

"Hah." Pulling out her chair, Maria grinned at her best

friend. "Since I've been feeling absolutely miserable, I appreciate your attempt to be kind."

"I'm serious, you dolt." Whatever else Rhonda might have been about to say was interrupted by the arrival of their waiter. They ordered the crab, avocado and mango tower to share and each ordered a glass of merlot. For dinner, they both had the eight-ounce filet. Maria ordered hers rare, while Rhonda's was medium.

They talked about everything and anything, with one exception. Maria really appreciated her friend steering clear of the painful subject of her short-lived fling with Ryan Howard.

After they ate, Rhonda said she wanted to go back to the same bar where Maria and Ryan had met. At first, the pang of longing she felt had Maria considering suggesting somewhere else, but there were only a few really good places on the island.

"Sure," she finally said, hoping her expression didn't reveal her inner turmoil. Since they'd be arriving well before the hordes of younger tourists descended on the place, she figured it would be fine. And who knew, maybe Rhonda would be her good luck charm and she'd actually meet someone.

Despite their fairly early arrival, the place seemed packed. Maria pushed through the crowd of gyrating bodies, scanning the perimeter for an empty table. There were none, but two seats had just opened up at the bar.

Maria and Rhonda reached them before anyone else could snag them.

"Whew," Rhonda said. "I'd forgotten how much work this is."

They both ordered wine, figuring to keep up the trend they'd started at dinner. Maria took a lazy look around the place but, as usual, didn't see anyone even remotely interesting.

When she swiveled back to face Rhonda, her friend laughed. "I looked for you, too. Maybe someone will come in later."

"Maybe. At least I have you to dance with." Long ago, both women had stopped worrying about what other people might think. If they wanted to have fun, then they would. Plus, since Rhonda had gotten married, she wasn't comfortable dancing with other men. Maria admired that.

A commotion over by the entrance made them both look. Maria's heart plummeted to her feet as Ryan strolled in, his arm around a stunning and slender blonde woman who had to be a model. Behind the two of them were several other young and beautiful couples, her friends, no doubt.

"Uh-oh." Rhonda winced. "I can see from your expression that you're still not over him."

"I'm fine." Maria almost snarled the words, watching as the man who'd claimed to be over the moon about her laughed down into the gorgeous face of his companion.

He couldn't see her. Not here, without a date. Biting down panic, she swiveled her chair so she faced the bar again, keeping her back to the rest of the room and him.

"Do you want to leave?" Bless her heart, Rhonda had gotten out her credit card to pay their tab.

"No." Deep breaths should help her calm down. "I refuse to let him ruin our night."

Luckily Ryan and his entourage headed for some sort of private room the manager must have reserved for them. They disappeared behind a door.

"Thank goodness." She gave Rhonda a weak smile.

Rhonda shook her head. "When you're ready to leave, just say the word and we're gone."

Maria nodded. She cast a quick, almost desperate glance around the place, noting some new arrivals who hadn't been there before. One of them was a tall, strikingly handsome man with close-cropped dark hair wearing what appeared to be a custom-made suit. He must have come here straight from work. Maria approved. He noticed her studying him and smiled.

"Well done," Rhonda said approvingly. "He's heading this way. I'll be your wing-woman if you need me to."

When Mr. Tall, Dark and Handsome reached them, he included both women in his smile. "I'm Darryl," he said, holding out an elegant, long-fingered hand. "Darryl Pride." His aura proclaimed him a Shifter, though Maria couldn't tell what kind.

"Maria Miranda," she said, smiling back. "And this is my friend Rhonda."

As usual, Rhonda made a show of displaying her wedding ring. "Pleased to meet you," she drawled, shooting Maria a quick nod of approval.

Darryl returned his gaze to Maria. She noticed he had unusual-colored eyes, a grayish-hazel. His cheekbones were set high in his face, making him look both exotic and dangerous.

"Would you like to dance?" he asked, his tone formal, contrasting with the sparkle in his eyes.

A slow song had just come on. Normally, Maria would have said no. But the image of Ryan smiling down into his gorgeous date's face made her feel reckless.

"Yes," she said, and hopped off the bar stool. "I'll be right back," she told Rhonda, who waved her on with a smile.

As his arms went around her and they began to move on the dance floor, she couldn't help but make comparisons to Ryan. While Darryl might be as tall, he wasn't as broad shouldered nor as muscular. And he smelled of expensive men's cologne rather than sea and sand and wind.

At first, she wasn't sure how to hold herself and moved stiffly. She didn't usually slow dance with someone she didn't know. Even her inner dragon, usually so vocal, had gone silent.

From the corner of her eyes, she saw a flurry of movement. Ryan and his entourage moved out on the dance floor. He swept his beautiful companion into his arms and moved her close, gazing down into her upturned face with the same intense look he'd given Maria.

A small part of her died when she saw that. As she and Darryl glided past, Ryan raised his head and saw her. As their gazes met, he flashed her an impersonal smile. She let her eyes drift right past, as though she didn't recognize him. And then, even though she knew it was wrong, she pressed her body against Darryl and looked up at him, smiling as though she found him the most perfect man on this Earth.

Darryl blinked, clearly stunned, and then reacted instantly. He leaned down, as if he meant to kiss her. She turned her head at the last moment so his mouth grazed her cheek instead.

And caught Ryan giving her a look of lazy amusement before turning his attention back to his date.

Anger, hurt and, yes, jealousy all churned inside of her. For one instant she wanted to continue this game of trying to make Ryan jealous, but then what would be the point? They had no future. While Darryl, who actually was the first man in a long time besides Ryan to even cause a glimmer of interest, might just be The One.

She'd never know if she used him to play some futile game.

"Sorry," she said, stepping out of his arms. "I don't actually know you all that well." Taking his hand she led him back to the table. As soon as they arrived, Rhonda got up and headed to the lady's room to give them the privacy they needed.

"I don't understand," Darryl began, his aristocratic features still composed.

"I know you don't. It's not your fault. I really would like to get to know you better, maybe over dinner or something." She blushed as she realized she'd just asked him out. Holding her breath as she waited for his answer, she knew she wouldn't blame him if he said no.

"I'd like that," he replied instead. "May I have your number?"

"Sure." Digging in her purse for a pen, she scrawled the info on a cocktail napkin and passed it to him. "Give me a call when you'd like to set something up."

The intensity in his unusual eyes sent a shiver up her spine. "I'll do that," he said, and turned and disappeared into the crowd.

Rhonda magically appeared just as two or three men approached the table. She glared at them as she took her seat and waved them away. Unbelievably, they went.

"So?" One brow raised, Rhonda took a sip of her wine. "Did you two click? You looked pretty into him on the dance floor."

"He's okay." Careful to avoid looking back that way, Maria summoned up a smile for her friend.

"Good." Rhonda swore as she caught sight of something on the dance floor. "Don't look," she ordered.

"I already saw." Maria didn't bother to keep the misery from her voice. "He saw me, too."

"Well, at least you were dancing with a good-looking guy," Rhonda said. When her rapid defense failed to summon even a ghost of a smile from Maria, Rhonda downed the last of her wine. "Do you want to get out of here?"

"I'd like nothing better."

As they pushed through the crowd, the slow song ended and a pulsating dance beat began.

They made it outside without incident.

"What now?" Maria asked, trying to put a brave face on, but not really caring.

"I know the perfect place for what ails you." Rhonda grabbed her arm. "Come on. A double scoop of Ben & Jerry's ice cream will make anyone feel better."

Ryan tried. Honest to hounds, he gave it his best shot. His date Anastasia or Amanda Something—a model who was not only hot, but she was Pack. Her brother was even a Pack Protector. She'd jumped at his offer to go out, even shrieking at him when he'd called. This, he'd thought, was how the women he dated usually acted. Not like Maria.

The instant he'd walked into the bar—*their* bar— he'd seen her sitting at a small table with a pretty human woman. Lust instantly zinged him at the sight of her, which he promptly quashed. He also felt a pang of regret, wondering if seeing him with another woman might hurt her, before he'd remembered Maria had been the one to send him away.

Later, after he'd had a couple of shots of ice-cold Patrón, he'd allowed Anastasia or Amanda to drag him out on the dance floor. The instant he'd caught sight of Maria slow dancing way too close with that tall, handsome man, he'd wanted to stride over there and pull the other man's hands off her smooth skin.

He'd seen the way that guy had looked at her, as if he wanted to eat her up. Ryan knew exactly how that felt.

Every muscle in his body was tight. His date had sensed something and snuggled up against him in an effort to turn his attention back to her and what she was offering.

As if her too-thin, curveless body could tempt him after Maria's.

The instant that thought occurred to him, he winced.

"Ryan?" Now his date frowned prettily at him. Since they were the same height, she didn't even have to look up. "Are you all right?"

No. He was not all right. He nearly said that, before realizing he needed to shake this off and try to get on with his life. He could not keep pining for a woman he couldn't have.

The music changed, lucky for him, and he headed off the dance floor. Anastasia pouted, and then grabbed the first man who passed by and dragged him out there to dance with her. Ryan felt only relief. It had been a huge mistake to ask her out.

Back in the private room provided by the club, he looked around at the crowd of partiers, every single one of them there for the free drinks or the notoriety or the possibility of getting into a billionaire's inner circle. Not because they liked him or were his friends. Hell, most of them barely even knew him.

With sudden stark clarity, he saw how he'd been living his life ever since his company had taken off and the money had started flowing. As if nothing mattered but having a good time. And with that realization, he understood why someone like Maria wouldn't want a future with a man like him. If he wanted to ever have a chance with her, he needed to make some changes. And fast. Before someone else snapped her up.

Glancing once more around the room, he went to find the manager, where he closed out and paid for the tab. He left directions that his tab was now closed and anything his date and her friends ordered would be on them.

And then he left the bar and headed to his beautiful, but lonely, beach house to think and plan. Maria had agreed to remain friends. Maybe they could build on that.

Darryl called the very next day, his calm and polite tone at odds with his apparent eagerness. He asked Maria to dinner the following evening, suggesting a small Italian place that only the locals knew about. Since any restaurant blessedly free of tourists sounded wonderful, plus she seriously wanted to give Darryl a chance, she agreed. He said he'd pick her up around seven, but since she didn't know him, she arranged to meet him there, instead.

She knew she should call her father and let him know the latest development, but she hated to let him—and the always expectant Council—down, so she didn't. She decided to wait and see how things went before saying anything.

But she could, and did, call Rhonda. The two of them had had a long talk over their ice-cream cones, and Maria had poured out a carefully edited story of her father's pushing and her feeling that her biological clock might have gone into overdrive. Rhonda, a perfect listener, had simply patted Maria's shoulder and nodded at the right times. She knew Maria didn't expect solutions. She just wanted someone to hear her. And Rhonda had fulfilled that role beautifully.

"I'm glad you're going out with him. He's nice looking. Just make sure you stay in a public place, okay?"

Maria smiled. "I know. I always do. I'm so glad we had our girls' night."

"Me, too. Ryan Howard showing up might have put a damper on things, but at least you met someone, right?"

"Right." Maria tried to sound a lot more optimistic than she felt. "I'll keep you posted on how everything goes."

Chapter 13

The next day at work, the morning passed in a blur of solid, back-to-back appointments, bridal parties in various stages of planning and a few prospective clients. Maria ate a hurried lunch in her office and had barely washed down her sandwich when her cell phone rang.

Ryan's number flashed on the screen. She froze. She took a deep breath, aware she had to sound nonchalant.

"Hello?" she answered, with what she thought was a cheerful lilt to her tone.

"Good afternoon." The husky sound of Ryan's voice sent a jolt right to her core. "Just checking in to see how my favorite wedding chapel owner is doing these days."

Briefly closing her eyes, Maria had to remind herself to inhale and exhale. "I'm fine. What can I do for you, Ryan?"

His immediate silence had all kinds of carnal images running through her head. She fanned herself, refusing to speak again as she waited for his answer.

When he finally spoke, the teasing note had vanished

and his tone became serious. "Have you changed your mind about the two of us remaining friends?"

Friends? She hadn't truly meant it. Of course, she hadn't expected him to want to continue any kind of relationship with her anymore if she wouldn't give him what he wanted. "Of course not," she said, with an injection of warmth. "We'll always be friends."

"Great. I was hoping we could get together and catch up. Plus, you haven't even seen my new place. How about you come over for dinner?"

Oh, hell. The man seriously didn't ever give up. What was it with him? Maybe he still considered her a challenge. Yet, even so, part of her wanted to agree. Talk about temptation. With every fiber of her being, she longed to give in.

Though she would have given much to be able to do exactly that, Maria knew her absurd fixation on Ryan Howard would destroy her ability to find and meet the man she needed. Which wasn't him. She had to figure out a way not to love him anymore.

"I can't," she answered, telling herself to remain strong. "I...er, have a date."

Her words hung out there in the air for a moment while she tried not to squirm. And then, just as she remembered she had no reason to be uncomfortable, she heard Ryan sigh.

"Well, good," he finally said, his speech clipped and unemotional. "I'll let you go." And he ended the call.

She stared at the phone. Had that been *hurt* she'd heard in his voice? Taking a deep, albeit shaky, breath, she tried to put it from her mind. She told herself she really liked Darryl. Or she could, if she gave him time. Like Ryan, Darryl was tall and dark and handsome. Unlike Ryan, he was ordinary. A regular, handsome guy with a charming smile. He was like the prairie, where Ryan reminded her of the sea. Maybe one would balance out the other. For the first time in a long time, she'd felt hopeful about the future.

Still, Ryan's call had brought that old ache back. She rushed through her afternoon appointments and went on a quick shopping expedition. Then she headed home to get ready.

Getting ready for their date, she took the dress she'd purchased that afternoon out of her closet and admired it. She wasn't a big shopper, but she'd seen this vintage pale yellow dress hanging in a window and stopped dead in front of the eclectic little shop in the Strand. When she'd gone in to look at it, she'd been delighted to see it was her size. When she'd tried it on, and found it fit as though it had been made for her, she'd twirled, enjoying the way the skirt flared out. The dress made her feel like a faerie-tale princess.

Of course, then she'd immediately thought of how Ryan would react if he saw her in it. Tears pricked the back of her eyes as she pushed the thought away, hating that once again she'd managed to ruin what could have been a perfect moment.

She met Darryl at DiBella's Italian Restaurant on 31st. As she'd told Rhonda, for first dates, she always brought her own car and met in a crowded place. He'd made reservations and was already waiting for her, looking handsome in khaki slacks and a button-down shirt. Out here, his aura seemed stronger, more powerful. She toyed with the idea of asking him what kind of Shifter he actually was, and decided against it. At this point, she didn't really care. If something came of their relationship, she'd ask then.

Over dinner she'd learned he was an only child, a lawyer who'd moved to Galveston to open his own law practice and an avid angler. She'd been careful with what she'd revealed about herself, telling him she worked in event planning, was also an only child and was from Wisconsin. During the meal she was careful to only drink one glass of wine.

After dinner he'd suggested they go for coffee at The Mod Coffee House on Post Office Street, but she knew the place would be packed with tourists since it was close to the Strand, so she politely declined. As they said their goodbyes in front of the restaurant, she braced herself for him to try and kiss her, deciding that, if he did, she'd offer a hug instead.

But he didn't. Darryl didn't even shake her hand. He cocked his head and smiled at her. "I'd like to see you again," he said.

She should have been thrilled, she supposed. Their date had been all right. Nothing special. No fireworks, but no bad feelings, either. She recalled that, when they met, he'd reminded her of the prairie. She'd enjoyed herself while visiting there, but she'd never stopped yearning for the sea.

Sadness filling her, she caught herself on the verge of offering excuses. She had a sudden, horrible feeling that this would be her life from now on. Safe and bland, no excitement, just security. Like the smooth glass the ocean became, right before a storm.

But she knew her people would say that was enough, as long as she had a child. Or two. Continuing the Drakkor race was important. Anything beyond that didn't matter.

"Give me a call and we'll see," she finally responded. Then she hurried to her car, got in and locked it before starting the engine and driving away.

Was it possible to force oneself to fall in love? Maria found herself contemplating that after her second, and then her third, date with Darryl. His striking appearance made other women sit up and take notice, and while Maria occasionally caught herself admiring the classic lines of his profile, she never felt that electric zing of attraction she did with Ryan. Not even once.

And therein lay the problem, she suspected. It might be entirely possible that Ryan Howard had ruined her for anyone else.

After her fourth date with Darryl, she began to suspect he felt about the same way she did toward him. Lukewarm. When she'd rebuffed his initial attempt to kiss her, he'd been a perfect gentleman. Sure, his hand might linger a bit too long on her shoulder, but he never did anything else to suggest he considered her anything but a friend.

That night, after visiting Moody Gardens and having dinner out, he'd dropped her off at her house—they'd graduated to that—and given her a quick hug. The kind one bestowed on a sister or brother. After watching him drive off, she'd gone inside and opened a bottle of her favorite wine.

All her life, she'd loved two things. The ocean and weddings. Which was exactly why she lived in Galveston and had chosen to run a wedding chapel as her career.

And now, it was just possible she loved another. Ryan Howard. A man who could never love her back.

Maria didn't drink much, and when she did, she usually only had a single glass of wine, maybe two. Somehow, without realizing it, she managed to drink a little more than half the bottle. And instead of making her feel better, the alcohol only made her want to cry.

This was ridiculous, she decided. Grabbing her cell, she found Ryan's number and punched Call before she had time to chicken out.

After the third ring, she began to think maybe she should hang up. After the fourth, she was just about to do that, when a decidedly feminine voice drawled "Hello?"

"Wrong number," Maria mumbled, her heart pounding.

She ended the call, feeling sick. Clearly, Ryan had already moved on. If this wasn't a gigantic hint from the cosmos, she didn't know what was.

Putting down her wineglass, she headed for the kitchen, where she poured herself a tall glass of water. Dehydration would be her enemy. She needed to feel better so that tomorrow after work she could meet Darryl for their next date and see about taking their relationship to the next level. After all, a girl couldn't get serious about a man without knowing how he kissed, could she?

The party Ryan had originally arranged for several of his top performing employees, as well as Jeff and David, the other guy who'd been supposed to meet Maria, had somehow morphed into a monster—pounding music, scantily clad models dancing on the table, and way too much alcohol. Since he knew he couldn't let any of these people actually drive, he'd already resigned himself to letting them bunk there for the night. Actually, he wanted to leave, but didn't dare leave his house and furniture unsupervised or he felt sure there'd be another fire or worse.

So he tried to stay away from the loudest group of revelers, which meant staying outside on one of his several patios. Mostly he watched strangers having fun inside his house, on the outside looking in, with no desire to join them. Odd how this, something he used to find highly enjoyable, now made him feel lonelier than if he'd been all alone. And he didn't really understand why.

It just no longer seemed enough, somehow.

Blowing out his breath in a snort, he gazed out over the darkness, unable to tell where ocean separated from sky, and wondered yet again how Maria was doing. No doubt she'd been seeing a lot of her new guy—the very thought made his stomach clench and his chest feel too tight.

He'd brought Timothy down from Austin and had him handle the party. Arranging such things had become one of Timothy's specialties. Hounds knew he'd had enough practice over the years.

Spying Ryan alone, Timothy hurried outside. "What's wrong, boss?" he asked, frowning with worry. "Why are you out here by yourself? Don't you like any of the models I invited?"

"They're fine." Ryan gave a dismissive wave of his hand. "They're all very beautiful women. Jeff and David seem thrilled."

"They are. But what about you? You seem a little…off."

Ryan nearly laughed at his assistant's description. "I am off. I find myself thinking there must be more than this."

Now Timothy looked alarmed. "You wanted a more extravagant party? I'm sorry, I thought—"

"No." Ryan turned away, gazing out at the blackness, wishing the clouds would move out so he could at least see the stars. "That's not what I meant. I'm just…" He looked to see Timothy staring at him, his face scrunched in worry. "Never mind. It's nothing to do with you. I guess I'm just not in the mood for a party tonight."

"Do you want me to make everyone leave?"

Ryan thought about it. "No. Let everyone have a good time. Just make sure no one destroys my house. I'm going to go for a walk on the beach."

Though Timothy nodded and attempted a smile, he appeared almost apoplectic with concern. "Will do."

Beyond caring, Ryan waved and headed down the stairs to the sand.

Away from the house, though he could still hear the thump-thump of the base from the music, he finally felt his soul settle. He breathed in, loving the hint of salt in the air. Though he was probably setting himself up for a world of hurt, he dug in his pocket for his cell phone, aching to hear Maria's voice.

The phone wasn't there. Nor in his other pocket. He must have left it on the kitchen counter in the house.

Gazing back at the brightly lit structure, he knew he couldn't go back in there just now. Maybe it was all for the best, a sort of omen from the universe. It had gone way past the time for him to figure out a way to live without Maria. Maybe he should cut his summer vacation short and head back up to Austin. There, he could always lose himself in work.

But here, with the sea breeze ruffling his hair and the comforting roar of the waves rolling onto the beach, his entire soul rebelled. He'd been a fool. It wasn't time to learn how to live without Maria. He needed to try and win her back. Yes, he wanted more than the shallow emptiness his life had become. He wanted her. He only hoped he hadn't waited too long.

Spinning around, his heart pounding, he sprinted back for his house. He'd locate his phone and call her. If she didn't answer, he'd swing by her house. They needed to give each other a second chance. Surely they could find some middle ground.

Snatching up his phone from the coffee table, he decided he'd just drive to her house and surprise her without calling. He grabbed the keys to his Jeep. Fending off two inebriated models, he located Timothy and told him he would be leaving for a few hours. His assistant nodded, his mouth turned down, and promised to watch over the house.

Then Ryan started the engine and headed toward Maria's. If her new boyfriend was there, he figured it was time they had it out once and for all.

* * *

One thing that bothered Maria about Darryl was the way he was always so agreeable. He never expressed an opinion of his own and instead agreed with everything she said. He wouldn't choose a restaurant and so she always chose where they'd go so she didn't have to spend twenty minutes mentioning places only to have him say "You decide."

A few times she considered trying to make him angry, just to see what he would do, but she found the idea oddly frightening. She could honestly say his bland exterior made her wonder what she'd do if he didn't know how to get angry.

But then, what kind of man was he? She knew little more about him other than what he'd told her in the beginning. He didn't make her laugh or cry; in fact, he didn't make her feel much of anything at all.

She'd spent the entire afternoon before their date pondering how to get him to kiss her. She'd finally reached the conclusion that she'd have to do it herself, wondering if he'd kiss her back or recoil in horror. Odd that she found the last strangely amusing.

In preparation for that evening, she'd taken extra care with her appearance. A few months ago, Rhonda had talked her into buying a dress, a formfitting, miniscule thing that Maria had never worn. Even the thought of putting it on made her feel as if she'd be approached by strange men wanting to hire her for the night.

Tonight, she'd made herself wear it to see if she could get a reaction, any kind of reaction, from Darryl.

Of course, her thoughts then drifted to Ryan. She knew what he'd do. His eyes would go dark and his breathing would hitch. He'd haul her up against him and kiss her until she was senseless.

Damn. Slamming the lid down on her fantasy, Maria shook her head at her own foolishness. All she needed to do was remember the breathy, slightly tipsy feminine voice answering Ryan's phone and she was good.

Dressed and nervous, she stared at herself in the mirror, wondering if she could walk in the five-inch stilettos. For one heart-stopping instant she panicked, considering changing into something more sensible. But she didn't. The time had come to find out if Darryl would be a viable prospect or if she needed to cut him loose.

Operation Kiss would happen tonight.

Darryl arrived promptly at seven. He was never late or early, something else Maria found mildly annoying. She let him in, standing in a semi-provocative pose so she could gauge his reaction.

His expression hardened. "You look nice," he said, swallowing hard. That tiny bit alone gave her hope.

"Thank you." She grinned. "I'm looking forward to tonight."

They had dinner and drinks and, at her request, went for a stroll on the beach. Though there was no moon and clouds obscured the stars, as usual she found the sound of the surf soothing. Even the ever-present bodyguards lurking in the background couldn't spoil the mood.

Finally, she tugged on Darryl's arm, making him look at her. When preplanning this moment, she'd thought about asking him to kiss her, but she decided to take matters into her own hands and kiss him herself.

Facing him, she stood up on her tiptoes and cupped his face with her hand. And then, her heart flopping in her chest like a fish out of water, she covered his mouth with hers.

Instantly, he deepened the kiss. Not entirely comfortable with this (and not really feeling it), she went along.

But when he tried to ram his tongue down her throat, she reared back. "Uh...that was nice," she managed. Unbelievably, she wanted to gag. If her breathing sounded fast, it was due to stress rather than arousal.

"Come here," he said, attempting to draw her closer. "I want to do it again."

She suddenly developed an urgent need for a drink of water. When she communicated that to him, he nodded and let her lead the way to a small bar and concession area near the chair rentals.

Fetching her a bottle of water, he handed it to her. "Here you go."

Staring at it in bemusement, she nodded. "Thank you." Her reply came out mechanical.

Increasingly, she felt worse and worse. Darryl, on the other hand, seemed to grow more and more exhilarated.

"You did it!" he exulted. "I knew if I played hard to get, you wouldn't be able to resist the challenge."

Confused, she eyed him. She felt a bit strange, weak even, though not from his kiss. That had been a bit like pressing her lips up against a mannequin.

"I did what?" she asked. Even her voice sounded weird, flat, as if the life had been sucked out of her.

"You kissed me. You did kiss me of your own free will, correct?"

She felt a prickle of unease. "Yes. I wanted to see how well we went together."

His laugh turned her unease into fear. "That no longer matters. You're mine now."

Staring at him, she shook her head. "I don't understand..." A wave of dizziness hit her. Had she been drugged?

"Not by anything you ate or drank," he replied, making her realize she must have spoken out loud. "But by my kiss."

"Whoa." Reaching out blindly, when her hand connected with the back of a beach chair, she used it to steady herself. "You're a bit overconfident there, Darryl. Honestly, I really don't feel well."

"I'm sorry." He took her arm. "Let me help you. I'll take you home right away."

Grateful, she leaned on him, aware that to anyone watching she must look drunk, but beyond caring. He assisted her out to the parking lot and then into his car.

Her head felt heavy. Fighting nausea, she closed her eyes.

When she next opened them, she was in total darkness. Confused, she suppressed her instant flash of terror. This reminded her of Eyrie. Except—she moved her arms and legs, stretching—she wasn't tied up and she wasn't hanging upside down.

But wherever she was, the darkness felt overpowering. Uneasy, she pushed to her feet and took a halting step forward, and then another, with her arms outstretched in front of her. Two more steps and she encountered a solid surface. Concrete, judging from the feel of it.

It took a while, but eventually she believed she'd made a complete circle of the room. All concrete. If a door existed, she hadn't been able to locate it.

Trying to think what could have happened, she realized the last thing she remembered was getting into Darryl's car.

Which meant one of two things. Either Darryl was holding her prisoner for some reason, or something had happened to him and Doug Polacek had gotten hold of her.

The instant Ryan stepped out of his car, he knew Maria's house was empty. The windows were completely dark and the lack of bodyguards approaching his car was his first clue. Checking his watch, he realized the hour was still early for Friday night, and if she'd gone on a date with that guy it could be hours yet before she returned home. If she came home at all.

Even that thought had his inner wolf snarling. He briefly debated whether or not to wait it out, and decided against it. He didn't want to go home, not to the noisy party and inebriated guests. He briefly considered changing and letting his wolf hunt, but his highly charged emotional state as human would make him too unpredictable as wolf.

He decided to drive over to the Strand, pick a bar and have a drink. If he was lucky, he'd be fortunate enough to happen upon Maria and her date.

Decision made, he turned to walk back to his Jeep. Just as he did, a black sedan came screeching around the corner, slamming to a halt right in front of him.

Both of Maria's Pack Protector bodyguards jumped out.

"What are you doing here?" Colton Richards snarled.

Looking from one to the other and noting their disheveled appearance, Ryan raised a brow. He didn't get a sense of urgency, rather more of confusion. "Shouldn't the better question be, why aren't you protecting Maria? Is everything okay?"

When Colton cursed, Ryan began to worry. "Seriously. Where is she? Is she out on a date with that guy?"

"Darryl Pride," Colton answered, his jaw clenched. "We were guarding her inside the concession area while they were at the bar, when all of a sudden both of us fell asleep. It couldn't have been a roofie. We didn't have anything to eat or drink."

A chill snaking up his spine, Ryan stared. "Do you know if Maria is all right?"

"No." Colton met his gaze, his own eyes bleak. "The next thing we knew, someone was shaking us awake and telling us to go home and sleep it off. Maria and Darryl were nowhere in sight. We checked his place, a rental over by the ferry, but no one is home. So we came here."

Sheer black terror swept through Ryan. "You need to alert the Council." Pulling out his cell phone, Ryan pulled up Maria's number. "I'm trying to call her now." But the call went directly to voice mail.

"Same thing happened to us," Colton said. "If Polacek has her, he has Darryl Pride, too."

"Or," Ryan heard himself utter the unspeakable. "Has anyone ever considered that maybe Darryl Pride might actually be Doug Polacek?"

After a moment of stunned silence, Colton cursed. "It's possible. They have the same initials. And it'd be very easy for him to wear a disguise and change his appearance."

His appearance. For the first time Ryan realized he had no idea what Polacek actually looked like.

"Were you ever actually given a photo of him? I know Maria wasn't."

Colton and the other guard exchanged a glance. "No, but I'm pretty sure just about every Drakkor knows what he looks like. We have strictly monitored email groups set up, and ever since we first learned of him photos and information have been distributed."

"But you have no way of knowing if Maria read those emails."

"Well, no," Colton admitted. "But why wouldn't she? I know her father made sure she was kept abreast of what was going on. He had to. It's a sacred charge, looking after a female Drakkor."

Because of their baby-making potential. While he understood, Ryan couldn't help but feel the need to enlighten Colton and his man. Maria might be what her people needed, but she was also so much more. He swallowed hard, pushing down the urge to speak. His two fellow Pack members would think he was crazy.

And they'd be right. He was. Crazy about Maria.

"We've got to find them," he said. "Mobilize your Protectors. I'd appreciate it if you'd patch me through to Maria's father. The Drakkor have magic, you know. Some more than others. There's an enclave of really powerful ones up in Boulder, Colorado. We need them to help us fight Polacek and get Maria out safely."

Chapter 14

An undeterminable amount of time passed before Maria heard a sound. Faint, at first, then growing louder. Footsteps. The scape of some kind of metal door opening. Then light flooding in from above her, temporarily blinding her.

"Hello?" Darryl's voice. Squinting, she saw his face peering down at her. She wasn't sure if she should feel relieved or worried. Since he didn't appear to be held captive, she went with the latter.

"Darryl, what's going on? Why am I down here?"

He moved away and she could no longer see his face. Her heart stuttered. "Please don't leave me here in darkness."

"What, no magic? Can't you get yourself out?" When he reappeared, he lifted his hand in a mocking salute. "Let me see how powerful you are. I've heard stories about your abilities. Prove them true."

Magic. Stories. Her heart sank. "Who are you, really,

Darryl?" Though she asked, she had a sickening suspicion she already knew.

His answer confirmed her fears. "Doug Polacek. Pleased to meet you. And you, my pretty, are my second female Drakkor captive. Though I have to tell you, Tracey isn't doing so well these days."

An instant of stark terror before rage consumed her. Good. Exactly what she needed to bring her magic to life. Stretching, she summoned up her power and willed it to flow through her veins and fill her.

Instead, nothing happened. Nothing at all.

She gave a little cry, nearly collapsing but caught herself at the last moment. "What have you done to me?" she asked, her tone laced with fury.

His smile almost seemed a leer as he waved his hand, bringing her up to the opening, though not out of the concrete cube. "I've taken away your magic, that's what. And doing so was surprisingly easy. Taking little Tracey's was a tiny bit more difficult."

She gaped at him. "How? I didn't even know such a thing was possible."

"There are quite a few things you don't know. Now, will you behave yourself if I let you out for a little while? Of course, there's not a whole lot you can do."

Not trusting herself to answer, she settled for a nod.

"That's what I thought." He wiggled his fingers again, and she flew up through the opening, out of what she now realized was a cement coffin.

He snapped his fingers and she found herself gently lifted and propelled along a hallway, up a flight of wooden stairs and then into what looked like a small waiting room. He lowered her onto a threadbare couch.

"Why are you doing this?" she asked. "I understand you want to father a child, but after all this time, surely you understand you can't. As for me, while I'm able to conceive, you know darn well there has to be love involved between both parties."

Though his expression had momentarily darkened at her reminder of his shortcomings, when she finished speaking, he shot her a twisted smile.

"Don't you see?" The earnestness in his voice matched his fierce expression. "You can love me. I can love you. The magic of such a love will enable me to get you with child. I can redeem myself and everything I've done. I will make good on my failures. And I can still be the savior of our people."

Heaven help her, she almost felt sorry for him. This man, who'd done so many horrible things, committed so many unspeakable atrocities, honestly believed he was only trying to help. He also refused to believe he was sterile.

And then he laughed. "And if you won't love me, I'll make you. I only hope you can last longer than Tracey."

Her blood ran cold. There lay even more proof of his madness.

"Darryl," she began.

"Doug," he cut her off. "I realize that's how you think of me, but I only told you my name was Darryl so you wouldn't realize who I was. Now that you know, call me by my real name." Icy contempt flashed in his eyes. Wow. And this man honestly believed they could love each other? That told her he knew nothing about love.

"Okay. Doug. I thought I knew you, but everything you told me was a lie. I knew Darryl, not Doug. How can you expect me to fall in love with someone I don't really… know?" Or care for.

Voice heavy with sarcasm, he moved closer. "Because love is like that. I saw how you were with *him*." He spat the word. "You loved Ryan Howard. Don't even try to lie and deny it."

She opened her mouth and then closed it. She needed to be supercareful not to antagonize this man. As long as he thought there might be the potential of a future with her, he wouldn't hurt her.

Or so she hoped. But then, everything he'd mentioned about Tracey...

"I've learned something else," he told her, his tone once again optimistic and light. "A lot, actually. In my travels abroad, I found a book in a Shape-shifter bookstore in London. I think that tome had been there for centuries. It's really old and was dusty. I found it back behind stacks of several other hardbacks."

She nodded, not really sure where he was going with this.

"The proprietor of the shop acted surprised when I tried to purchase it." He laughed. "You know what? The old bat refused to sell it to me. She claimed it was too valuable and needed to be returned to the Drakkor Council. So I killed her and then burned the shop down."

The casual way he spoke the words made Maria feel sick. Clearly, he didn't consider murder—or arson—a big deal.

The book, she reminded herself. He wanted her to ask about the book. "What was the book about?"

He fixed her with a piercing glare. "Drakkor. It was filled with prophecy about our people. And there were some magic spells, too. It was written by some guy who apparently was a contemporary of Nostradamus."

She couldn't hide her shock. "The French astrologer from the 1500s?"

"Yes, that same one. Only he prophesied about human-kind. This book was written by a Drakkor named Lucian

Lefivre, and seems much more straightforward than Nostradamus's ramblings. It's taken me some time to translate the French. But it works. That's how I cast the spell to have a kiss steal your magic."

His almost palpable excitement scared her. Again, she tested her bonds. Though he'd claimed to have taken away her magic, she wasn't entirely sure she could believe him. Either way, even if she still had magical abilities, his apparently were stronger than hers.

Still, she didn't panic. She remembered the lessons at Eyrie. She'd get free. She was strong, she was confident. Even without her magic, she'd figure out a way. It was just a matter of time.

Meanwhile, just in case he'd told the truth, she really wanted to see this book. If it told how to use a kiss to steal magic, surely it said something about how to restore it. "May I take a look at this book?"

Gaze narrow, he studied her. "No. Not until we love each other."

Which meant, at least as far as she was concerned, never. She had to press her lips shut so no sound escaped.

"We've got to find her," Ryan announced for maybe the third time, pacing back and forth so swiftly it even made him dizzy. Colton Richards gave a tired nod, lifting one finger to indicate he wasn't finished with his phone conversation. Since Maria's father was on the other end of the call, Ryan kept his mouth shut. No doubt the tongue-lashing Colton was receiving from the older man was painful. After breaking the bad news, Colton hadn't been able to get a word in.

And Ryan still needed to talk to Mr. Miranda.

In the meantime, standing around doing nothing was killing him. He had money, lots of it, and virtually unlimited resources. He'd promptly offered it to the Pack Protectors, just in case they needed helicopters, jets, hell, even an army. After a faintly incredulous look, Colton had politely thanked him and said he'd let Ryan know if there was anything he could do.

Which meant they didn't want or need his help. Yet, aside from Maria's father, Ryan doubted anyone cared more about Maria's safety.

Gritting his teeth while waiting for Colton to wind down the conversation, he wished *he* had magic. More than that, he needed some sort of telepathic connection that would enable him to find out where Polacek had hidden Maria. And if she was all right.

With every fiber of his soul, he knew she had to be. He believed he'd somehow feel it, right in his chest, in his heart, if any harm came to her.

"Eyrie," he said out loud, finally having had enough. "Let me have that phone." Snatching it out of Colton's hand before the other man could protest, Ryan cleared his throat.

"Mr. Miranda, you don't know me, but I'm a friend of your daughter's."

"Ryan Howard," the other man said, surprising him. "I know who you are. My daughter spoke highly of you."

After thanking him, Ryan outlined his plan. Instead of immediately discounting it, or asking him how he had so much inside Drakkor info, Maria's father didn't waste time. "I'll contact the Council immediately. If we bring together all of those with strong magic, I think you're right. We should be able to locate them."

"I hope so, sir." Handing the phone back to Colton, Ryan walked off. He couldn't believe he'd been such a stubborn fool. If he'd let go of his pride earlier and called her before she'd gone out with Darryl, she might still be safe.

"No sense in blaming yourself." Colton's large hand

came down on his shoulder. "At least that's what I'm telling myself and my men. All we can do is move forward at this stage and hope for the best."

Hope. Such a fragile thing. Ryan needed more than hope. He wanted certainty. He wanted Maria right here, right now, in front of him smiling her beautiful smile. Unharmed and safe.

"The Drakkor Council is in charge from now on," Colton continued. "We Pack Protectors haven't been called off, because they know there are no better trackers. Why don't you head on home and get some rest. We'll start again in the morning."

Ryan thought of his house, packed with revelers, and shook his head. "I think I'll just get a hotel room," he said. "I'm going to need sleep to make it through this ordeal."

Colton gave him a long look. "You seem to care an awful lot about Maria. I thought you two had broken up."

Instead of answering, Ryan shook his head. "Not the time or the place, okay?"

One corner of Colton's mouth twisted. "Look, I know how you feel. I lost my chance with a woman who loved me because I couldn't let down my guard. If we get Maria back..." Clearing his throat, he corrected himself. "When we get her back, you might just get a second chance. Don't blow it."

Ryan nodded. "I don't intend to."

Though the thought made bile clog her throat, Maria understood what she'd have to do. No matter what it took, she'd have to convince Doug that she loved him, or at least had started to care for him. If she intended to have any hope of saving herself or Tracey, she had to get him to let her see that book so she could regain her magic.

"Where is Tracey?" she asked, wiping her cheek with

the back of her hand in a futile attempt to clean the dirt from the concrete room off her face.

"None of your business."

His mercurial moods followed no pattern that she could tell. Holding eye contact, she spoke calmly. "I need to see her and make sure she's all right."

"Why bother? Once we're in love and you carry my child, she's dead."

Damn. A sudden thought hit her. "Why? Why settle for one child when you could have two."

A spark briefly illuminated his flat gaze. "Explain yourself."

"You know in the old days, kings and sultans had an entire harem. Why shouldn't you have more than one wife? And more than one child."

"Because she won't love me!" he shouted, spraying her with spittle. An instant later, he calmed himself. "My apologies. I generally have better control over my emotions." He took a deep breath and then fixed her with a piercing look. "The situation with Tracey is frustrating. I'm sorry for taking it out on you."

This apology surprised her at first, until she realized he was back to playing a role in hopes she would fall in love with him.

This gave her another idea. "Any man I love must be compassionate." She manufactured a tremulous smile. "If Tracey is hurt or in pain, please allow me to help her. Think about it, Doug. If you truly want to have us both love you, that is."

Instead of answering her, he spun on his heel and strode away.

The instant he'd disappeared from sight, she attempted to push to her feet. But whatever invisible bonds he'd used continued to hold her, even in this different location.

She looked around the room, curious. Mismatched, utilitarian furnishings reminded her of an underfunded medical clinic or charity waiting room. Clearly, they were not in a regular home, at least not on Galveston Island. Any attempt to dig too deeply would result in hitting water, so an underground room like the one Doug had held her in would be impossible.

Unless he'd taken her inland, farther north. She had no idea how long she'd been unconscious.

After noting the shabby furniture, she studied the way the cracks in the ceiling ran down the wall and along the concrete floor. No water seepage that she could see. They were definitely off Galveston Island.

Since she couldn't move, even to stretch her legs, she began trying to develop more concrete plans. Clearly, this wasn't going to be something she could do quickly. Unless somehow the Drakkor Council rescued her, it appeared she'd be here awhile. She needed to make sure she stayed alive, and figure out a way to get him to let her help Tracey. Assuming, she thought, as a shudder snaked up her spine, the other woman was healthy enough to survive.

A sound interrupted her contemplation. Blinking, she glanced back the way she'd come, spying Polacek heading toward her with a motionless shape levitating ahead of him. As he grew closer, Maria saw this was a person, bruised and battered, dressed in rags and so filthy her skin seemed gray. Tracey. Unless he had more than one woman held captive.

When he reached the area where Maria sat, Doug slowly lowered his burden to the floor. As her body connected with the concrete, a cry of pain escaped her.

Maria's heart stuttered. "Tracey?" she asked, her gaze going from Polacek to the other captive, who made no response when Maria said her name.

"Yes, this is Tracey. You wanted to see her. See what you can do with her," he demanded. "She stinks."

At his words, Maria felt the bonds around her loosen. She stretched and gradually got to her feet, suddenly unsure if her legs would hold her. To her relief, they did.

Slowly approaching the still and silent shape, she ignored Polacek as she reached out to smooth matted and lank hair away from Tracey's face. "It's all right now, Tracey. It's me, Maria Miranda. I'm going to try and help you."

The morning after the big party, Ryan called Timothy bright and early, waking him. He told his assistant to get everyone out of the house immediately. Once they were gone, Timothy was to hire a cleaning crew, offering top dollar if they could arrive immediately and finish within two hours.

Micah, Brandon and Roger would be arriving from Colorado the next afternoon. Maria's father, Javier, would also fly in, from Wisconsin, arriving at roughly the same time. Colton Richards would pick them all up at Bush Intercontinental Airport and take them to Ryan's large beach house where they'd be staying.

Ryan wanted the house superclean for his visitors.

Being the miracle assistant that he was, even with a hangover, Timothy came through. By the time Ryan arrived around eleven, no trace of the party from the night before remained.

For the twentieth time, he checked his watch. The house was empty; Ryan had sent Timothy back to Austin with Jeff and David. All of the spare bedrooms had fresh linens and the kitchen had been completely restocked. Amazing what paying a premium could do.

The planes should already have landed, Ryan thought.

He'd offered to send his private jet to collect all or some of them, but the Drakkor Council had politely declined. Ryan guessed they preferred to take commercial flights, for whatever reason. At least they'd accepted his offer to provide a place to stay. With them here, at least Ryan would be involved in the decision-making process as to how the rescue would go.

And how fast. Maria had already been in that monster's clutches for way too long. Ryan wanted her out now.

Standing outside on the front deck, Ryan tried to hide his impatience as he watched the black, government-issue car turn into his long drive. He'd given Colton the key code to operate the metal gate, but the system had been set up to alert him inside the house when it was used.

After parking, Colton got out and opened the back door to help out the elderly man from Colorado. Ryan suppressed a flash of anger, remembering what Maria had told him Micah had done to her when she'd first arrived at Eyrie.

A short, pudgy man emerged from the front passenger side, his dusky skin and jet-black hair so reminiscent of Maria's that Ryan knew this had to be her father.

Ryan hurried down the stairs to shake his hand. "Ryan Howard. Pleased to meet you, sir. I wish it were under different circumstances."

"I know who you are." The exhaustion and pain in the older man's eyes spoke volumes. "Though she never would admit it to me, my daughter cares for you."

Ryan lifted his chin. "I'm willing to use my nearly unlimited resources to find her."

"Oh, quit your bragging." Micah gave him a good-natured slap on the back. "We all know you're a rich billionaire. It isn't money that will help us find that young lady. It's magic."

Behind him, Colton met Ryan's gaze, his own stating plainly he thought Micah might be short a marble or two. Ryan gave a slight nod. He didn't care about what Micah was or wasn't. Only the possibility that the older Drakkor could use his magic to save Maria mattered.

Once everyone had been ushered inside his house, Ryan offered drinks and snacks. He'd stopped by the market and picked up some veggie trays along with cold cuts and cheese. Everyone appeared to be hungry, so Ryan and Colton hung back and watched while they ate. Javier Miranda had a few bites and grabbed a can of soda before coming to stand next to Ryan.

"I see you care about my daughter," Javier began.

Meeting the older man's brown eyes, so reminiscent of Maria's, Ryan smiled. "She's very important to me."

At his words, Javier looked crestfallen. "I see."

For the life of him, Ryan couldn't figure out what he'd said wrong. "I take it you have someone else in mind for your daughter?"

This time, when Javier met Ryan's gaze, he gave a clear challenge. "I do, actually," he said, crushing Ryan. "Someone who loves her."

The weight on his chest eased slightly. He couldn't tell Maria's father how much he loved her yet. He wanted to tell Maria first.

At the sound of her name, Tracey moaned, but still did not open her eyes. The closer Maria got to her, the worse the stench of urine and feces and vomit became. From the mottled bruises and cuts all over her face and body, Maria could tell Polacek hadn't been gentle with her.

Anger filled her, tempered by fear. A cold knot formed in her stomach as she realized that if she didn't play her role right, Tracey would die. Maria bit down hard on the inside of her mouth to keep from turning around and clawing at him. Such a foolish action would only result in losing what tiny bit of freedom she'd gained.

Once she felt certain her expression was impassive, Maria turned and met Polacek's gaze. "Why have you let her get in this shape? Several of these cuts are infected. She needs to be cleaned up."

At her words, his expression clouded with rage. "She wouldn't cooperate. Why should I help her in any way if she won't help me?"

Hanging on to her self-control, Maria took a deep breath. "Remember what we talked about? Do you want to be a king or not? If you intend to have your own harem, you can't be letting your women suffer like this. Remember, there are very few of us left."

His nostrils flared. "Maybe so, but there are other women, other species. All a child will need is Drakkor blood. My blood."

Maria looked down so he wouldn't read contempt in her eyes. Clearly, he still didn't understand the truth about his infertility. She wasn't foolish enough to try and make him, not right now, when both she and Tracey were at his mercy.

"I can help you, Doug." She used a soft voice, speaking as one might to a recalcitrant child. "But you must help me get Tracey clean and comfortable. I'm assuming you have soap and medical supplies?"

Arms crossed, he grudgingly nodded. "I'll show you where everything is, but don't expect me to help. And, Maria, don't even think about trying to get away. I've enclosed this entire place in a cloaking spell, one I learned from that book. No one will be able to find us and no one inside can leave."

Ninety minutes later, Maria had a freshly bathed Tracey moved to a cot covered in clean sheets. Despite his words,

Maria had convinced Polacek to help as she couldn't move Tracey alone. Tracey certainly couldn't move herself; she never really regained consciousness.

Aware of Doug lurking in the background as he had the entire time she was fussing with Tracey, Maria finally made eye contact with him and summoned up a half-hearted smile. "At least that odor is gone. Now, tell me, what have you been feeding her?"

His casual shrug didn't fool her. "I gave her what dragons in the wild eat. Insects and rodents."

Bugs and rats. Swallowing back bile, Maria nodded. "And has she been eating any of that?"

"She's still alive, isn't she? I'm assuming she ate. I didn't stick around and watch. I've been keeping her in one of those concrete boxes, just like you were in."

Horrified, she thought back to how long ago she'd learned Tracey had been taken. While she didn't remember how many days or even weeks that had been, she knew it had been a long time.

"She's been in the box all this time?" she asked.

"Of course not. At first, I treated her exactly like I am you now. I explained what I expected of her and she refused. I fed her and worked magic on her and buttered her up like a croissant hot out of the oven, but she wouldn't even try to love me." Again he lifted one shoulder in a shrug. "So she went down in the box. I planned to leave her there until she changed her mind. But then I started focusing on you and getting you to date me and like me so you'd kiss me. I guess I forgot she was in there."

Appalled and horrified, his callous cruelty incensed her. She hated being at his mercy like this, but knew she could show no reaction to anything he said.

"Um, any idea how long it's been since you fed her?"

"No." He gazed up at the ceiling as if thinking. "Maybe a week? More or less."

Deep breath. Calm, even breathing. "May I ask a favor?"

Her deference pleased him, at least judging by the quick smile he flashed at her. "Go ahead. I can't promise I'll grant it, but I'll listen."

"Can you get me some food for her? Nothing too solid, maybe some chicken broth and crackers? And water? I think she really could use something to drink."

He went silent. Maria braced herself, not sure whether he'd erupt in anger or decide to be gracious and honor her request.

"I'll see what I have," he finally said. "You will not be able to leave this room."

Maria nodded. "Thank you." Watching him, she held completely still until he'd gone back up the stairs.

Part of her wanted to test him. She still couldn't believe that something as simple as one kiss could rob her of all her magical ability. But now she had Tracey to consider, and until she was well, Maria had no plans to go anywhere.

Tracey moaned and Maria leaned closer, brushing still-damp hair away from her freshly scrubbed face. While Maria had no idea of Tracey's age, freckles dotted her creamy pale skin. "It's going to be all right, Tracey," Maria murmured. "It's me, Maria Miranda."

At the name, Tracey visibly struggled to open her eyes. Maria's heart ached for the other woman and she had to swallow back her increasing fury at the beast that had done this to her.

He returned with a battered metal cup and handed it to Maria. "Broth," he said, his tone full of disgust. "I warmed it as best as I could."

Dipping her pinky into the liquid, which was lukewarm, Maria managed a smile. "Thank you."

She managed to get a little of the broth into Tracey, before the battered woman turned her head and retched. Doug had placed a plastic cup of water on the floor, and Maria raised it to Tracey's lips. "Drink. It's water."

Tracey drank greedily, but she'd only taken a couple of gulps before she turned her face away, signaling to Maria that she'd had all she could take.

Maria put the cup down and opened her mouth to speak, but Polacek grabbed her arm and yanked her up to her feet.

"Enough of this," he said. "She'll be fine."

"I'm not too sure about that," Maria began. "She needs more help than I can give her. Medical help."

His hard stare had her fighting not to squirm. "Now you want me to kidnap a doctor?"

"No. Of course not. I meant—"

"I know what you meant." His twisted grin made her stomach sour. "And it's not happening. Now. You've spent enough time coddling her. Your attention needs to be on me."

Chapter 15

Of course it did. Remembering she had a role to play, Maria nodded. "You're right. I'm sorry."

He ducked his head, giving her a nod to let her know she'd pleased him. "You mentioned you wanted to see the book?"

Instantly, all of Maria's fatigue fell away. She knew better than to reveal her excitement, so she merely nodded. "Sure."

He narrowed his gaze in speculation. "You read French, then?"

"No." She tried to think of something she could say. She wasn't sure why she felt the need to see this book so strongly, but she did. "I don't speak or read French. But maybe if I could see it, plus your translation, I might be able to help. You know what they say about a second pair of eyes."

He wanted to believe her, she could see it in the muscle

twitch in his cheek and the flash of eagerness in his un-usually colored eyes. Still, he didn't move.

"You may not see the original," he finally declared. "It's far too valuable for me to take a chance of you destroying even one page."

She managed a nod, careful to hide her disappointment.

"But I can let you take a look at my translation," he continued. "I have more than one copy of that."

She thanked him, well aware she'd have to take what she could get.

He fetched his notes with great fanfare, carrying them with as much reverence and delicacy as if he considered them a holy object.

Motioning that she should take a seat on one of the rickety plastic chairs near the metal table, he placed the stack of papers in the middle.

"Once we're truly in love, we'll be able to read each other's thoughts the way true mates do," he said, apropos of nothing.

Maria smiled. "True." She itched to reach for the book, but didn't dare without a signal from him that it would be all right to do so.

When he leaned closed, trailing his finger down her throat to her shoulder, she shuddered, closing her eyes and praying he thought her shivers were from ecstasy.

"What a pair we will be," he mused, smoothing her hair away from her face. Relief flooded her that he hadn't continued to slide his hand downward, toward her breasts.

"May I look at the book?" she asked, her breathlessness not from arousal but from repugnance. She marveled that she'd ever found this man attractive enough to date.

"You may." His indulgent smile told her she needed to act grateful.

"Thank you so much," she said. "I can't wait to see what's in there."

He let her read undisturbed for at least thirty minutes before coming back for her. At least Maria thought half an hour had passed. She didn't know for sure, as she didn't have a watch or a clock and he'd confiscated her phone.

"Did you find anything, love?" he asked, leering at her with a peculiar blend of lust and hope.

Terrified that he would decide they were in love and make an attempt to rape her, Maria made a show of pretending she was close to finding something important in his translation of the book.

"I'm almost there."

He sighed. "I'll wait." And he did, reading over her shoulder and breathing in her ear. She suppressed the urge to jerk away, managing to hold herself still and continuing to peruse the pages.

"I just need a few more minutes," she said, every time he grew bored and tried to drag her away so they could "spend time getting to know each other better."

What she really wanted to do was get back to Tracey, but she knew he'd not allow that for very long.

So, for now, the book claimed all of her undivided attention. "There's something here," she said again, not entirely lying, either. "Right now it's eluding me, but I know if I continue to read, whatever it is will become clear."

He yawned, not even bothering to cover his mouth with his hand. "Fine. You have thirty more minutes. I promise you can look at it again tomorrow, but you and I have got to have some together time."

The idea made her feel as though she had insects crawling all over her skin. "Okay," she managed, praying she'd stumble across something exciting enough to distract him.

And then she struck gold. But the instant she read the

passage and realized how it applied to her, she knew she could never tell him.

True love's kiss. Of course. Nearly every fairy tale, every myth, had some variation of this theme. Whatever spell Polacek had used to take away her magic with a casual kiss, could be invalidated if she could kiss her true love.

She read the passage again, wondering if the love had to be reciprocated for this to work. Of course, no more details were given, and the next paragraph went on to another subject.

"Did you find something?" Gaze sharp, Polacek watched her intently.

Staring blindly at the page, she started to shake her head, but then she read the first paragraph of the next page and smiled. "I believe I did," she said. "Though I'm not sure you're going to like it."

Since Colton was put in charge of the search, Ryan was allowed to attend the briefing along with the Pack Protectors, Maria's father and the three Drakkor mages from Eyrie.

"The Galveston police force must be kept in the dark about this," Colton said. "We'll have to learn everything we can about Darryl Pride without alerting the local authorities."

Which made perfect sense. Even though working outside the realm of the law would hinder them somewhat, they couldn't take the risk of humans learning anything about Shifters or magic.

"We do, however, have a Pack member working as a police officer here in Galveston. His help has been invaluable in conducting our investigation," Colton said.

A man wearing a Galveston police uniform stepped forward from behind the large group of Pack Protectors and gave them all a mock salute. "Dennis Rocho at your service," he said.

After the chorus of welcomes and thank-yous died down, Colton continued. "Here's what an initial investigation has revealed. Since Doug Polacek is an attorney, we checked to see if Darryl Pride worked as a lawyer anywhere in Galveston or on the mainland. Granted, he would have had to forge a law license, which might draw too much unwanted attention. This is probably one of the reasons we can't find any record of him working in the legal field."

"Do we know how long ago he arrived in Galveston?" One of the other Pack Protectors asked.

"As far as we can determine, right before he started dating Maria Miranda. We have been able to learn he was renting a motel room in Texas City under the name Darryl Pride."

"Excellent work," the senior Drakkor from Eyrie named Micah spoke, his deep voice resonating around the room. "What I'd like to know is how Polacek even learned of Ms. Miranda's whereabouts in the first place."

As if on cue, everyone except the three Drakkor mages turned and looked at Ryan.

Micah appeared puzzled.

"She was dating a celebrity," Javier explained, pointing at Ryan. "Him. The paparazzi caught her out with him and her picture was on television and in magazines. I'm sure Polacek saw her on *TMZ* or *Access Hollywood* or something."

Ryan refused to feel guilty, despite the reproachful stares nearly everyone in the room directed his way. "I didn't know," he said quietly. "I value my own privacy and had no way of foretelling that they'd find me here. Believe me, if I'd been aware of Maria's situation, I would have taken extra precautions to keep her out of the spotlight."

At his words, some of the open hostility vanished from the Drakkor's faces. To Ryan's gratitude, Maria's father reached over and squeezed his shoulder in support.

Colton cleared his throat. "Understood. Now, if I may proceed. We've been viewing traffic camera videos from around the Strand and the pier area. Restaurant surveillance has shown Ms. Miranda and Doug Polacek getting out of a late-model black Dodge Charger. We were only able to get a partial on the plate, but Dennis here has quietly put out an APB on the car, stating the driver is a suspect in an arson investigation."

Since Colton looked right at him and dipped his chin, Ryan knew he meant the fire at the first beach house.

"So you're looking for his car," Javier put in. "That's helpful and all, but I need to know what else you are doing? Has anyone ever gotten any leads on the other woman he kidnapped, Tracey Beauchamp?"

Stone-faced, Colton shook his head. "A different unit is involved in that rescue operation, but as far as I'm aware, they have nothing. We will of course, furnish them whatever information we obtain."

"Maybe you should tie the two together," Micah said, his arms crossed. "Clearly, the rouge Drakkor is collecting our few remaining women. Can I assume the others have been placed under heavy guard?"

"Most assuredly." Colton nodded. "And I think—"

"Good," Micah interrupted. "Now, if you're done blathering about what little you've managed to accomplish, the three of us have work to do."

Though Colton narrowed his eyes at that, he nodded, still clearly respectful. "What's your plan?"

"As soon as darkness falls, we're shifting to Drakkor

and taking to the sky. We'll split up—less chance of us being seen. And we'll find him, you can bet on that."

"Will you use magic to look for him?" Ryan asked.

"Of course," Micah snapped, glaring at him. "No doubt he's using magic to shield himself, which will actually make it easier to find him. Magic gives off an aura, visible only to the eyes of others with magical ability. If this Polacek is using magic to keep those women captive, we will find it."

"I'm going with you." Javier stood. "I have a fair amount of magic of my own. I want to do whatever I can to help find my daughter."

Micah considered, then slowly nodded. "As long as you agree to follow my orders."

"Of course."

Now Micah looked at Colton. "I'll need you or someone familiar with this area to take us to the best place to change into our dragon form."

"I know where that is." Ryan stepped forward. "I'd be honored to take you. That's where I go to shift. Maria, too." He smiled sadly. "She is truly a beautiful dragon."

Now Micah and his cronies, as well as Maria's father, all stared at him. "You've seen my daughter change?" Javier asked.

"Yes." He decided not to tell them that she hadn't known it at the time. "Now, if you're ready to head that way, let's go. The sooner you start searching, the quicker we can get Maria back."

"Well?" Polacek demanded. "You've been at it long enough. What did you find in the book that I'm not going to like?"

Taking a deep breath, Maria swallowed. She couldn't

tell him the truth, but she had to say something. Something that contained at least a kernel of truth.

"There." She pointed to a page with a trembling finger. "I'm sure you saw it, but it talks about the end of the Drakkor species."

Eyes narrow slits, he glared at her. "I did. It's a bunch of prophetic nonsense."

"Oh." She didn't have to feign her disappointment. "May I continue to read? I'm sure if I keep at it, I'll find something."

"I doubt it," he said, his expression both disapproving and calculating. "But go on. I've got more important things to do to occupy my time."

She nodded and went back to the book, glad she'd managed to keep her breathing even and hadn't revealed how hard her heart pounded.

And soon she lost herself in the pages.

Though Maria had no idea of the time or whether outside the sun or the moon lit up the sky, she had no choice but to believe him when Polacek announced it was bedtime. Hearing the word spoken in his silky tone made her entire body clench with worried revulsion.

She did a whole lot of fast-talking, reminding him of the courtship necessary in any relationship before there could be love. She also told him she didn't want to go too fast.

Somehow, by some miracle, he bought it and bid her good-night. As he walked away, he told her he thought he might spend the night with Tracey instead.

Though she knew doing so might put her right back into his sights, she grabbed his arm. "Please don't. She's in no condition for anything like that. If you want her to come to care for you, you must let her heal."

Gaze steely, he eyed her. "You're full of demands for a prisoner. Be grateful I don't put you back in the cement box. You do understand that I call the shots here, don't you?"

Swallowing back a gag, she let her hand trail down his arm. "Of course I do. I'm only trying to help you so you can have your harem and we can have our babies."

Still studying her, he finally nodded. "Fine. I will sleep alone. For now. And before you ask, no, you may not spend the night taking care of Tracey. She's survived this long without you, so I have no doubt she'll heal quickly. Good night."

And he left her, locking the door behind him.

Relieved she'd managed to talk him into letting her sleep alone, she tried to get comfortable on the threadbare rug she'd been given to place on the cold concrete floor for use as a sleeping place.

Her body and mind were exhausted, but she couldn't shake the feeling there was something she'd overlooked.

Finally she must have dropped into slumber because suddenly she saw Ryan. Looking achingly handsome and decidedly concerned, he stood on the edge of a deserted peninsula and stared up at the moonlit night sky. She swore she could feel the sea breeze and taste the salt of sea spray on her skin. She saw them then—four dragons, launching themselves into the air. Recognizing her father, she gasped when she realized the others were Micah, Brandon and Roger.

Along with Ryan, who clearly didn't sense her presence, she watched until they were nothing but specks blending into the black velvet of the starry sky.

For a breathless second, she fancied she could hear his thoughts. The others would use magic to search for her, while Colton and the Pack Protectors used whatever human law enforcement tools were at their disposal. Yet Ryan, despite all his money and vast resources, could do nothing. He'd been relegated to standing by helplessly, waiting for others. Not something he was used to. Even now, his worry over her safety mingled with his sense of urgency that there had to be something he could do.

But what?

Aching for his touch, she reached out toward him, unsurprised when her fingers went right through him instead of caressing his skin. She knew she had only come in spirit form while her physical body slumbered.

Still, she'd take what she could get. Drinking in the sight of him, she noted new hollows in his face, though that might have only been a trick of the darkness.

As he turned to go, she noticed he'd taken the others to Corps Woods to shape-shift. Holding her breath, she watched as Ryan, now alone, initiated the change into wolf. This was different than the whirlwind way the Drakkor changed, no puff and swirl of smoke, but rather a thousand twinkling lights like fireflies.

When he'd finished and stood in front of her, a magnificent wolf with gray fur made silver by the moonlight, she felt a sense of awe.

And then wolf-Ryan lifted his head and howled at the moon, the sound so full of pain and anguish tears stung her eyes.

The agony woke her and her dream vanished. Raising her head, she blinked as she took in her surroundings. The chill from the cement floor had seeped up through her mat and into her bones. She began shivering, wondering how Tracey fared and how long it was until morning. She couldn't help but dread it. Who knew what the next day would bring?

Somehow, she must have fallen back asleep. The sound of a cheery whistle woke her. Stunned, she listened as Polacek whistled "It's a Beautiful Day in the Neighborhood," as if this scenario was a horribly twisted episode of the old television show *Mister Rogers' Neighborhood*.

"Breakfast is ready, honey," he said, smiling at her as if he hadn't done anything to her and she wasn't actually his captive.

Struck dumb, she collected herself to realize she needed to smile back. "Sounds great," she chirped, wincing as she climbed to her feet. Part of her body ached so badly she had to hobble instead of walk.

Polacek didn't appear to notice. He continued beaming, holding out of plate of some unidentifiable substance that might have been oatmeal or really old scrambled eggs. Her gut cramped at the thought of eating them.

Still, afraid to anger him, she accepted the plate. "That looks good. What is it?" she asked. Her heart skipped a beat as his smile slipped.

"Grits," he told her. "I found a box of instant grits. I made you two packets and Tracey two packets."

"What about you? Aren't you having any?"

Now his smile had definitely vanished, replaced by a black scowl. "I went out for my meal. Once the two of you start being nicer to me, I might start bringing you back some of my leftovers."

On cue, her stomach growled. "I'm really hungry," she began, eyeing the plate and trying not to gag. "But I've never been fond of grits." And especially grits that looked like they were ten years old.

"Suit yourself." He shrugged, back to the easy-going man of earlier. His mercurial moods were alarming, since she had no idea what might set him off. "I'm going to go take a nice hot shower."

She would have just about killed for a shower. "I'd love—"

"Not yet." Interrupting her, he began circling around

her like a dragon inspecting its prey. "All privileges must be earned."

Earned. Mind racing, she managed a nod. "I understand," she said, ducking her head so he wouldn't read the fury in her eyes.

Once again, she tapped into that emotion, willing her magic to fill her. And once again, she was met only by emptiness.

Lifting her chin, she saw he still waited, watching her. As soon as her gaze met his, he smiled. "Have a nice day," he said. "I'll see you later."

"Wait." She nearly ran after him. "What about Tracey? Can I check on her?"

"I'm taking care of that one myself. She'll be fine."

Fine. Right.

Horrified, she realized that while she'd been thinking he'd reached the door. "What about the book?" she asked, noting how he instantly stiffened. "May I study your notes while you're gone?"

If he truly wanted her to suffer, he'd deny her. As he considered her request, she could only hope his desire to gain knowledge was greater than the urge to hurt her.

"I'll bring it to you after my shower," he finally said.

"Thank you." She stood still while he closed the door and listened to the sound of him locking it. It was only then she realized what he'd just said. Despite the utilitarian nature of this concrete place, if there was a shower nearby, it might be someone's home. And if they were close to restaurants or fast-food establishments, they were in a town or city.

Texas City? Houston? Or had they gone farther north?

She thought of her father and the Drakkor mages, wondering if they'd be able to find her, hidden by not only concrete, but a cloaking spell. Once again, she realized her best hope lay within Polacek's translation of that book. If she couldn't get her magic back—and how could she if she needed true love's kiss?—maybe she could find some sort of remedy to make Polacek's magic invalid, too.

After changing to wolf, Ryan let out his pent-up emotion in one long howl. As he finished, he swore he saw movement in the corner of his eye and spun around, but nothing was there. Just to be certain, he sniffed the breeze, looking for any telltale scent. Nothing but sea and salt.

He hunted that night, letting smaller prey go in his search for something that would relieve at least some of the pain. Of course, he found nothing, and he finally left the rabbits and toads and squirrels to their own devices and shape-shifted back to human.

In his mercurial rise to wealth, Ryan Howard had few regrets. He believed in treating others the way he expected them to treat him. He didn't cheat or lie or steal, or step on other's backs in the climb to the top. Talent and hard work had gotten him far. And even though people who didn't know him might find fault with the way he conducted his love life, he'd been up front and honest with every woman he'd dated.

Except Maria.

Sure, he'd believed that the same old stock recitation of his desire for no strings had been true. At the time, it had been. Until his desire had somehow morphed into something deeper. Something…more.

Driving his Jeep too fast, he found himself on her street, heading toward her tidy little house. Of course the place sat dark and unoccupied, but even so, he pulled up in front and parked.

Maria had made that house into a home. All the money

in the world hadn't been able to do that with any of the numerous houses he owned.

It had begun to rain, a light mist, just enough to make the roads slick. Ryan drove carefully, glad he'd left the top up on his Jeep. Interesting how his first thought had been that the sea had begun to shed tears. He wasn't poetic by nature, so he figured this new insightfulness had to be because he'd begun to see the world through Maria's eyes.

He couldn't believe how much he missed her. Hoping and praying she was safe wasn't enough. There had to be something he could do, somehow. If only he knew what.

Finally, he pulled back onto the street and headed toward his beach house.

There, he found Colton and Javier Miranda in the kitchen, strategizing over bourbon on the rocks.

Ryan poured himself a glass and took a seat at the table. "When did you get back?" he asked Maria's father. "You just left."

"I know." The older man winced. "I'd barely gotten a mile out into the gulf when an old wing injury had me turning around and heading here. I'd only hamper them. As much as I don't want to, I'm going to have to sit this one out. My Maria is far too important."

"She is," Ryan agreed. Missing her so strongly he ached, he tried to figure out some other way he could help. "Surely there's something I can do," he said, looking from one to the other.

"Sorry." Colton clapped him on the back. "But I have to tell you, the Pack Protectors expressly forbid you hiring your own private investigative firm, which quite honestly is what I'd want to do in your shoes."

Ryan swore, hating that the other man had guessed his plans.

Even Maria's father vetoed the idea. "This is a Drakkor matter," he said sternly. "We're working with the Pack Protectors, but there is no need to involve any others."

Hands once again tied, Ryan nodded. "How's the search going, then?"

Colton shook his head. "On the ground, we've found nothing. The three Drakkor disappeared—I assume to keep searching."

"They have more power and stamina than I do," Javier admitted. "I had to return here while they continued on."

Colton tossed off the rest of his drink and stifled a yawn with his hand. "Well, I'm off to bed, gentlemen. I've got to be up early in the morning to meet with the head of the Protectors and give him a report to take to the Drakkor Council. Good night, all."

Ryan murmured something suitable and continued sipping his bourbon. Any second now, he figured Maria's father would make his excuses and leave, too. Ryan wondered if the older man blamed him for his daughter's capture. Certainly it seemed as though some of the others did.

"Why are you still here, son?" Javier asked softly. "I mean, it's nice of you to offer us the use of your place and all, but a busy man like you? Why stick around?"

"Ouch." The word slipped out before Ryan had time to consider what he'd say. "That really hurts."

"Does it?" Curiosity shone in Javier's gaze. "Again, I ask why?"

Truth. He realized he didn't care if anyone believed him or liked him or even cared how he felt. And though he'd planned to tell Maria first, keeping everything inside made him feel as if he could burst.

"Because I love your daughter," he said quietly. "It feels good to finally say the words out loud. I'd actually planned to tell her first, before I spoke to you or anyone."

Chapter 16

"You love her?" Javier repeated slowly.

Bracing himself for derision or anger, Ryan glanced at the older man, stunned to see a broad smile creasing his face.

"You truly love her?" Javier asked again.

"Yes."

"And she doesn't know?"

A bit puzzled, Ryan nodded. "That's right."

After a long drink of his bourbon, Javier wiped the back of his hand across his mouth. "Any idea how she feels about you?"

Ryan inhaled, deciding he might as well take a leap of faith. "I believe she feels the same way."

Javier whooped, throwing up his hands and then jumping from his seat to embrace Ryan. "You have no idea how happy that makes me."

Feeling warm inside for the first time in days, Ryan

nodded. "So, I guess that means I have your permission to…"

"Yes! Yes, of course."

Ryan wondered why Javier was dancing around the room, acting as if he'd just won the lottery. Sure, Ryan might be rich, but there was no guarantee Maria would even want to enter a committed relationship with him.

Suddenly suspicious, Ryan eyed the man. "Is there something you're not telling me?" he asked.

"No! Yes. Oh, I don't know. All I can tell you is that you and my daughter have a lot of talking to do."

"Once she's found." Ryan's quiet statement had the effect of instantly calming her father. "We need to find her, or none of this matters."

"We will." Javier looked more confident than he sounded. "Micah and the other two mages from Eyrie are among the oldest and wisest of my people. Their magic is unrivaled. They're so revered that rarely are they called on to help. But when needed, they spring into action. In addition to helping us find Doug Polacek, they trained Maria and the other women."

He sounded so proud that Ryan almost didn't tell him what Micah and his crew had done to Maria. But then he figured her father had the right to know.

"Did Maria speak much to you about her time at Eyrie?" Ryan asked. "You know I took her to Boulder and waited while she learned how to harness her abilities."

Javier's eyes widened. "She didn't give me many details, and certainly not that."

Ryan shrugged and polished off the last of his drink. "Well then, maybe I shouldn't have said anything. I'd feel funny discussing this without her knowing. In fact, I think I'm going to turn in. There's no telling what tomorrow might bring."

Frown changing to a yawn, Javier did the same and pushed to his feet. "I'll see you in the morning. If we're up at the same time, I make a mean scrambled egg breakfast burrito."

Ryan smiled and headed toward his room.

The rain picked up during the night, occasionally accompanied by booming thunder and flashes of lightning. Ryan couldn't sleep, and he tossed and turned all night. Finally, just before dawn, he gave up and jumped in the shower. Thinking of Javier's breakfast, he got dressed and headed down toward the kitchen. The sun had risen, but barely made a dent in the gray and rainy sky.

Javier was already there, looking freshly showered, too, and sipping on a mug of hot coffee. "There you are," he said, smiling. "Let me get some caffeine in me and then I'll get cracking on those burritos."

"Sounds good." Ryan poured himself a cup. "What all do you put in them?"

Before Javier could elaborate, a crash from outside had both men jumping from their seats. Ryan rushed to the French door and yanked it open. Brandon, the youngest of the three Drakkor from Eyrie, lay sprawled in an exhausted heap in the misting rain, his body rapidly changing back from dragon to man.

He raised his head as soon as he saw Ryan. "Micah needs your help. He's located the rouge Drakkor, though we've yet to make ourselves known. Micah has made some sort of plan, and it involves you."

That had been faster than Ryan dared hope. Joy flooded him that he could finally assist. "Of course. Tell me where I need to go and I'll find a way to get there."

Pushing himself up off the wet deck, Brandon shook his head. Javier tossed him a towel, so he could not only dry off, but cover his nakedness.

"You'll have to come with me. I'll fly you."

On the back of a dragon. In the books he'd read, there'd been a few references to this ancient custom, which had died out centuries ago.

The idea thrilled him. But eyeing Brandon, he doubted the young Drakkor had enough strength to fly anywhere himself, never mind with a passenger.

"You need to rest," he said. "Get a good night's sleep and we'll head out first thing in the morning."

"No time." Brandon took a deep breath. "Though my beast needs to eat. Do you have any steak around? Preferably raw?"

Ryan laughed. "I'm Pack. Of course. How many do you need?"

"Three or four, preferably four."

"Coming right up." But before he went inside, he hesitated. "Should I wake Colton? Do the Pack Protectors need to get involved?"

"Not at this time," Brandon said. "Micah was very specific about that."

After fetching the meat, Ryan watched as Brandon effortlessly changed shape again. The swirling smoke that enveloped him when he started his change was different than the flickering, multicolored lights that appeared when Ryan or anyone he knew shifted into wolf.

Brandon's scales contained a multitude of orange and rust-colored hues. Ryan had come to appreciate that every dragon had different colors, and he found all of them beautiful.

Brandon beckoned with one huge claw. Ryan glanced at Javier, uncharacteristically uncertain.

"Just walk around to his back and climb up his tail," the older man advised. "There are ridges there that you can use as steps. You take a seat right behind his head. There's a slight indentation there where you can sit."

Ryan nodded, doing exactly that. When he grabbed hold of one of the spines that protruded, the soft texture of the supple hide surprised him.

"Go on," Javier urged. "From what Brandon said, it sounds like Micah needs you there as quickly as possible."

"What about you?" Ryan asked.

"I'm still not feeling well. Since I doubt my wing will let me make the trip, I'll stay here and keep the Council informed. Now go."

Hoping like hell he wasn't hurting Brandon, Ryan climbed quickly, taking a seat in the spot Javier had indicated. "I'm ready," he said quietly.

Immediately, Brandon rose, spreading his massive wings and launching himself into the air. Glad it was still early, Ryan clutched a flap of hide and held on.

Either the author of Polacek's book enjoyed rambling and repeating himself, or the translation was off. Maria frowned, wondering if she'd miss something if she began skimming. The repetition had become boring, but she was terrified, too.

Upstairs, she could hear a lot of clanging, which meant Polacek was up to something. Again she thought about Tracey and wondered if the other woman would survive.

She had to figure out a way to get her magic back. The possibility that the answer might be in this book told her she needed to pay attention. So she forced herself to keep reading.

Every twenty minutes or so, when she stretched, she'd make an attempt to locate even a tiny kernel of magic inside of her. Each time she felt only emptiness.

Polacek returned after she'd been at it a while—might

have been hours, she had no way of knowing. Her stomach growled, reminding her she'd had nothing to eat in a long time. Yet just the thought of those nasty-looking grits was enough to banish her hunger.

"I brought you lunch," he said, sounding more like the man she'd come to know as Darryl Pride. "I picked up some chicken. I think you'll like it." He held up a red-and-white box with a familiar logo on it. Heaven help her, her mouth started to water. The smell alone made her want to swoon.

"Thank you," she said, somehow managing to keep from rushing at him and snatching the box out of his grasp. "I really appreciate it."

After he placed the box down on the table, he pushed the book away. "Wouldn't want to get it dirty. Go ahead and dig in."

Wondering if, when she reached for the food, he'd jerk it away, she moved slowly. When she opened the top and saw fried chicken, fried okra, and mashed potatoes and gravy, she nearly cried. Not to mention the perfect, mouth-watering biscuit that came with every meal. He also carried a drink, with ice and everything.

"This is really nice of you," she told him, still hesitant. When he pulled out a chair and sat next to her, a bit too close, she knew she'd better not move away. A horrible thought occurred to her. Did he think he could so easily buy her with a meal?

"Eat." His soft order contained a hint of steel.

So she did. It was the best chicken she'd ever eaten. Crispy on the outside, moist and tender under the skin. She tried to eat slowly, knowing she'd make herself sick if she gulped her meal, but even though she alternated between the meat and the veggies, it wasn't long before she had nothing left but bones. And even those she picked clean.

The drink was diet cola, something she used to love and had weaned herself off of several months ago. It, too, tasted like ambrosia.

When she'd finally finished, she forced herself to turn and look at him. "Thank you again," she said, meaning it. "How is Tracey?"

Just like that, the indulgent look vanished from his face. "Tracey is not your concern."

Stunned, she scrambled for an answer. Before she could think of one, the entire building gave a violent shake. Earthquake?

Cursing, Polacek leaped from his seat.

"What is it?" she asked, wondering if she was about to die here, after all.

"No idea," he snarled, rushing toward the door and unlocking it. She held her breath, hoping in his hurry he might forget to secure her in her room, but then she heard the sound of the key turning in the lock.

Again the walls and floors shook. This time she also heard a low rumble, like an avalanche or something worse. She stood, knowing she had nowhere to run, no place to hide.

A screech sounded, so loud she had to cover her ears. And then another. And one more. A fleet of incoming jets approaching? No. Suddenly, she knew that sound. A dragon. More than one.

The Drakkor Council must have found her. Now they'd battle Polacek.

Oh, how she needed her magic. She paced and spun, cursed and pleaded. Dug deep within herself time and time again. But whatever he'd done to her still held, and she had a feeling it could not be broken, except by the one thing she didn't have. True love's kiss.

There was another thud, and a huge crack appeared in

the cement floor. Not large enough for her to fit through, though she had a feeling if the assault continued walls would soon begin to fall. When they did, she'd need to protect herself and be ready to escape.

But not without Tracey. She had to find Tracey and get her out to safety.

Amazed and exhilarated, Ryan hung on for dear life as Brandon powered through the night sky. The light rain had ended as soon as they left the coast, and the best that Ryan could tell, they were heading out over the gulf, but in a northeast direction. Louisiana?

As they flew, Ryan knew he had to stay awake. He didn't dare sleep and run the risk of falling from the dragon's back. They flew fairly low, staying out of radar, he supposed. Anytime a ship's lights appeared on the horizon, Brandon veered and took evasive action.

The sky remained dark, and even though he'd lost track of time Ryan began to wonder when the sun would start to rise. He figured they'd reach their destination before then, as the Drakkor went to great pains to keep from being seen.

Finally, the water of the gulf gave way to land. Brandon continued to fly, keeping above the treetops, massive head swinging left and right as if looking for something. Ryan hoped he hadn't lost his way.

More time passed. An hour? Two? No longer sure of his bearings, Ryan tried to guess where they were, but failed. Brandon stayed away from larger cities or towns, though judging by the lights in the home windows, the topography had become hilly. Oklahoma? Arkansas?

Finally, they landed in an empty lot, in a downtrodden, dangerous-looking area of whatever town they were in. The nearest building, made of cinder block and corrugated metal, had boarded-up windows and graffiti scrawled all over the front.

He'd expected the Drakkor to do battle as dragons, but the instant he climbed off Brandon he began a swift change back to human. Micah and Roger stepped from the shadows of the building and handed him clothing. While Brandon hurriedly dressed, Micah walked up to Ryan and smiled at him. "I'm glad you came. You're going to come in handy pretty soon. I do need to ask you to stay out of the way so you don't get hurt."

"I can fight," Ryan told him, letting a bit of the anger show through in his voice. "Even though I'm not Drakkor, I'm a good shot." He let the other man see his pistol, which he kept holstered on his belt.

Micah's silver brows rose, but he nodded. "How quickly can you change?"

"Not as fast as you," Ryan responded. "But fast enough. Do you think I can help more as wolf?"

"I'm not sure. This will be an intense battle. Our primary weapon is magic. Once it begins, Polacek will only be expecting magic. He will not anticipate you, whether you're man or wolf. Keep watch and the instant you see an opening, take it."

"Understood. Is this the place?" Ryan asked, pointing at the abandoned factory.

"Yes." Micah spun and strode away, head up, shoulders back, in the manner of a general about to lead his troops to war.

He reached the other two men. In unison, they faced the building and raised their hands.

An explosion of light and fire, oddly silent, lit up the darkness. The building shook so badly some of the boards fell from the windows. Ryan started forward, but Micah barked out his name, stopping him. "Not yet."

Again the mages moved as one, stepping closer and once again raising their arms. More light, more fire, though this time something dark swirled over the brightness and attempted to extinguish it.

"He fights back," Micah said, his grim voice nonetheless determined. "We will need to increase our efforts."

It was three against one, which meant this Polacek must be powerful with magic, indeed. Despite this, Ryan hoped he could be the one to find him and make him pay for what he'd done to Maria.

Even thinking of this made his blood boil.

All three Drakkor had their arms up, battling the swirling black mist. At first it appeared they were at a standstill, but gradually their light began to push it back. And somehow they did all this in silence, apparently so the battle wouldn't alert any humans who might be nearby.

Again Ryan moved closer to the building, watching Micah for a signal. If Micah didn't give one soon, Ryan planned to go anyway. No way was he staying on the sidelines while the woman he loved was in danger.

"When you find Maria," Micah yelled. "Kiss her before you do anything else. Do you understand me?"

Mystified, impatient, Ryan nodded. "Tell me when to go in."

"Now!"

Blood pounding, Ryan went. Darting in between one of the cracks in the metal, Ryan saw that this place had once been some kind of manufacturing plant. A rat scurried by, no doubt terrified by the shaking.

He did a quick check. As far as he could tell, there was no place here to hide a prisoner. He eyed the black smoke, illuminated by the light it battled, noting the way it rose from a hole in the floor. He realized there had to be a basement, which meant they were way farther north than he'd originally guessed. The damp soil and low freeze depth made the construction of basements impossible in the Deep South. Four feet down and the builders would hit water.

The building shook again. Wood rained down on him, along with damp pieces of something. Crouching low, he ran toward the place where the smoke seemed to originate. A tiny hole in the floor. Not big enough to be any sort of entrance. Which meant there had to be a door and a staircase somewhere.

There. On the other side of the room, ten feet from the other wall. A door. Behind it, Ryan suspected he'd find a staircase.

He yanked it open, barely pausing as he crept down the steps. If not for the magical battle waging above him, he would have been trying to make his way in total darkness.

Hoping Polacek would remain occupied by the fight, Ryan went looking for Maria.

No sign of Polacek. So far, so good. A huge fissure had cracked open in the wall, allowing Maria to escape. The only problem was light. As in, there was none outside of her room.

Creeping along, she tried to stay away from the walls, afraid they'd collapse on her. What she'd give for her magic back, as not only would magical ability aid in finding Tracey, but once she had, she could join in the battle to take Polacek down.

Since she had no magic, all she could do was try and locate the other woman and get her to safety.

A high-pitched keening sound made her grimace. Tracey? Daring to use her voice could be dicey. On the one hand, she might accidently alert her captor to her location. On the other, if Tracey were semiconscious, perhaps she could make a sound so Maria could find her.

"Tracey?" Her whisper sounded as loud as a shout. Luckily, another great shudder shook the ground, and she heard a roar as whatever was above them collapsed.

Great. Praying she hadn't just been trapped in here, she continued her forward motion.

"Tracey?" She tried again, a little louder. This time a muffled whimper rewarded her. *That way*, she thought. Another crash shook the ground and she crouched low, crab walking until she thought it was safe to stand. The complete darkness made it impossible to see and she considered attempting a change into dragon so at least she'd have her fiery breath for light, but decided against it. She had no way of knowing if there were any gas leaks due to the battle and the last thing she wanted was for the entire building to explode.

So she continued on, feeling her way along step by step, until her fingers encountered what appeared to be an opening. A doorway?

"Tracey? If you can hear me, make a sound. Any sound. I'm trying to reach you but I need some help."

Silence. Maria held her breath. And then, another tiny whimper, sounding as if it came from the opening right in front of Maria's hand.

Exhaling, Maria counted to three and then dove inside, clearing the opening as more cement and metal rained down on where she'd been standing.

Maria inched forward, praying she didn't encounter spiders, or worse, rats. "I'm right here," she said, aware that she had no actual plan of action once she found the other woman. If Tracey had been able to walk…

"Maria?" Tracey's voice sounded stronger this time. Maybe Polacek had actually been feeding her. "Where are you?"

"Judging from your voice, around five feet away. Have you regained your strength?"

"A little. He's brought me edible food ever since you shamed him. I've tried to eat. I feel a little better, a lot less weak."

"Great." Again, Maria moved closer. She wondered if she'd be able to help Tracey up and support her if they made a break for it. Hopefully so.

"How'd you get out?" Yep, definitely sturdier. "And, Maria, what on earth is going on?"

"I don't know. From the sound of it, Polacek is under attack. I'm thinking they came to rescue us. So I need to ask you, can you access your magic?"

"My what?" Tracey's voice wobbled. "I have no magic."

"You do. We all do. I don't have time to explain too much, but I need you to reach inside and see if you can access it."

"I can't," Tracey responded instantly, telling Maria she hadn't even made an attempt.

"Do you want to live?" Maria had no choice but to speak harshly. "We have no other options, unless you think you can jump up and run. Can you do that?"

Silence. Tracey finally responded in a very small voice. "No. But I swear to you, I don't have any magic. At all."

Speaking quickly, Maria gave the other woman an abbreviated version of what had happened to her. "The male Drakkor worked hard to convince us we were less, somehow. Just like the fertility issue," she finished.

Another loud crash, and then the entire building seemed to groan. "We're running out of time. I need you to reach deep inside yourself and yank your magic into life. And then I need you to connect to the other Drakkor outside and find out what needs to be done."

"I can't," Tracey began.

"You will," Maria interrupted. "Do it. Do it now."

Just like that, the darkness that had enveloped them vanished, lit by a glowing light emanating from Tracey's trembling fingertips. Wearing a stunned expression, Tracey looked at Maria and grimaced. "Wow."

"Yes, wow." More explosions sounded. It seemed as if the battle might be getting more intense and drawing closer. "Now, please do as I asked and reach out toward whatever Drakkor are outside. Just be careful and don't let Polacek know you're doing it."

"I'm not sure exactly how I can—" Tracey began. Something she saw in Maria's face stopped her. She jerked her head in a quick nod. "I'll try."

The light wavered and wobbled as Tracey closed her eyes, apparently to better concentrate. Though she hadn't been trained at all, desperate times called for desperate measures and Maria hoped she'd manage to make it work.

An immense roar sounded outside, echoing all around them. Tracey's eyes popped open. "I think I did it," she whispered, her voice amazed and ragged. "There are three of them. Ancient and powerful Drakkor. Now that they know where we are, they will try to get to us."

"We're not going to wait for them," Maria told her. "I need you to try and stand. You and I are getting out of here right now."

"Maria?" Another voice, so familiar and beloved that for a heartbeat Maria thought she might be hallucinating.

"Ryan?" She gasped out his name, wondering if this was yet another of Polacek's cruel jokes. "Ryan, are you really here?"

He rushed through the doorway, yanking her against him for one hard and fast hug. Glancing at Tracey, who barely sat upright, he took in the situation.

"We don't have much time. Can you walk?"

Instead of answering, Tracey tried to push herself to her feet. She failed miserably.

"Come on." Ryan didn't hesitate. Slipping one arm under Tracey's, he helped her to her feet. Maria hurried over and did the same on the other side.

"How long can you keep up projecting that light?" he asked as they moved out of the doorway and turned left.

"I don't know," Tracey answered. "I guess until it stops."

"What about Polacek?" Maria asked.

"I think he's pretty busy at the moment." Ryan flashed a grin.

They rounded one corner and then another. Maria vaguely recognized the area—she'd been there with Polacek when he'd first let her out of the concrete cell.

"Stairs," Ryan said, pointing. "This is going to be the hard part."

They'd managed to shift and shuffle and push Tracey up halfway before a mighty roar made the wooden staircase tremble.

"Get. Back. Here. Now." Polacek appeared, hair disheveled, expression crazed. "Those are my women. Mine. I'll kill you for even daring to touch them."

Ryan glanced at Maria. "Can you use your magic?" he asked. When she shook her head, his eyes widened.

"Oh, yeah," he said. "I forgot. Micah told me to do this." And he leaned in and kissed her. Just once, a quick press of his mouth on hers, but it was enough.

Chapter 17

Power filled her. So much, so strong, Maria felt as if her entire body had begun to glow. Just like that, her magic had returned. She used it to send both Ryan and Tracey the rest of the way up the stairs, ignoring Ryan's struggles to resist. "Go," she ordered, moving them all the way outside where the others waited. And then she turned to face Polacek. Alone.

"You fool," he sneered, clearly unimpressed. "Thinking that tiny display you somehow engineered using Tracey's puny magic to help you will be able to stop me. After I deal with you, I'll just bring them back—along with the others."

She smiled. "You think?"

At the sight of her confident smile, rage mottled his skin. "Oh, you're going to suffer for this. And now, the others will writhe with pain, as well. I've already taken down those idiot Drakkor who thought to try and stop me. And now you've just earned yourself a long stay in a concrete cell."

"Really?" Cocking her head, she waited for him to draw closer. He'd just given her an idea. Her magic might be strong, but she knew the Drakkor from Eyrie would make her stronger, if they could combine theirs with hers. So she reached out and connected with Micah, who'd already linked to Brandon and Roger. Quickly he let her know that they'd pulled back and were waiting for Ryan to get Tracey and Maria out before obliterating the building and Polacek. When she let him know what she needed, he agreed instantly.

As Polacek neared, all three mages poured their strength into Maria. She continued to smile, waiting for Polacek to touch her. Somehow she knew he'd prefer his hand on her skin first, so he could physically subdue her before using his magic.

She was right. As his fingers dug into her arm, she turned her head and met his gaze. Then, the strength of the magic making her feel drunk, she zapped him with a blink of her eyelashes. His snarl froze, transforming his face from handsome to hideous as she instantly immobilized him.

Fury and frustration combined to make his eyes appear to glow. He managed to force a single word out through his unmoving lips. "How?"

"Well, I managed to get my magic back," she said, letting herself gloat, just a little. "And those 'idiots' you say you vanquished? Turns out you didn't. They're outside waiting for us. You're going back to prison, if you're lucky. If not, I imagine they'll kill you. But no worries. Unlike you, they're not vindictive. I'm sure they won't make you suffer."

With a wave of her hand, she suspended him a few feet above the floor, still unable to move.

"Come on, you coward," she said, delivering the insult

as she sent him up the staircase ahead of her. "It's time for you to go back to prison."

"Or die." Micah's voice, reverberating all around them. "We may have no choice but to eliminate him. He's nothing but a danger to both himself and to others."

"See?" she told Polacek. "You can't say I didn't warn you."

As soon as Maria reached the upper level, Micah and Brandon stepped in to take charge of Polacek, who soundlessly cursed them but still couldn't move. Roger and Ryan had lowered Tracey to the ground and crouched over her, clearly trying to assess her ability to travel.

Flexing her fingers to release the last lingering magical residue, Maria watched Ryan, drinking in the sight of him. She wasn't entirely sure why he was here, but if she'd had any doubt about whether she really loved him, she knew the truth. He'd kissed her and restored her magic. Furthermore, Micah had told him to do that, which meant the mage knew how she felt despite her never having said a word. She could only hope he hadn't said anything to Ryan. That would be beyond mortifying.

Ryan looked up and their gazes locked. The tenderness in his gaze confused her, but she moved toward him, drawn like a sea lion to the sun. Her heart jolted and her entire body tingled as he met her halfway, sweeping her up in his arms. She held on for dear life, stunned to realize she was on the verge of tears and telling herself that, no matter what, she would not cry.

"Did he…?" he asked.

She shook her head. "No."

Then he kissed her again. This time, there was nothing quick about the movement of his mouth on hers. Slow and drugging, his lips were a promise and a vow. A jolt went through her, making her wonder if she dared to hope, dared to believe. Her emotions whirled as she fell into his kiss, the heat intensifying until she thought she might pass out. Or rip his clothes off right there in front of everyone and have her way with him.

Lifting his head, Ryan gazed at her hungrily, as if he could read her thoughts. "Don't ever do that to me again," he rasped. "How do you think I felt, leaving you alone to face that monster?"

"You gave me back my magic. I'm fine."

"Gave you back…how?"

Instead of answering, she kissed him again. He didn't need to know that she loved him. Apparently true love's kiss could be one-sided. Lucky for her.

As they melted into each other, Micah cleared his throat. "If you two are done with your excessive display of PDA, we need to get going."

Flushing, Maria turned and nodded, gratified when Ryan kept one hand on her shoulder. Though she wanted to lean into him, she forced herself to stand slightly apart, remembering what Micah had prophesied.

"Tracey isn't able to fly," Micah continued. "I think shape-shifting will harm her, so she will remain human and ride on top of Roger. I will take Polacek with me, since I'm the strongest. Ryan, you have a choice. Brandon can carry you as he did before, or you can ride on Maria."

The idea made Maria feel dizzy. Chills of excitement shivered up her spine as Ryan's broad smile left no doubt as to his choice.

"Of course," Micah said, sounding more pleased than she'd expected. "Now, let's all move outside and change so we can make our way back. I've notified the Drakkor Council. They'll take charge of Mr. Polacek once we are back in Galveston. It will be up to them whether he lives or dies."

Maria followed everyone out of the building. Night time, then. Good. They'd be better able to shield themselves in darkness. Yet how long had she been...

"The battle raged for one night and one day," Micah said, correctly interpreting her expression. "We had to put up a cloaking spell so no humans saw. Now we change, and once we're in the air I'll remove the spell."

Nodding, she stepped around and behind a large tree and hurriedly undressed. Normally, the Drakkor had no shyness about being nude in front of each other, but the odd combination of the three mages, Polacek and Ryan gave her a fierce need for privacy.

Breathing deeply, she shape-shifted into her dragon form, scooping up her human clothing and tucking it into a little pouch on her stomach. When she came out from behind the tree, she saw the others had done the same.

Ryan approached her, his handsome face alight with wonder. At her? Refusing to glance around and see what could have caused this expression, she lowered her head, not sure where he planned to sit for the journey home. When he climbed up her back, knowing exactly where to step for the best leverage, her surprised pleasure made her give Micah a huge, toothy Drakkor grin. To her amazement, Micah grinned back.

Once Ryan had taken a seat and moved around until he felt secure, she glanced at the others and nodded. One by one, they pushed up into the sky, leaping up and giving one huge thrust of wings. And then another, until they were high above the earth.

Though Ryan, at over six feet tall, had a large build, she barely felt his weight on her back. Pure joy filled her as she pushed the wind under and behind with her massive wings, using her huge tail for guidance. Though, as a dragon, her shape was big, her body had been designed for flight. In the air, she felt graceful, like a breeze dancer. Carrying the man she loved, sharing this with him, brought her pure happiness untainted with regret.

They flew low, keeping close to the water and avoiding all ships. She wasn't sure where they'd been but the ocean air energized her. Eventually, she saw the lights ahead beckoning, their welcoming brightness speaking of home. Galveston. Part of her heart, along with the sea.

They came in fast, landing on a private beach outside a beautiful and massive house. Hoping the total darkness kept them hidden, Maria waited until Ryan slid off her back before initiating the change back to human.

She kept her back to him while she hurriedly dressed, her entire body heating at the thought of him seeing her naked while with the others.

Finished and fully clothed, she turned. As she opened her mouth to speak, everything went black.

Ryan watched in stunned disbelief as, one by one, each Drakkor dropped to the ground, unconscious. Since Micah went first, Ryan was able to catch Maria before she hit the sand. Cradling her on his knees, he glanced at the others, bracing himself for Polacek's vengeance.

When it didn't come, he realized Polacek hadn't broken free at all. In fact, he lay unconscious with the others. Only Ryan had been unaffected by whatever magic had felled the Drakkor.

But who? Who was powerful enough to do this?

At the sound of footsteps coming down the stairs, he looked up. It was Maria's father, moving swiftly.

"Javier, what's going on?" Ryan asked. "We just landed, they changed, and then they all fell."

"I know." Javier spoke in a flat tone. "I managed to hide

the strength of my magic abilities from them all. I'm actually pretty damn powerful."

Perplexed, Ryan stared. "But why? They freed Tracey and your daughter, and recaptured Polacek."

"Yes, I know. And the Drakkor Council is spineless and weak. I know full well once they regain custody of that monster, they'll send him right back to prison." Shaking with rage, the older man strode over and kicked the unconscious Polacek in the side.

Ryan winced.

"The Council is on their way here," Javier continued. "And my spell won't last too much longer. Polacek doesn't deserve to live. He's not only dishonored my family, but the entire Drakkor race. That, in addition to the laws he's broken by shifting to dragon where humans could see, is enough to earn him the death penalty."

"Maybe, but isn't that for the Council to decide?"

"They've already decided." Spitting the words, Javier glared at each and every one of the downed Drakkor. "I spoke to them right after Micah notified them of Polacek's capture. Since I'm not on the Council, my opinion holds no sway with them."

"Which means what?" Ryan asked. "Are you planning on acting as Drakkor judge and jury here?"

"And executioner." Javier pulled a pistol from a holster at his side. "Look away if the sight of blood bothers you."

Trying to remember what he'd read, Ryan wondered if ordinary bullets could kill a Drakkor. For his kind, regular bullets could cause harm, but not a mortal wound. Only a silver bullet or fire could kill a shape-shifting wolf.

Evidently, that didn't hold true for Drakkor.

"Wait." Ryan spoke fast. "What about you? Have you thought about that? Won't you go to prison? How will that affect Maria, knowing her father is a murderer? Have you thought about that?"

Already bringing his weapon up to aim, Javier's arm never wavered. "She'll understand. She'll know I had to avenger her honor. Tracey's, too. All of our people deserve justice for what this man has done to our women."

It dawned on Ryan what the other man believed. "Listen to me," he said. "I asked Maria. Polacek didn't touch her." He wasn't sure about Tracey, but now was not the time to mention that.

"What?" Javier swung his head to look at Ryan, though he kept his weapon pointed at the still unconscious Polacek. "Don't lie to me. Not now."

"I'm telling you the truth. I asked Maria. She told me. And she wouldn't lie."

Baring his teeth, Javier turned back to his enemy. "Yes she would. She wouldn't want the man she loves to know another man had raped her."

Man she loved? Filing this away for later, Ryan took a step toward Maria's father. "Think about what you're doing, Javier. Do you never want to know your grandchild? To spend your time locked up, not able to bounce that special child on your lap?"

This time, his words registered. Slowly, Javier lowered his gun. "How could I not have realized?" he muttered. "Of course. You and my daughter are meant to be together. She will bear children. Hopefully more than one. I can't destroy—"

A shot rang out. Polacek jerked once, blood seeping from a wound in his chest.

"Heart shot," an unfamiliar man's voice declared, satisfaction ringing in his tone. "He won't be bothering anyone again."

Stunned, both Ryan and Javier squinted into the darkness. "Who's there?" Ryan called out, hoping he and Maria weren't next. "Show yourself."

Nothing but silence met his request. Holstering his pistol, Javier rushed over and checked Polacek's pulse. "He's dead."

Ryan shook his head. "At least it wasn't at your hand. Now, you'd better wake everyone up or you're really going to have a lot of explaining to do."

After a wave of Javier's hand, everyone began stirring, except for Tracey. Whatever weakness or illness she suffered, the deep sleep was no doubt a blessed thing.

The instant Maria regained consciousness, she smiled to find Ryan's face so close to hers. Then, as she realized what had happened, she frowned and struggled to get to her feet.

Around them, all the others began stirring.

Spotting Javier, Maria's expression cleared. "Dad!"

Wrapping his arms around her, Javier gave her a tight hug. "I'm so glad you're all right."

Before she could answer, Micah and his crew discovered Polacek. "Who did this?" Micah demanded. "Javier, you'd better start talking."

Ryan could tell Javier briefly considered attempting to hide part of the truth. "Just tell them," he urged quietly.

Maria's face fell. "Please tell me you didn't kill him, Dad. I don't know what I'll do if—"

"He didn't," Ryan put in. "I was conscious and saw the whole thing."

Speaking quickly, Javier told everyone exactly what had happened, including keeping the strength of his magic concealed.

This, more than anything, clearly infuriated Micah. "Do you realize we could have used your help?" he demanded, glaring at Javier. "If you are truly so strong that you can do this, your absence could have cost us all our lives, including your daughter's."

Javier bowed his head. "I had faith that you could handle him, but I see now I was wrong. I focused on vengeance, and by doing so I became nearly as evil as him. I offer my sincere apology and regret."

"That may not be enough," Micah declared. "Of course, the Drakkor Council will need to decide your fate."

Javier nodded. "They will be here soon."

Stepping forward, Ryan faced Micah. "What about finding out who actually killed Polacek? Don't you think that's more important than prosecuting someone who did nothing?"

Before Micah could respond, headlights from a vehicle illuminated the beach.

"That will be them," Javier said, sounding both pugnacious and defeated. "They've sent two representatives to collect Polacek."

As the car pulled up to the beach house and parked, the headlights cut off.

"We need to go meet them," Micah declared. "Javier, you will come with us."

"We'll stay here and watch over the body," Ryan put in, reaching for Maria. "We can't just leave him lying here on the beach."

But Maria sidestepped his hand. "I need to go with them. I've got to make sure my father is represented fairly."

"What about Tracey?" he asked. This question made Maria falter, however briefly.

"Watch over her. We need to make sure she gets qualified medical help. The Drakkor Council will know what to do." And she took off after her father.

Just like that, they were gone. Leaving Ryan alone with the dead man and the still-unconscious woman.

"Hey, Howard." Colton's voice, drawing nearer. "What's going on? I was jogging down the beach when I heard what sounded like a gunshot. Is everything okay?"

"Not really." Pointing, Ryan watched for Colton's reaction as he spotted Polacek.

Colton swore. "Is that...?"

"It is."

"Damn. You'd better get out of here. The last thing you need is for paparazzi to show up. I can see the headlines now."

Ryan didn't move. "I appreciate the sentiment, but this is my private beach. I have signs posted. The instant one of them sets foot on my property, I can have them arrested."

"Or shot." Colton might have been joking, but then again he might not. "Who killed him?"

When Ryan told him, Colton whistled softly. "That's what our Pack Protectors used to do, before the reform. Our job was to eliminate any threat to the Pack. I wonder if the Drakkor have people like that."

"That would explain what happened," Ryan said. "And why no one seemed surprised or concerned that some random guy appeared out of nowhere and gunned him down."

"Who's that?" Colton knelt down near Tracey. "Why is she still unconscious?"

Even after Ryan explained, Colton didn't leave Tracey's side. "She needs medical attention," he said.

"I know." Even as he spoke, Ryan saw Micah heading back their way. "Here comes one of the Drakkor now."

When Micah reached them, he jerked his head in a nod of acknowledgment and waved his hand in Tracey's direction. Immediately, her inert form lifted a few feet above the sand. Micah wiggled his fingers and began propelling her up the sand toward the others near the waiting vehicle.

"Where are you taking her?" Colton demanded.

"To be healed," Micah answered.

Both men watched silently as the older man marched away, magically pushing Tracey ahead of him.

Once he'd reached the vehicle, he must have moved Tracey inside. Ryan shrugged, and glanced back at Colton.

"I'm sure they take good care of their own," he said.

Colton nodded. "What about your girlfriend?"

Just hearing Colton refer to Maria like that made Ryan happy. Maria didn't know it yet, but she was about to become a whole lot more than a girlfriend. Assuming, that is, that she said yes.

Of course, Colton didn't need to know that. "She's with her father, talking to the Drakkor Council. Javier might be in a little bit of trouble."

"I doubt that," Colton said, his tone certain. "What he did sounds right up their alley. Those Drakkor can be pretty damn fierce."

"I hope they send someone to collect the body."

As soon as the words left Ryan's lips, smoke began to swirl around Polacek's inert form. "That's what happens when they change," he told Colton, who also watched intently.

"Surely once he'd dead, he can't become a dragon." Colton scratched his head. "That would be freakishly strange."

They watched, and when the smoke cleared, instead of a dragon's body, nothing at all remained.

"He's gone." Ryan glanced back at his house, slightly mystified. "Do you suppose they...?"

"We'd better hope so." Colton sounded grim. "Or else we've all got a helluva big problem on our hands."

"Come on." Ryan had already started forward. "Let's find everyone else and see what they say."

No sooner had the words left his mouth, when the vehicle that had arrived moments earlier, drove off. "I guess the Council is gone," Ryan said. "Though I'm sure Maria can tell us what's going on."

But when they reached the house it was completely empty. Apparently the vehicle that just left had taken every Drakkor away. Including Maria.

Maria didn't understand why the Drakkor Council wanted her spirited away, but her father and the three from Eyrie immediately agreed. They all piled into the one vehicle, a minivan with three rows of seats, refusing to give her a chance to even say goodbye to Ryan. Micah had suspended a still-unconscious Tracey a few feet above Maria's lap.

They drove fast, as if they were fleeing something. Screeching around corners, the driver accelerated rapidly, apparently intending to get on I-45 and leave the island.

Only when they'd gone a fair distance from the beach house did Micah explain. "The Council has received information that there is a vigilante Pack Protector on the loose. That's who killed Polacek. We could not take any chances with your safety. Once we know for certain Colton Richards is clean, we'll brief him and he can fill in Ryan."

Ryan. Even the sound of his name filled her with longing. Anger rose in her, making her magic begin to bubble in her veins. Her aura reflected this—even she could see how unsteady it was, shifting and changing color like a thunderstorm over the sea.

"Maria." A note of caution in her father's voice. "Get yourself under control."

She took several deep breaths, trying to clear her mind, and after a moment she thought she'd regained some sort of balance. A quick glance at her father confirmed this as he gave a small nod.

Now, to deal with the rest of them. She'd just about had enough of other people telling her what to do.

"Where are you taking me?" Maria asked. "And maybe you can also tell me why I've gone from being Polacek's prisoner to yours."

"We're headed somewhere safe," Micah said. "Don't worry, we're not driving all the way to Colorado."

"Or Wisconsin," her father put in. "I have to say, I don't think it's a good idea to separate my daughter and Ryan right now."

Micah chuckled, staring at her. "I told you that you wouldn't end up with him."

She stared right back. "Well, you're wrong."

"They won't be separated for long." This from one of the Council members, the one driving the van.

"I think you'd better give me a time frame," Maria demanded. "Because this whole capture and run thing is getting really old."

"Maria," Micah snapped. "Be careful. You are speaking to a member of the Drakkor Council."

"You know what, I don't care. I'm fed up. I'm one of the four remaining females of our people. I should be allowed to have a say on what happens in my life."

Dead silence. A quick glance at her father revealed Javier had begun to perspire, something he always did when nervous. Micah's pursed lips and prolonged silence told her he thought she'd done it. Clearly, they all expected she'd brought the wrath of the Council upon herself.

"She's right," the man in the front passenger seat finally spoke, his voice deep and rich with authority. "While we have an obligation to keep you safe, we don't have the right to do it against your will."

"Good." Leaning forward, Maria spoke directly to him,

ignoring the others. "Then stop the car and let me out. Now."

The backseat occupants erupted in protest. But the man—she never got his name—made a small gesture to the driver and the van pulled over.

"Maria, please." Her father, his expression afraid, stretched out his hand to her.

Taking it, she squeezed lightly. "I'll be all right. Trust me. My magic is strong."

Ignoring Micah, who pleaded with her to reconsider, she got out of the car and headed back down the road toward the beach house. She wasn't entirely sure what she'd find when she got there, but she no longer wanted to fight her destiny, no matter what Micah or his cronies claimed to have known or seen.

Chapter 18

After finding her gone, Ryan's control slipped. His beast, raging and snarling, mirrored the fury and anguish inside him. Baring his teeth, he growled.

For the first time in his entire life, Ryan didn't struggle to rein in his wolf. He let the change rip through him, tearing his clothing as his bones elongated and his body went through the rapid transformation from man to wolf.

And then, running full out, as fast as his four legs could carry him, he went after her.

"You'll never catch up to that car!" Colton shouted after him. But Ryan didn't even look back. He simply didn't care. He was done sitting around and letting others take action. Maria and he were mates—he saw this clearly now—and no wolf let his mate be taken from him without a fight.

He ran and ran and ran and still he saw no sign of that car. At this hour, the infrequent traffic made it necessary for him to duck and hide whenever he saw headlights coming toward him. If any of the locals—or hounds forbid, a tourist—were to report seeing a large wolf running down the road, he wasn't sure how animal control might react.

Finally, slowing to a lope, then a trot, and finally a walk, he conceded defeat. Once again, Maria was gone. And once more, he'd failed to save her.

As he sat on his haunches on the side of the road, aching, a howl building up in his throat, he spied someone coming on foot. The breeze carried her scent in his direction.

Maria?

Disbelieving, he got to his feet. Taking care to stay in the shadows, he padded toward her. When they were maybe twenty feet apart, he moved into the light.

She stopped, the moonlight turning her dark hair silver. Only then did he realize he was still wolf, but it didn't matter. He'd seen her as dragon, the time had come for her to see his lupine side.

Still closer he came, and she held her ground. When he reached her, she dropped to her knees, right there on the pavement, and burrowed her fingers deep in his coat.

"Ryan," she said, her voice certain. And then she gathered him to her and wept.

He held himself completely still, not entirely sure how to react. Her tears brought him pain, even though he sensed they were tears of joy.

Finally, she pulled back, wiping at her streaming eyes with the back of her hand. He nuzzled her, tasting the salt, and padded a short distance away, back into the shadows. Once there, he rapidly began to shape-shift.

Only after he'd changed back to human did he realize he had no clothing—what he'd been wearing lay in shreds in the driveway of his beach house.

"Ryan?" Maria, moving toward him. "I'm not letting you out of my sight again."

"I'm naked," he said, warning her. Also, as always happened in the instant after the change, he was fully aroused.

"Good," she growled, her voice sexy and breathless and so, so happy. "I've been dying with wanting you."

When she reached him, her eyes widened. "Well, you are definitely as happy to see me as I am you."

To his amazement, she began yanking off her clothes, only stopping when her naked skin was gleaming.

He hauled her up against him, his arousal almost painful. He inhaled sharply, flesh pricking as she climbed on top of him, taking him into her in one smooth motion. They came together with as much heat as summer lightning. Her lush curves molded to his as she began to move, riding him.

He claimed her mouth with his. She gave herself freely to his passionate kiss, just as she gave her body, with abandon.

Release loomed close—too near, too fast. He gripped her waist, attempting to slow her down. But she only shook her head, arched her back, her shapely breasts taunting him, and continued to move.

With each motion, his heart beat with the pulse of her name. A tormented groan escaped him as he lost the battle for self-control.

No. Unwilling to let this end, he rolled, so that her body now was under him, the sensual beauty of her naked body stealing his breath.

"Ryan," she began. Kissing away her protests, he began again to move, this time with agonizing slowness, determined to prolong the ecstasy.

She cried out, urging him faster, first with her hands and then with her entire body. His control snapped, and he gave himself over to the movement, to her, to the shuddering, shining moment of ecstasy as they reached the pinnacle together, the pleasure explosive, yet pure.

Love. This, he thought, tucking her curves into him as he held her. This was love. True love, the stuff of fairy tales and legends. The kind he'd never believed in until now.

Trembling, she clung to him, her body still damp from their lovemaking.

Finally, she moved away, collecting her clothing from the grass. "Now what?" she asked him, once she was dressed.

He faced her, unashamed of his nakedness, hoping she could see the love he felt in his eyes. "Now we discuss the future."

Her laughter made him smile. "No, I meant more immediately. How are we going to get you back to your beach house without any clothes? If someone sees a naked man strolling down the road, you know they're going to call the police."

"Then I'll just have to make sure no one sees me."

Once they reached his gate, which still sat wide-open, he hurried over to where he'd shape-shifted earlier, hoping there might be something salvageable he could put on. But, since he hadn't taken the time to remove anything when he'd changed to wolf, every bit of his clothing had been torn or shredded.

He held up the tattered remains of his shorts and put them on. "At least it's better than nothing."

"It looks like you are worried for nothing," she said, looking around. "It seems as if everyone is gone."

Making love with Ryan had sealed the deal, as far as Maria was concerned. No longer would she worry about her father, or the Drakkor Council, or anyone else for that matter. Ryan might never love her in return, but that no

longer mattered to her. She loved him with every bit of
her heart and that would have to be enough. She'd enjoy
being with him for as long as he wanted her.

Back at his new beach house, it appeared as if everyone
had vacated the premises. Which meant the Pack Protectors were out hunting their own rogue. And she and Ryan
were alone. Though she knew better than to let down her
guard, she wanted one night with him before returning
home, one morning to wake up with him beside her.

Inside the house—which truly looked amazing—Ryan
locked the doors and closed all the blinds. When he turned
to face her, his expression serious, she tried to figure out
the best way to tell him what she'd decided.

"We need to talk," he said. "About our relationship."

"Shh." She put a finger to his lips. "There's no need.
After all of this happened, I realized you're right. You've
been right all along. I want the same thing you want, for
however long it lasts. Let's just enjoy our time together
while we can. Life's too short to worry about nonsense."

He frowned. "But you said you need to find your mate.
What about your destiny? Your burning need to have a
baby. What about that?"

If her laugh sounded a bit brittle, she pushed the thought
away. "There's no need to worry about me getting pregnant. See, that's part of my destiny. Both parties need to
be in love for a pregnancy to occur. And since neither of
us loves the other like that, it simply won't happen."

She expected to see relief in his eyes, maybe even joy.
Instead, his frown deepened. "Maria, what about you?
What about what you want?"

"I just told you what I want. You. On your terms, exactly the way you stated you wanted it. No strings attached.
That will be enough."

"What if it isn't?" Gently, he cupped her face with his large hand. "I know you want more than that."

Confused, not understanding why he no longer seemed to want her at all, she realized she might have misunderstood what had driven him to rescue her.

"What about you, Ryan?" she asked. "Not too long ago, you had no problem telling me what you wanted out of life. I get that, but maybe I need to know more. What is it you truly love? Money? Power? Freedom?"

"You," he answered instantly, his gaze unwavering and certain. "I truly love you."

She heaved a sigh. "I've already told you, you don't have to say you love me to get me to be with you. I want to. No need to lie. Not now, not ever."

His eyes narrowed. "You don't believe I love you."

"I'm pretty sure I know what you really mean by that," she said. "I get that you clearly like your freedom. You don't want to be tied down, because you believe you'd run the risk of eventually growing bored."

He only shook his head. But then, she'd known he wouldn't refute her statement.

She could understand this. But through loving him, she'd also come to see a relationship could be so much more. Unlike land, which sat solid and unchanging, she'd come to understand love would be much like her beloved ocean. Always there, but sometimes stormy, with crests and waves. Other times, calm and smooth as glass.

But she couldn't teach him this. It was, she believed, something he'd need to learn for himself.

"Ryan, I love you." She gave him the most precious gift she could give, though once again he'd never know. "I love you enough to give up my search for a mate, at least until you get tired of me."

He stared at her as if she'd spoken in a language he

didn't understand. "I can see I have some convincing to do," he finally said, his smile so sensuous her knees went weak.

Both intrigued and tired of playing his game, she leaned into him for a long, deep kiss. "Convince me again," she said.

And so he did.

The next morning, Maria woke to bright sunshine. Cradled in Ryan's arms, she could hear the constant roar of the sea outside. Home. Surf and sun and sand, the screech of seagulls wheeling above the waves, and the man she loved sleeping next to her. Life couldn't get any better than this.

Smiling, her entire body humming with happiness, she slipped from the bed and padded to the bathroom. The luxurious appointments rivaled any expensive hotel and she grinned to think her own bedroom would fit easily inside this one area. Perks of dating a billionaire, she supposed.

The thought dimmed her smile somewhat. If Ryan had been an ordinary person, she suspected their relationship might have been a lot less complicated. Ah, well. Reminding herself to enjoy him as he was, she exhaled, refusing to allow any negative thoughts. She loved Ryan for what he was. Heck, any other woman would be thrilled to date a celebrity.

Though she'd showered the night before, she wanted to feel fresh after a night of vigorous lovemaking, so she stepped under the hot water and lathered her hair. The exotic tile and frameless glass stall was big enough for two and she entertained a fantasy of Ryan joining her. Once she'd finished, a bit disappointed that he hadn't, she towel dried her hair and put on one of the short, fluffy bathrobes she found hanging near the shower.

There were even new, unopened toothbrushes and tubes

of toothpaste. Realizing that Ryan was well prepared for guests dimmed her enthusiasm somewhat, as she knew she wasn't generous enough to share him with another woman. He was hers, and she knew they'd need to discuss relationship terms. Exclusivity would be her deal breaker.

Back in the bedroom, she saw that Ryan still dozed. For a few moments, she watched him sleep, her heart full. She didn't want to wake him, so she quietly closed his door and went to explore the rest of his house. As she'd expected from her brief glimpses of the night before, the place looked amazing, decorated in a beach theme with touches of the sea, which she loved.

When she reached the kitchen, she stopped and stared, awed despite herself. A marvel of granite and copper, it could have been the showpiece of a cooking show or any home improvement magazine.

Locating supplies, she made a pot of coffee and checked to see if he had breakfast food in the refrigerator. No surprise—a carton of eggs sat next to plastic-wrapped, thick-cut bacon. He also had country-style bread for toast and three kinds of jam. She saw orange, apple and tomato juice.

Again she realized this place had been stocked for guests, maybe a party. She bit her lip, remembering Ryan's lifestyle. Though she'd been certain before, doubt crept in now. Not about how she felt. She loved him with all of her heart. But she also knew it would be only a matter of time before he found someone else and moved on.

She needed to figure out a way to keep her heart from breaking when the inevitable happened. Right now, she needed to keep busy so she didn't overthink things.

Deciding to make a breakfast quiche, she found what she needed and got to work. Once she'd popped that in the oven, she poured herself a cup of coffee and went out on the patio outside the kitchen to drink it and watch the wind stir up whitecaps on the sea.

A few minutes later, Ryan found her there. She smiled when she saw him. "Grab a cup of coffee and pull up a chair," she invited. "Breakfast is in the oven."

He held up a mug. "Got it. By the way, the kitchen smells delicious."

Something in his tone alerted her. A certain hesitation, maybe. A thrum of urgency coloring his deep voice.

"Is everything all right?" she asked, trying to sound lighthearted even as all her insecurities came rushing back. Would he send her away so soon? Surely not.

"Yes. No." He raked his fingers through already disheveled hair. "This isn't going to work."

Though her heart plummeted all the way to the soles of her feet, she managed to keep her expression emotionless. Which wasn't easy, considering her throat had become clogged with pain. "What do you mean?" she asked, dreading the answer.

His eyes were like the sea during a storm. "This pretending. You don't want a casual type of relationship, you never have." He gazed intently at her. "And, Maria, you deserve more than that. You deserve it all—a husband, a home of your own, children."

Something lifted inside her. Relief, mingled with the pain. Sooner might actually be better than later. Though she didn't know how she would bear it, after all she'd been through, she needed to stop selling herself short.

Knowing he was right, and that she deserved to find happiness on her terms, she nodded. She'd wanted to be with him so badly, she'd let love cloud her judgment, even though she knew deep inside such a shallow relationship would never be enough for her. "I know," she said in a very small voice. "I also love you. I don't know how to reconcile the two."

He came closer, carefully setting his mug down next to hers. "You don't have to. I want to be all that for you, if you'll let me."

Disbelieving, she couldn't speak as he dropped to one knee in front of her, gazing up at her with love plain on his face. "I don't have a ring—we can pick that out together—but Maria Miranda, will you do me the honor of being my wife?"

His wife? Since they'd decided on honesty, she could be nothing but. "Ryan, if you're serious, what about your prenup? Didn't you once tell me you could never get involved without that?"

Shaking his head, he kissed the back of her hand. "My darling dragon-lady, being with you has taught me there are a lot more important things than possessions. Even if I were to lose half of everything I own—the houses, the cars, the jets, the yachts—none of that comes close to how much it would hurt if I lost you. I don't think I could survive that kind of pain."

His words mirrored the way she felt. Oh, how she wanted to believe. With every fiber of her soul. Yet one more issue—perhaps the most important of all—held her back. "What about children?" she asked softly. "You know I have to get pregnant. More than simply have to, I really want to have a baby. Honestly, I'd like more than one."

Silence reigned while their gazes locked and held. The sound of her heartbeat mingled with the waves outside, so loud in her ears she wondered if he could hear it.

"Of course I want children. Plural. I'd be honored to help continue the Drakkor species." His devastating grin, that confident sexiness, made her suck in her breath. "Not to mention how great it would be to have a little mini-you and mini-me running around. I can give them everything, Maria." He spoke earnestly, clearly aware of how much this meant to her. "The best education, a lovely home, toys. They'll want for nothing, our kids."

Our kids. Her heart began to sing. "What about love, Ryan? I know you can give them material possessions, but love matters the most. That's more important to me than anything else."

"Love?" Pushing to his feet, he caught her around the waist and pulled her close. His beloved scent, spice and pine and masculinity mingled with the salty air, went straight to her head. He held her, chest to chest, near the wooden railing, while below the sea continue to roll onto the sand. "As much as I love you, how could you even think I'd love them any less? I'd love them equally," he said. "I'd say maybe even more, but I don't know how that would even be possible."

Still, she hadn't yet told him everything. "Before I give you your answer, there's one more thing you need to know." She took a deep breath and met his gaze. The tenderness in his eyes warmed her. "Love is what I needed all along. Female Drakkor can't conceive at all if there isn't love on both sides."

He grinned, sexy and roguish and…hers. "Then I'll have you pregnant within a week," he promised swiftly. "Now, please. Put me out of my misery and accept my marriage proposal."

Now she let go, allowing the joy to sweep through her, so much so that she felt she might burst if she didn't change to dragon and take to the sky. Later, she would, but for right now she had to give her man his answer.

Wanting to tease him, she bowed her head and pretended to have to consider. Finally, with love and happiness still filling her, she raised her head and laughed. "Ryan, the answer is yes. It's always been yes."

He claimed her or she claimed him—later each would tell the other they'd been the one to initiate the kiss. It didn't really matter, not right then, as their lips and hearts and bodies came together, and laughing, they stumbled back to bed.

It wasn't until the smoke detectors began shrieking that she realized the quiche had burned.

The next morning, Maria and Ryan were lounging in bed when Ryan's cell rang. "Colton Richards," he told her, giving her a quick kiss on her delectable mouth. "I've got to answer this."

Smiling drowsily, she gave a languid wave of her hand and closed her eyes.

He stepped outside onto the balcony. "What's up, Colton? Have you caught whoever killed Polacek?"

"We have." Colton sounded grim. "Turned out, he's not Pack, after all. He's a human who once dated Tracey Beauchamp. She broke up with him and he'd been stalking her. When he saw her leave with Polacek, back when she was captured, he assumed they were lovers. It's a bit strange, but he was out for a stroll when he saw the two of them again on the beach after y'all got back. He says he didn't think, just reacted. He killed Doug Polacek in a jealous rage. How's that for irony?"

"Wow." Stunned, Ryan shook his head. "I assume the Drakkor Council is going to handle this?"

"I think so, especially since we don't have a body. The Drakkor vaporize when they die."

"I know. I saw." Ryan sighed. "At least it's over. Thanks for letting me know."

"No problem." Colton hesitated. "So you and Maria are together again?"

"Yep. As a matter of fact, we're going to get married."

"Congratulations." Colton didn't sound surprised. "I'm glad the two of you came to your senses."

"Keep it under your hat for now. I promise once we've nailed down specifics, you'll receive an invite to the ceremony."

"Thank you." Colton cleared his throat. "Do you have any idea how Tracey's doing? The Drakkor have closed ranks around her and I can't get any info."

"No, but I can find out. I'm sure she's recovering. Maria's been keeping in touch with her, I think. I'll ask her."

"Great. And would you mind doing me one little favor? Have Maria ask Tracey if she'd mind contacting me once she's well. For whatever reason, I haven't been able to get her out of my mind."

After a second of initial surprise, Ryan laughed. "Definitely, my friend. And best of luck with whatever happens between the two of you. Finding the right person really is a great and wondrous thing."

They ended the call and Ryan went back to his own right person and proceeded to show her exactly how happy she made him. Later, when he told her about Colton's interest in Tracey, Maria smiled and said she'd noticed the way Colton had looked at her.

The next several days were a whirlwind of activity. They drove to Houston, where Maria selected a stone and she and Ryan worked with a custom jeweler to create her ring. Ryan paid the man double to complete the work quickly. For himself, Ryan chose only a plain, platinum band.

They discussed the wedding. When and where. He wanted an elaborate ceremony, but she still shrank from the idea of paparazzi and incessant media coverage, and told him she preferred something quieter, with only their families and closest friends. Indulgent, he agreed to her request, though he suggested they have their wedding on a private island he owned in the Bahamas. Stunned, she only stared at him and shook her head.

"We could fly everyone in and that way there'd be no stolen photos, no drones or paparazzi hiding in the bushes or trees," he told her. "If you want privacy, that'd be our best option."

She promised to consider this idea, since all her family were Drakkor and could fly themselves. "But the truth is, ever since I opened my wedding chapel, I've dreamed of having my own wedding there, here in Galveston," she confessed. "Maybe that's silly, and I know it's not as fancy as it could be on some remote Caribbean island, but that's always been my dream. That's really what I want."

He kissed the tip of her nose. "Then that's what you shall have."

They chose a date three weeks in the future, after Maria checked her schedule and saw her wedding chapel had nothing booked that day. She confided in Kathleen, who reacted by jumping up and giving her a big hug. "I just knew you two were meant to be together," Kathleen said, after being sworn to secrecy. "Now let's get together and plan you the best wedding ever."

Three weeks passed in a blur. Even though she'd been staying with Ryan at his beach house, the night before they were to be married she planned to go home to sleep in her own home, telling him it was bad luck for the groom to see the bride right before the wedding.

Ryan hated that idea, but went along with it. Their wedding day was still far enough off, by four days, for him not to think about that just yet. There were other, more pressing worries. First and foremost was the weather.

All the forecasters were talking about the storm, a Category 4 hurricane that might or might not make landfall in Galveston. Already in the gulf, this storm had three projected trajectories. Galveston, Brownsville or somewhere in between. Everyone in Texas prayed for the area in between, a sparsely populated, rural area where the wind and water would do much less damage. While the island had not been formally evacuated, everyone remembered Hurricane Ike, which had leveled parts of Galveston in 2008. All roads heading north were already clogged. Quietly, he began to make alternate plans.

Meanwhile, the people of Galveston tried to prepare as best they could.

Those who owned businesses from the Strand to the Seawall began boarding up windows. Homeowners did the same, and plywood sold out in a matter of hours. Everyone everywhere on the island existed in a state of heightened anticipation, dreading that moment when they knew for certain the hurricane would be headed toward them.

Nervous as a sea crab far from water, Maria worried and fretted. She had numerous conversations with her father, the gist of which, Ryan gathered, was Javier trying to soothe her.

The day before the wedding dawned cloudy and windy. The sky and the sea both roiled ominously, and now a mandatory evacuation had been put in place. The hurricane would be hitting Galveston in roughly nine hours.

Chapter 19

Even with the ominous clouds and the angry wind, Ryan could feel the change in the barometric pressure. Both exhilarating and nerve-racking, this almost sixth sense lent an even stronger sense of urgency to their rushed preparations. Working alongside Maria and Kathleen, he nailed sheets of plywood over the windows of her wedding chapel. When they'd finished, Maria grabbed his hand and said a quick prayer that her building would be spared.

"Come on," he told them. "We're finished here. We've got to see what we can do to fortify your house, Maria. What about you, Kathleen?"

"I live in an apartment," Kathleen answered. "I've already packed my most precious belongings."

"I closed my hurricane shutters this morning," Maria added. "That's about all I can do to my house." When she turned to face him, she wasn't entirely successful at hiding the panic in her beautiful brown eyes. "But, though I hate to admit it, we need to start making phone calls and cancel the wedding."

Pulling her close, he kissed the top of her head. "I've already had Timothy contact everyone."

Her dejected nod had him cupping her chin with his hand, lifting her face to his. Though he'd worried he'd find tears, there were none. "But our wedding isn't canceled."

She gasped. "What?"

"I've arranged for a different location. Timothy went on ahead to get everything set up. We're only postponing it one day."

"One day? But that's not long enough for people to change their travel arrangements."

Shaking his head, he brushed a light kiss against her lips. "Your family has let me know they've taken care of their own." Which meant they'd fly themselves as dragons. "As for everyone else, I've got them taken care of. Tickets are purchased and all travel is arranged."

Maria nodded. But then, as the rest of what he'd told her sank in, she narrowed her eyes. "You say you've moved our wedding? To where?"

Though she'd find out soon enough, Ryan simply smiled. "It's a surprise. Now grab your bag. Since Houston's closed all the airports, I've hired a helicopter to pick us up at John Sealy Hospital. It'll be here in an hour."

Maria didn't move. "But…"

"Come on. We'll stop by your house on the way so you can grab your things. Since I forewarned Kathleen, she's got her bag with her. Your friend Rhonda will also meet us there."

"Good. I couldn't very well have a wedding without my maid of honor. Still, I don't think I'll ever get used to what money can do," Maria muttered, climbing into his Jeep. Then, gazing out the window at the ominous sky, she brightened. "If my Corvette gets flooded, will you buy me a new one?"

He grinned. "Of course. You can even have it painted turquoise if you like."

Her answering laugh was music to his ears.

Maria grabbed her overnight bag and the plastic bag containing her wedding dress, which she took great pains to conceal from him, then they headed to the hospital. The chopper had already arrived and the pilot waited for them near the door going outside to the heliport.

"I'm glad you're on time," he said. "Your other passenger is already here. If we'd waited too much longer the first band of the storm would have made it too dangerous to fly."

Once they stepped onto the luxurious helicopter, Rhonda jumped up from her seat and gave Maria a hug. "Isn't this exciting?" she asked.

Maria glanced at Ryan, the corners of her sensual mouth lifting. "Yes. Yes, it is."

The two women sat next to each other and began chatting. Ryan gathered Maria's friend was thrilled to have a break from her husband and small child for a couple of days. They'd evacuated and were staying with his family in Fort Worth. Kathleen joined in the conversation, while Ryan merely watched and listened, content.

Despite the buffeting wind, they lifted off without any problems. Once aloft, the first band of the hurricane—monstrous clouds clawing at the roiling sky—could be clearly seen.

"This is going to be a bad one," the pilot remarked. Maria winced, clearly thinking of her little wedding chapel, not to mention the other businesses on the Strand and near the seawall that had already endured hurricane damage and flooding in 2008. If she remembered right, several sections of beach houses had been obliterated.

"Where are we going?" Maria finally asked, earning conspiratorial grins from the other two women.

Brushing her unruly hair away from her face, Ryan kissed her cheek, loving the delicate way she shivered. "To Austin."

"Is that where we're getting married?"

"No." He shook his head. "My jet is being fueled as we speak. We're catching a flight out of Austin-Bergstrom to Sea-Tac in Seattle. I've got a sweet little place on Bainbridge Island. Since there's a three-day waiting period, I took the liberty of obtaining the license when I first learned about the storm—that's what I had you sign the other day when Kathleen notarized it."

She tilted her head. "I wondered if there was something we'd missed when we got our Texas license. Smart man, to take such a precaution."

Please by her compliment, he smiled. "Thanks. I know this isn't where you wanted to have our wedding, but I promise you Timothy will do his best to make everything as beautiful as possible."

"With only two days' notice?" This came from Rhonda, watching the interaction between them with interest.

"Money can accomplish a lot," Kathleen said, sounding satisfied. "Plus I've been consulting with Timothy to make sure everything is the way Maria would want it."

Maria's eyes widened as she looked from her friend to her receptionist and finally back to Ryan. "You know what," she declared. "I think I'm just going to try to relax and enjoy everything. I have complete confidence that between Timothy and Kathleen, everything will be perfect." As they continued northwest, she rested her head on his shoulder.

Damn, he loved this woman. He kissed the top of her

head, amazed that even now her hair smelled so sweet, like tangerines.

"Where are you two going to live?" Rhonda asked. "I know your company is in Austin, Ryan."

Instead of answering, Ryan decided to see how Maria responded.

"You know, I've been thinking about that." Maria replied. "I know we have to live in Austin so you can run your company, but I'd like for us to spend as much time in Galveston as possible."

"You know, I've got a bunch of trusted employees who keep my company running. If they need me, I can always teleconference if we're not in Austin."

She brightened. "So we can live in Galveston? I don't do well if I spend too long away from the sea."

He laughed, aware his new bride had no idea yet of how many properties he owned. Houses they would soon own together. "I assure you that won't be difficult, no matter where we stay. Most of my other properties are near various oceans, except my ranch in Jackson Hole. Besides the island I just bought in the Bahamas, and this waterfront place near Seattle, I recently bought a property off the Maine coast. We can travel anywhere you want to go."

"What? Nothing in Europe?" she asked. Then she laughed, but he'd heard a note of consternation in her voice.

"What's wrong?" he asked, wrapping his arms around her as much as he could manage with the seat belts.

"I'm not sure I'll fit in to your world," she told him. "I'm just a regular person, not some fancy-schmancy rich socialite."

Her words made him smile and kiss her neck. "I love you so much it hurts. Maria, you know me. I'm just a regular guy who happened to have worked my ass off to make my money. I don't hang around phony people, believe me."

Maria let out a huge sigh. She closed her eyes and, with him still holding her, promptly fell asleep.

The trip to Seattle passed in a blur. Maria felt a little sad to have to abandon her dream of getting married in her wedding chapel by the sea, but the fact that Ryan had arranged that they'd still be married near the ocean cheered her immensely.

Beyond that, she felt a profound sense of relief that all the particulars had been handled by Kathleen and Timothy. Instead of stressing over the wedding, she could focus on what was important—her love for her husband-to-be.

On the private jet out of Austin—Private. Jet. Maria couldn't believe it—Ryan broke out a bottle of expensive champagne for the women, leaving them to go have a word with his pilot. Kathleen sidled over to her, holding a delicate flute. "Timothy did ask me what we'd set up in Galveston," she said. "He's promised to try and keep things as close to that as he can."

Running her finger down the rosewood armrest, Maria nodded. "At this point, all that I care about is actually getting married. As long as I have my groom and my dress, I'm good to go."

Kathleen nodded, taking a sip of her champagne. "What are you going to do with the wedding chapel after you're married? Are you planning on selling it?"

"No, of course not." Horrified that Kathleen would even think such a thing, Maria reached for her own champagne flute. "That's why I promoted you and gave you a raise. I want you to run it for me. And if the hurricane takes it out, we'll just rebuild. That business was a dream of mine. I'm not about to let it go just because I'm getting married."

"To one of the richest men in the world," Kathleen added, her voice wistful as she glanced up at the door to the cockpit where Ryan stood, his back to them as he talked to the pilot.

"And the handsomest, too," Rhonda chimed in, raising her glass in a salute.

"He's just Ryan to me." Maria touched her glass to Rhonda's and then Kathleen's. "I'd love him even if he were an unemployed beach bum."

Rhonda sniffed, swiping at her eyes with her cocktail napkin. "I know. That's what makes it so perfect."

After they arrived in Seattle, where it was actually sunny and warm, contrary to what Maria expected, two limousines waited to whisk them away, Kathleen and Rhonda to their hotel, and Ryan and Maria to the ferry, for the trip out to Bainbridge Island.

"I think I should stay with Rhonda," Maria said, panicking a teeny bit for the first time since they'd left Galveston. "You know what they say about the groom seeing the bride right before the wedding."

"I'd rather you come with me." Ryan kept hold of her arm. "I don't want to take a chance that, for whatever reason, you don't make it to Bainbridge tomorrow for the wedding. I promise, you can stay locked in your room, or I can stay in mine, and that way you don't have to worry about me seeing you."

Exhausted, she nodded. "They both need to be there in the morning. I need their help to get ready."

"They will be," Ryan promised.

Waving goodbye to the other women, she let Ryan help her into the limo. She dug her phone out of her purse and she checked to see if there were any stories about the hurricane online.

"It's still a ways out yet," Ryan said softly, his breath tickling her ear. "Notice they're now predicting it will veer south. Hopefully, when it does make landfall, it won't be anywhere near Galveston."

She nodded, leaning into his strong chest, her fears and tension melting away.

"I promise you we'll have a beautiful wedding," he continued. "I'm sorry we couldn't have it in Galveston, but—"

She kissed him, cutting off his words. When they finally came up for air, aroused and giddy, she smiled. "None of that matters, my love, as long as you are there with me."

Though doing so was more difficult than she would ever have anticipated, she and Ryan spent the night apart. Despite her exhaustion, she slept fitfully, throwing back her sheets and getting out of bed as soon as the sky began to lighten. Her wedding day! A day she'd dreamed of since she'd been a little girl.

Hurrying to the bathroom, dizziness made her grab the edge of the counter to keep from falling. She caught sight of herself in the mirror. Too-bright eyes, flushed complexion…more than just the ever-present fatigue she'd been noticing. Great. She groaned. All she needed was to be getting sick. "Not today," she said out loud, determined to will this away.

She took another step, and a second wave of dizziness hit. As she struggled to recover from this, her eyes widened in horror and she rushed toward the commode, barely lifting the lid in time before the entire contents of her stomach came back up.

Gross. Since she'd been a toddler, she'd done everything and anything to keep from throwing up. The fact that this had happened so rapidly, and the way she'd had absolutely no control over it, frightened and appalled her.

This, too, shall pass. A hurricane hadn't been able to stop her wedding. A little queasiness in the morning wouldn't, either.

Rinsing out her mouth, she brushed her teeth. Mouthwash helped, though even the minty taste made her feel queasy again.

And then it dawned on her. Could this be morning sickness? Could it be possible that she might be pregnant?

Closing her eyes, she thought of all the times she and Ryan had made love. She didn't use birth control; she'd never had a need. And though in the beginning Ryan had used protection, there'd been a few occurrences of impetuous passion, and he hadn't.

If she'd ever needed proof he loved her—which she didn't—getting pregnant would confirm it without a doubt.

To her stunned disbelief, her eyes filled with tears. Tears? And then she decided. Even though she never, ever cried, this time she'd make an exception. Letting them flow, she allowed herself to become a blubbering mess, because this time the tears were from joy rather than sorrow.

Finally, she blew her nose and dashed at her eyes with tissue. She looked a fright, but she knew time and makeup would take care of that.

A baby! She and Ryan were going to have a baby! She'd fulfilled her destiny, after all. Now all she had to do was make it through the wedding. She'd tell Ryan and Javier later.

Taking a deep breath, she stepped into the shower, determined to hang in there until the queasiness faded. She'd call Timothy and have him bring up some fruit and crackers. Maybe some ginger ale, if they had it.

The light repast did the trick. Wearing a white robe, Maria smiled and nodded as a hairdresser tried to tame her wild black hair into some sort of updo. Rhonda and Kathleen would be there soon to help her with her makeup.

A soft tap on her door made the hairdresser freeze.

"Go ahead and see who it is," Maria directed. "If it's

the groom, send him away. If it's my maid of honor and my friend, let them in."

"It's not either," a familiar voice said. Micah. "I need a moment with you. May I come in?"

"Sure." When he stepped into the room, wearing a fitted gray suit, she almost didn't recognize him. He'd even trimmed his white beard, which made him look even more distinguished and dapper.

"I just need a moment of privacy," he continued.

The hairdresser took the hint. "I'm going to take a five-minute break. I'll be back."

Micah waited until she'd left before he cleared his throat. "I need to talk to you about my prediction."

"No." Maria held up her hand. "This is my wedding day. I refuse to allow you ruin it. I'm sorry you don't feel Ryan and I belong together, but we do. We're getting married, whether you like it or not."

He nodded, covering his mouth to hide a slight smile. "I was wrong," he said. "I never saw any vision or prophecy about the two of you. I told you that in a moment of peevishness, after you bested me. I wanted to let you know I'm sorry."

"Sorry?" Blinking, she stared at him. "Do you have any idea how much damage you almost caused?"

"Did I really?" When she opened her mouth, he held up his hand. "Sometimes we work harder for things we consider forbidden."

Narrow-eyed she considered his words. "Maybe so," she allowed. Finally, she realized that this, too, she needed to let go. "Either way, I forgive you. I don't want anything to cloud this day."

His gaze dropped to her belly, as if he already knew the spark of new life resided there. She held her breath, praying he didn't ask. No matter what, she knew she had to tell Ryan first.

To her relief, Micah dipped his chin. "Thank you," he said. "I wish you many blessings and much happiness."

And he left the room.

Staring after him, Maria wondered at the weight she felt lift off her shoulders. She hadn't even been aware of it, but Micah's prophecy had sat festering in her mind ever since he'd told her.

Now, with that gone, she had nothing to cloud her happiness.

Three hours later, hair and makeup done, Rhonda helped her into her dress. Eating had done wonders to settle her stomach, and she vowed to focus on her wedding and Ryan on this most special of all days. There'd be plenty of opportunities later to run out and buy a pregnancy test.

"It's time," Kathleen said softly. "Oh, and Ryan said to tell you another friend of yours—Tracey Beauchamp—was well enough to attend, as well. He thought you might like to know."

Smiling, Maria thanked her. "I'm so glad. She's been in the hospital. I know Ryan's friend Colton is very interested in her. I hope Timothy seated them near each other."

Rhonda peeked out around the curtains. "I can't tell. For a small and intimate wedding, there sure are a lot of people."

When Timothy had told Maria the wedding would be outside near the waterfront, she'd been thrilled. It helped knowing that if she couldn't get married in Galveston, she'd still be near the sea. Before going to bed, she'd watched the news and had been elated to see the hurricane had not only been downgraded to a Category 3, but it had come ashore south of Galveston, in an unpopulated area where it had done little harm.

Part of her had wanted to rush back home and have her wedding there. But Timothy had worked his behind off, and guests had begun arriving the day before. She'd be married in Washington State. The location didn't matter. The man—and possible baby—did.

A soft knock sounded on her door. Kathleen opened it to let Javier in. "Are you ready?" he asked, his gaze searching his daughter's face. "You look ready. You're actually glowing."

Smiling up at him, Maria nodded. "Thank you. And, yes, I am ready." She took his arm and let him lead her down the long hallway, toward a door leading to the outside.

Rhonda and Kathleen hurried on ahead, to take their places as part of the wedding party, while Maria and her father hesitated, waiting for the music to start and cue them.

And here it was.

The instant they stepped through the door, Maria smiled with joy. Everything, from the bright blue, cloudless sky—which she'd heard was something of a rarity in this area—to the calm, mysterious ocean, glinting in the sun, was perfect.

Tiny white lights adorned the trees, winking magically so the shaded areas turned into a wonderland. There were flowers—oh, the flowers—tulips and daisies and carnations and more. So many she wondered if Ryan had bought out a flower shop.

Chairs had been set up facing the water, with a beautiful wooden pavilion at the end. The hushed guests all turned to watch her as she approached, their faces lit up with awe.

Music continued to play softly while wind chimes gently tinkled in the breeze as she made her way up the stone pathway to where her groom waited, devilishly handsome in his cream-colored suit. Tall and confident, his dark hair glinting in the sun, his craggy features full of love as he watched her move closer.

She was his. And he...he was all hers. Now they would make it official.

Her heart was hammering in her chest as she approached, but her nervousness vanished when her gaze met Ryan's. He smiled, his eyes glowing, alight with happiness.

Feeling as if she floated toward him in a dream, she took her place across from the man she loved, waiting impatiently while the preacher said the vows.

"I do," she responded, when her time to do so came.

"I do," Ryan said, his fierce gaze never leaving her face.

"I now pronounce you, Ryan Howard and Maria Miranda, husband and wife. You may now kiss the bride."

So he did. Or she kissed him. Years later, when they told the story of their wedding to their beautiful daughter, born exactly eight months and three weeks from that day, each would say with a grin that they'd been the one to initiate this kiss. And then they'd laugh and kiss each other again.

* * * * *

1015_MB515

MILLS & BOON®

n o c t u r n e™

AN EXHILARATING UNDERWORLD OF DARK DESIRES